May Day

A Curse, in Black and White

SCOTT

ARCHWAY
PUBLISHING

Archway Publishing books may be ordered through booksellers or by contacting:

Archway Publishing
1663 Liberty Drive
Bloomington, IN 47403
www.archwaypublishing.com
1 (888) 242-5904

ISBN: 978-1-4808-8045-0 (sc)
ISBN: 978-1-4808-8046-7 (hc)
ISBN: 978-1-4808-8044-3 (e)

Library of Congress Control Number: 2019911458

Print information available on the last page.

Archway Publishing rev. date: 09/04/2019

"A curse on him who is lax in doing the Lord's work!
A curse on him who keeps his sword from bloodshed!"

Jeremiah 48:10

Chapter 1

The tinkling whisper of feminine laughter, and an occasional name shouted out in greeting were the only sounds drifting up from the meadow below. To the ears of the concealed man, what he was hearing could more easily have passed for sounds of a large family picnic than of preparations for a black mass.

Hermano pushed up the left sleeve of his army field jacket and checked the time. It was so dark in the covered trench that he had to hold the watch a few inches from his face to make out the luminous hands.

Seven o'clock.

Sundown was supposed to be a little after six, so he felt that it should be dark enough outside by now to risk raising his cover.

The trench was about six feet long by three feet wide. He was dug into the side of a hill, so the upside end of the trench was about five feet deep, and the downside end was closer to four feet. It was covered by a 4 x 8-foot sheet of quarter inch plywood which had been well-camouflaged with an attached pile of assorted brush and leaves.

Using a small spade, Hermano had begun quietly digging the trench around midnight the previous evening. Since he couldn't risk leaving a telltale pile of fresh dirt laying around, he had shoveled it into a five-gallon plastic bucket. He had then carried the bucket a couple of hundred yards back into the forest and scattered the dirt each time it was filled. It was slow work, but he was finished and had his plywood covering prepared by around 5 a.m.

By 5:30 he was stretched out on the floor of his covered trench. Exhausted, he had slept until 6 p.m.

Last night's work, though, was nothing compared to the previous six months he'd spent in preparing for it. Six months earlier, on Halloween night, he had secretly observed a black mass near Kansas City, Missouri. Once the black mass had degenerated into a drunken orgy, he had slipped around to the parking area and recorded the license numbers of all the twenty or thirty vehicles. There had been three vehicles with out-of-state license plates—two Kansas and one Colorado. The Ford Bronco with Colorado tags had been registered to Jake Hart, a resident of Colorado Springs.

Hermano had spent the past six months in Colorado Springs, following and studying every aspect of Jake Hart. For the past three months Hermano had been employed as a waiter at Jake's favorite coffee shop, A Touch of Scorpio, in Old Colorado City. In late March, Hermano had learned that Jake's primary duty to the satanic church was to secure sites for their black masses.

As Walpurgis Night, the last night of April, had approached, Hermano had quit his job and had begun keeping Jake under 24-hour surveillance.

The previous morning, he had followed Jake about ten miles north on Rampart Range Road. There, Jake had left the road to drive east on a little-used dirt trail which had disappeared into the national forest.

Hermano had driven a couple of miles farther and then, leaving Rampart Range himself, had hidden his old Jeep fifty feet off the road and behind a thick curtain of trees.

On foot, it had taken Hermano about three hours to locate and scout-out Jake's campsite, which was about a half-mile east of the road. Jake had pitched his tent on the west side of a meadow that was circular in shape and about fifty yards in diameter. Except for some wildflowers, the meadow was clear and unusually smooth. The north, east, and south sides, sloped gently down to converge at a half-moon section of barren level ground on the west side. The half-moon section occupied about a fourth of the clearing and Jake's tent was pitched on the far side of that. The clearing was ringed-in with a thick growth of Aspin and Fir trees, giving the whole scene a vague amphitheater look.

Hermano had located a good spot to dig his trench--near the tree-line on the far east side, and then had hiked back to his jeep. It was the 29th of April and Beltane didn't begin until sundown on Walpurgis Night—the 30th—so Hermano wasn't in any particular hurry. He had driven back to Colorado Springs to buy a sheet of plywood and pick up the rest of his gear and was back at the meadow just before dark.

Hermano pulled a small, flat metal box from his jacket pocket and, having opened it, began applying powdered charcoal to his face and neck. His American-Indian ancestors would have preferred war-paint, but they would have approved of the final ghostly effect that the coal dust had on Hermano's appearance. Once he was confident that no light would be reflected from his face and neck, Hermano slowly began raising the downhill end of his camouflaged plywood cover. After he had raised it about a foot, he propped a short thick stick under each of the two corners. Then, leaning against the end of the trench, he peered out the slit at the bizarre spectacle below.

Twelve large round stones had been evenly spaced around, and just outside, a white circle. The circle, about thirty feet in diameter, had been drawn on the level ground at the west end of the clearing.

Within the circle, its five points touching the perimeter, was a large white pentagram. At the pentagram's center, within its pentagon, a five-sided stack of firewood pyramided to a height of about nine feet.

A dark rectangular altar had been set up between the western-most point of the pentagram and the tree-line, near where Jake's tent had been. The altar, about eight feet long by four feet wide appeared to be made of some sort of dark, heavy wood.

Hermano had secretly observed six black masses prior to this one, but he had never seen anything like this. Rather than everyone being dressed in the usual black robes, the thirty or forty people who were conversing in small clusters on the west end were dressed in—not only black—but, also, white and green robes. There appeared to be about an equal number of each. The scene was illuminated by a half-dozen Coleman lanterns, which were hanging from tree limbs on the west side of the clearing.

Hermano's gaze was transfixed on a particularly imposing middle-aged man in a white robe who was standing near the altar. The rites hadn't as yet begun, and his head was still uncovered. It was his head, or more particularly—his hair, that interested Hermano. The man, who appeared to be about 6'4" or 6' 5", had a gray beard which was slightly forked and reached to mid-chest. His hair, long in back, was cut in a tonsure. That is, shaved foreword of a line drawn from ear to ear across the crown of his head. "A Druid!" Hermano whispered incredulously. The Druid, who appeared to be in an animated conversation with three of the black robed people was leaning on a six or seven foot "wand" with a crescent-shaped crook at the top.

Hermano was too far off to hear the conversation, but the Druid appeared to be on the verge of flying into a rage. He had been holding the wand with his left hand, but when he grabbed it with both hands, Hermano thought that he was going to start swinging.

Apparently, one of the other white-robed people thought so, too, because he quickly stepped up to the Druid and put a reassuring hand on his shoulder. Gently pulling him back near the tree line, the two conversed privately for a few moments.

Hermano sat down on the upturned 5 gallon can and pulled a granola-bar from his jacket pocket. He leaned back against the wall of the trench and thoughtfully began to munch his supper.

Beltane was originally a Druid holy day alright, but he hadn't expected to see any Druids here. He knew that Jake was a member of the Church of Satan—he was probably one of the black robed characters below. But that white robed man with the wand was definitely Druid, and it was logical to assume that the other white robed people were

Druids, also. The green robed people were probably bards, neophyte Druids.

"Damn", Hermano mumbled. This could be a real dangerous mixture—vitality and worldly wisdom. It didn't seem to be a very happy marriage, though.

Hermano's thoughts were interrupted by the sudden silence. All sounds from below had suddenly ceased. He stuffed the empty granola wrapper into his pocket and stood up to regain his viewpoint.

The scene was much more somber, now. All the participants, with the exception of the tall Druid, were standing about ten yards up the slope facing the ringed pentagram.

The tall Druid, now hooded, was slowly walking in a counter-clockwise direction around the ring. Wand in hand, as he walked, he chanted something in a language with which Hermano wasn't familiar. The chant would end with the word *"Belenos"*, which the Druid would shout each time he reached one of the twelve stones. Then, touching the stone with the crook of his wand, he would begin the chant again as the proceeded on to the next. It took him about fifteen minutes to complete the circle. As he touched the final stone he shouted, *"Hail Belenos, Hail Satan!"*

The entire group responded with, *"Hail Belenos, hail Satan!"*

Next, the tall Druid slowly approached the pile of wood in the center of the pentagram, all the while softly chanting the same thing that he had been chanting while consecrating the stones.

When he reached the pile of wood, he touched the crook of his wand to it and shouted, *"Hail Belenos, hail Satan!"*

Immediately, the pile of wood burst into flames. As the tall Druid stepped back with his wand held high, the crowd went wild. They began leaping and shouting, *"Hail Belenos, god of darkness! Hail Satan, God of darkness!"*

Hermano sat back down and searched through his jacket pockets for his notebook and pen. In a few minutes he would have to leave his trench and circle the clearing. The night before, he had located the only place large enough to serve as a parking area. It was a small meadow, about seventy or eighty yards west of this larger clearing.

Apparently, what was going on below was only a Beltane fire ceremony and he wasn't sure how much longer it would last. The way the participants were getting along, he doubted that it would go much longer. Hermano stood up and glanced out the slit. He was surprised to see what looked like the beginning of another ceremony. Or, since he wasn't familiar with the Druid fire festival, it could have been a continuation of what he had already witnessed.

Nine members of the group, three abreast and three deep, had taken positions within the circle—between the bonfire and the rectangular wooden slab. The tall Druid stood at the opposite end of the slab, facing the fire.

As Hermano watched, a small group of four or five black robed people solemnly entered the clearing from a point behind and slightly to the left of the Druid. They slowly approached the altar.

Hermano stepped back from the slit and stooped over pressing his shoulders up against the plywood while slowly freeing the two corner posts. Dropping them to the floor of the trench, he squatted slightly and lowered the plywood back to the ground. Turning, he stepped to the back of the trench, scooped up two longer posts, and stood on the bucket. Again, placing his shoulders against the plywood, he slowly straightened up, lifting the back of the plywood a couple of feet before placing the two-foot long posts at the corners. With one quick fluid movement he was out of the trench and at the tree line.

Glancing down the slope to make sure everything was as he had last seen it, he stepped into the forest. He had taken three or four steps when he stopped. Quickly, he turned and retraced his steps to the tree line. Those black robed people who had approached the altar had been laying something on it, and it had looked like- it was- a small child.

Hermano clenched his fists. A nude girl, about seven or eight years old, was laying on the altar. The tall Druid was still standing at the other end, but he had traded his wand for what looked like a short sickle.

He was holding the sickle aloft in his left hand. The Druid's right arm was extended horizontally over the child with his palm down. With a low, rumbling baritone, he began his invocation, "*Oh mighty Belenos, we invoke you in the name of Satan. Oh blessed Andraste, we invoke you in the name of the Prince of darkness. Oh clever Cernunnos, we invoke you in the name of Lucifer!*"

Hermano leaped from the tree-line and landed upright six or seven feet down the slope. With his right hand outstretched and his index finger pointing at the Druid priest, his voice cracked like thunder when he roared out, "*In the name of Jesus Christ, release that child!*"

Pandemonium erupted in the clearing below as everyone turned to look up at Hermano. The tall Druid pointed at Hermano, but before he had a chance to shout back, a huge dark shape materialized behind his back.

Several things seemed to happen at once. A fist-sized metallic object arced from the direction of the phantom to land in the midst of the nine who were on the Druid's side of the bonfire. At the same time, the Druid's head—hood and all—seemed to fly off his shoulders. The dark shape scooped up the child and was moving back toward the tree line when the metallic object exploded—engulfing the nine in a kind of white fire.

The phantom paused at the tree-line and hurled another metallic object over the bonfire. It landed just in front of the rest of the satanists, who had started scrambling up the slope toward Hermano. Hermano turned and leaped back into the forest a split second before it exploded. He dodged forty or fifty yards farther up the slope through the trees and veered off to the right to circle the clearing. The moon was waning, two or three nights past the full, so there was plenty of light to see by.

Hermano could hear screams coming from the clearing. He was tempted to go back and offer aid, but he was determined to find out if what he had just witnessed was really a rescue. There was still a little girl out in these woods somewhere, and he wasn't sure what it was that had her.

Hermano glided through the trees and brush like a creature born to the woods, and in less than ten minutes he was at the parking area. The air reeked with the smell of gasoline, but he didn't see anyone near the cars as he sprinted up the trail that led back to Rampart Range Road. He had run less than a hundred yards up the trail when he stopped dead in his tracks.

"Freeze!" The man was standing at a bend in the trail with a flashlight, pointed at Hermano's face, in his left hand and what looked like an Uzi in his right. The Uzi was pointed at Hermano's midsection *"What the hell's going on back there? And who are you?"*

Before he could answer, Hermano caught a movement out of the corner of his eye. Something big was coming out of the trees behind the man and to his right. Hermano could tell what it was this time—a huge bear of a man dressed all in black. His hands, held aloft, were clutching the hilt of a huge broadsword. *"You'd better speak up mother-----,"* the gunman's right arm, severed at the shoulder, dropped to the path. The big man swung again, and the gunman's head was gone, bouncing down the path behind Hermano. Hermano stepped back reflexively to avoid the blood, spurting three or four feet into the air from the man's neck. The guard dropped the flashlight and crumpled quietly to the path between Hermano and the phantom.

"I don't think you'd better pass the plate tonight, preacher."

The big man reached down and pried the Uzi from the dead man's fingers, sticking it into his belt. Next, he grabbed a ballcap out of the dead man's pocket and began wiping the blood from the blade of the sword. *"You got balls, preacher,"* he said, studying Hermano curiously. *"You want to get yourself and that little girl out of here alive?"*

Hermano nodded.

"There's another guard at the end of this trail—back at Rampart

Range. There's two more, a half-mile in either direction from there—you got a car stashed around here?"

Hermano nodded again, he had trouble finding his voice. *"A couple of miles north on Rampart Range."*

"Good, take the girl—she's over there," he pointed with the sword toward the north side of the path, *"five or ten yards into the woods.*

She's asleep—drugged or something. Do you know how to get to Woodland Park, just off Rampart Range?"

"Yes," Hermano was beginning to relax. He reached down and picked up the flashlight.

"Hit 24 and head back toward Colorado Springs. When you get to Cascade, look for the post office, it's on the left side of the highway. Across 24 from the post office there's a dirt road. Take the dirt road about two blocks and you'll see an old church on your right—it just says 'church' on the sign out front. It'll be unlocked. Lay the girl on one of the church pews and get out of there as fast you can. As you leave, honk your horn three times. It sounds silly, but—well, it probably won't sound silly to you—the preacher wants to be able to truthfully say that he didn't see who left her. Take care, I've got some unfinished business here. Watch out for those guards."

As quickly as he had appeared, the big man was gone, vanished into the woods to Hermano's left. Using the dead man's flashlight, Hermano quickly located the little girl. Still nude, and curled into a fetal position, she was sleeping soundly where the big man had indicated. Hermano took off his field jacket and quickly wrapped it around her. Picking her up, he carefully began making his way north, calculating a route that would bring them to Rampart Range at least a mile north of the cut-off.

He'd been walking less than five minutes when he heard a horrendous explosion from the direction of the parking area. He stopped and looked behind and to his right. A simmering red glow, which seemed to be gaining in intensity, caused him to remember the smell of gasoline as he had run through the parked cars. He hefted the child over his shoulder and began walking a little faster.

It was over an hour before he got to Rampart Range Road and by then he could no longer see a red glow in the south-east.

Apparently, the fire hadn't burned beyond the parking area. He rested for a few moments and then continued on to his jeep.

The drive to Cascade took thirty or forty minutes and Hermano found the "church" just as the big man had described it. The door was unlocked, and someone had left the heat on, so Hermano didn't feel guilty about retrieving his jacket. He quickly walked back to the Jeep, honked three times and drove off.

Hermano didn't know whether anyone at the Black Mass had recognized him, but he thought that it might be prudent to get out of Colorado Springs for a while. He'd been renting a room by the week at a Manitou Springs motel, so he drove straight there, picked up his belongings and drove back west on 24. He'd decided to camp up in the mountains for a couple of weeks. He wanted some time alone to think—and pray—about what he had witnessed tonight.

Chapter 2

Toby believed in leaving them dead or dying, and he didn't believe in leaving until his job was done. As soon as he had walked away from Hermano, it was as if a killing machine had been turned on. He was totally focused on exterminating satanists, and the more terrifying and painful their deaths, the better.

He moved as quickly and quietly through the woods as his six-foot six-inch, 300-pound frame would allow, and was back at the parking area in about five minutes. He had stood at the tree line and waited. It was only a couple of minutes before he saw a group of about a dozen black and white robed people straggle into the meadow from the opposite side. They stopped just inside the clearing.

"Lenny!" One of them called out.

"I think this is Lenny," the voice came from the tree line about ten yards to the group's right. A green-robed figure was bent over a body laying just inside the meadow. He jumped back away from it. *"His head's missing!"* He exclaimed.

The group was quiet for a full minute.

"Is he the only guard?" Asked the green-robed figure as he joined the others.

"Yeah, here. There's four more on the road. We'd better get out of here." One of the black-robed figures started for the cars. The others hesitated for a moment and then followed.

Most of the group piled into four cars-on the other side of the meadow from Toby. Toby wasn't concerned about having a clear field of fire, though. His intentions were to have a *whole* field of fire.

He had punctured all the gas tanks earlier, before rescuing the girl, and there had been plenty of time for the meadow to get completely soaked with gasoline.

He reached into a black canvas bag attached to his belt and pulled out a green cylindrical object about four inches high. He hadn't been too sure of the effectiveness of these old white phosphorus grenades until tonight. The first two had certainly been effective, though. He was preparing to pull the pin when he saw three more stragglers enter the meadow from the other side. Toby waited for them to get to their cars—then he pulled the pin and tossed the grenade. It landed in the center of the meadow and bounced under one of the occupied cars.

Toby stepped back into the forest just as the grenade exploded. He could hear screams as the meadow was transformed into a blazing inferno. Except for a little mopping up, this job was nearly complete.

He made his way back to the path and casually walked toward the point where he had left Hermano and the dead guard. He wanted to get the three remaining guards before he searched for any more stragglers, and the overheard conversation of the group he had just incinerated in the meadow had given him an idea.

Earlier, when he had decapitated the guard in the parking area, he had inadvertently destroyed the men's two-way radio. But when he had heard his name, Lenny, mentioned by the green-robed man, Toby had thought of a way to lure in the remaining guards.

When he reached the point where he had left Hermano, Toby stooped over the dead guard. A two-way radio, which appeared to be undamaged, was clipped to the man's belt. Toby reached down and picked it up, pulling out the antenna. He held it to his mouth. "*Security,*" he rasped, "*come in, over.*"

Silence.

"*Security, Lenny's been hurt-and Dr. Milton asked me to call you in, over.*"

"No names over the air," the voice cracked back from the radio.

"Sorry," Toby rasped. *"We've had a couple of accidents and now we've got a security problem. All of you're supposed to come in—and bring the wagon. Over and out."* Toby turned off the radio and, taking a handkerchief out of his hip pocket, wiped off any possible fingerprints. He bent over and reattached the radio to the dead man's belt.

Next, laying his sword on the path, he reached into his bag and took out another white-phosphorus grenade. Holding the grenade lever tightly against the grenade, he pulled the pin. Stooping over the dead guard he pressed the grenade lever against the man's breastbone and gently rolled him over onto his chest. Carefully pulling out his hand, he looked around on the path until he had located the dead man's head. Toby placed the head, face down, at the proper place above the shoulders, and, grabbing the severed arm, tossed it into the trees. Scooping up the sword, he then positioned himself about twenty yards up the path-and waited.

Toby was used to waiting. In the ten years that he had been warring against satanists he had done a lot of waiting. He sat down on a tree-stump beside the path and, sticking the point of the sword into the ground, held the hilt loosely in both hands. He never touched the sword that he didn't think about his niece.

He'd bought the sword for his niece. It wasn't that she was a tomboy, it was just that, aside from his brother and sister-in-law, she was the only family he had. From the time that she was born, he had made it a point of getting her a relevant souvenir from each place that he had been stationed. His last duty station, before his retirement from the military, had been in the Mideast. He had found the sword at a little shop in Beirut. The proprietor had assured him that it was an authentic antique sword, left in the Mideast during the Crusades. Toby wasn't an expert on antiquities, but he did consider himself to be an expert on weapons, and he had never seen a sword to compare with this one. The blade was super-hard and well-balanced-with a broad perpendicular hilt. The grip was crafted of bronze and shaped to resemble a coiled spring. The letters *I.N.R.I.*, each about an inch high, were slightly raised and arranged vertically on either side of the grip. They were arranged in such a way that if the sword was raised point-up, they could be read on one side, and if the sword was placed point-down they could be read on the other. He had felt that he was getting away cheap when the sword had only cost him a month's wages.

Toby was only thirty-eight when he retired from the Air Force. In the excitement of becoming a free bachelor with a comfortable income, he had completely forgotten about his intended gift. And then his niece was gone.

She had been snatched out of a busy shopping center in broad daylight in a little town north of Dallas, Texas. Toby had set up residence in Dallas, but for several weeks after the abduction, almost all this time was spent in Denton, the site of the kidnapping. His brother and sister-in-law had lived in Denton for years, but Toby was a relative stranger to the town. That didn't last long.

As hours dragged into days, with no apparent progress being made by the police department, Toby's patience gave way to anger. Anger at his brother for not pushing the police harder, and anger at the police for not trying harder. His abrasive treatment of everyone associated with the investigation had finally culminated in a violent argument between himself and his brother.

His niece was never found, and he didn't see or speak to his brother again for several months. He'd never forget the next time he saw his brother, though. It was the last time that he had seen him alive.

It had been ten years, but he remembered it as vividly as if it had only been last night. His brother had shown up at Toby's house in the early morning hours, so frightened that it had been several minutes before Toby could get him to talk. When he finally did talk, he told a story so bizarre that Toby could hardly believe it.

His brother had related that he and his wife were members of an organization called the *Church of Satan*. Their daughter, Toby's niece, had been a human sacrifice. Toby's brother talked for at least an hour, relating a story that Toby had thought was the raving of a lunatic. He had said that certain members of the police department, and other respected members of the community were involved. He named names, and he kept repeating that his daughter had been conceived to be sacrificed.

"It was her destiny," he had said.

Toby had listened for as long as he could stand it, but finally, in a fit of rage, he had kicked him out. His brother's parting shot had been to whine that his group was concerned about his mental stability and were planning to kill him. If Toby had believed his story, though-he probably would have killed him, himself.

The next day Toby had learned that his brother was dead. He and his wife reportedly had died when their house had burned-the night before. Toby had remained cool and calm. After the funeral he had taken a short vacation to collect his thoughts. Then, for the next several months, he had done a thorough investigation of everyone that his brother had mentioned. There had been 15 of them, and Toby had determined to kill them all. Slowly and methodically. He would not only kill them but would do it in such a terrifying way-one at a time-that the survivors would live in constant dread. Until it was their turn.

It was a strength of the organization that none of the members could be connected, either in business or socially. So, their strength became their trap. When he began killing them, the survivors couldn't seek police protection, unless they wanted to tell the truth-none did.

Their executions had taken several months. He had saved the high priest for last, a man who was so terrified by the time that Toby had gotten around to him, that Toby had had to chase him over half the country before catching him. Toby had cleaved him almost in half with the old broadsword. 'Old Henry', as he called the sword, had been his instrument of terror in most of the executions.

When it was over, Toby had tried to get back into the lazy life of "retired bachelor", but it was useless-his eyes had been opened. He was old-fashioned. A patriot. He had spent most of his life defending his nation from foreign threats, only to learn that the real enemy was right here at home.

About six months after he had killed the high priest, Toby began following up leads that he had obtained when investigating his brother's satanic church. He had killed scores of satanists since then. A few with the sword, but most of the executions he had made to look natural or accidental.

About a year earlier he had started watching a couple of philosophy professors at Louisiana State University, Dr. Milton and Dr. Olson. They were both satanic high priests, whose specialty was recruitment. Between the two of them, they had probably recruited more satanists than Toby had exterminated.

Dr. Olson had had two passions outside philosophy—young college coeds and deep-sea fishing. The combination had proved to be his undoing. Last summer, Toby had rented a boat from a retired Air Force major who lived in New Orleans. He had then berthed it in the same Marina where Dr. Olson kept his boat. Toby had stocked up with plenty of food for what he had thought was going to be an extended waiting game but, as it turned out, he had only had to wait for three days.

Early one Saturday morning, with one of his pretty satanic priestesses in tow, Dr. Olson had put out to sea for a weekend of indulging his passions.

Like some great shark following a school of tuna, Toby had trailed along behind, always remaining just barely in sight.

As it grew dark, Dr. Olson had anchored fairly close to the Louisiana shoreline.

Toby brought his boat to within 300 yards of Dr. Olson's before he killed the engine and dropped anchor. About four o'clock the next morning, Toby had quietly rowed over to the other boat in a small rubber dingy.

It was a warm summer night and Toby had caught them both sleeping on deck. He had killed the priestess out-right with Old Henry. But with cold detachment, he viewed Dr. Olson as a valuable source of information. After knocking him unconscious, Toby had dropped him into the dingy, which was tied alongside. He then began soaking the deck of Olson's boat with fuel. This accomplished, he had climbed back into the dingy and cast off. He had paused long enough to ignite Dr. Olson's boat with a flare gun, and then had rowed back to his own boat with Dr. Olson lying unconscious at his feet. He had left the satanic priestess to burn with the boat.

It had turned out that Dr. Olson had had an incredible amount of information. Toby had let him live for three days, tied to a heavy metal chair in the cabin, while he cruised south in the Gulf of Mexico.

Dr. Olson had witnessed the slaughter of his lover, so Toby hadn't had to resort to torture to make him talk. He only had to pull up a chair in front of him and start sharpening Old Henry.

Dr. Olson would immediately begin talking. Whenever he stopped talking-Toby would stop sharpening and begin glaring at him.

In three days, Toby had spoken only one sentence to him. On the first day, as soon as Dr. Olson, tied to the chair, had regained consciousness, Toby had said, *"When you finish telling me every detail about the Church of Satan and the people in it-I'm going to kill you."*

On the third day, Toby had just poured himself a cup of coffee and had sat back down in front of Dr. Olson, when the professor's mind snapped. Toby had leaned Old Henry, point down, against his leg while he drank his coffee and Dr. Olson's eyes seemed to transfix on the hilt of the sword.

"I-N-R-I?" He glanced down at the floor and appeared to be thinking. *"INRI! No! N-o-o-o!"*

He had begun thrashing around so much in the chair that it toppled over backwards. Still tied up, he had laid on his back-screaming curses at Jesus Christ as he continued to kick and strain at the ropes.

Toby leaned Old Henry against the bulkhead and, grabbing the legs of Dr. Olson's chair, began dragging him out onto the deck. Without hesitation, he picked him up, chair and all, and tossed him over the side.

Dr. Olson had been a veritable gold mine of information. Toby had figured that he had picked up enough names to keep him busy for years.

The biggest upcoming event, according to Dr. Olson, was a "fire festival" which was going to be held somewhere in Colorado on the last day of April of the coming year. Dr. Olson, Dr. Milton, a dozen or so other satanic high priests, and representatives of an organization which Dr. Olson had called "ID" were to be in attendance. Dr. Olson had called it a "marriage of philosophies".

Toby had been excited at the prospect of catching so many satanic high priests in one spot, but the fire-festival was still ten months off. Uncharacteristically inpatient, Toby decided to content himself with working off some of the lower-level names on Olson's list. In San Francisco, Los Angeles, and Salt Lake City he had eliminated an even dozen by Christmas.

After the first of the year, though, Toby had remained inactive until a month ago. At that time, he had bugged Dr. Milton's apartment and had begun listening-and hoping-for any sort of clue that would lead him to the site of the fire-festival. His patience had paid off five days ago, when he had overheard Dr. Milton make an airline reservation to Colorado Springs. The reservation had been for yesterday morning, so Toby had had three days to drive to Colorado.

Toby had arrived in Colorado Springs the day before yesterday and had been able to secure a motel room with a private telephone. Using the Yellow Pages, he had begun calling hotels to check on a reservation for Dr. John Milton. Fortunately, the Four Seasons Hotel wasn't far down the list, so it hadn't taken him long to learn where Dr. Milton would be staying. Relieved, Toby had grabbed an early supper and had turned in for the evening.

He had felt refreshed the next morning, and after breakfast he had driven to the airport to observe Dr. Milton's arrival. Toby had found a good vantage point near the receiving area for gate 18 and had watched as Dr. Milton was met by a young well-dressed man in his mid-twenties. The young man was clean-cut, and to all appearances, it was the young executive greeting a visiting business associate.

Toby had followed them from the airport to the Four Seasons, and when Dr. Milton was dropped off Toby had decided to stay with the young man. It had turned out to be a boring and apparently unprofitable afternoon.

The man had driven to a shopping mall and had spent the next four hours walking aimlessly from shop to shop, stopping occasionally to make a small purchase. Except for the clerks, the only person to whom the man had spoken had been a tall slender man in his mid-thirties who had been accompanied by a little girl. Their conversation had been little more than a greeting so, at the time, Toby hadn't placed much importance on it.

After the shopping mall, the young man had driven to a middle-class residence on the west side of Colorado Springs which, because of the man's casual familiarity with the place, Toby had assumed was his home. The man had had a key to the front door and after he had been inside for fifteen or twenty minutes, Toby had decided to drive his old station wagon back to his motel room and clean up before supper.

He'd gotten back to his room just in time for the five o'clock news. On the local news, the top news story had been the abduction of a seven-year-old little girl. Toby had sat and watched with rising interest as the newscaster described the apparent abduction, which had occurred that afternoon at a local shopping center.

Toby tensed up and scooted his chair closer to the television when he saw the man whom his man had greeted at the shopping center-the man with the little girl. He was standing near a fountain in the shopping center, talking with a television news reporter. The man explained that he had left his little girl in the toy section of a department store while he had looked for some fishing gear in the sporting goods section. When he had returned for his daughter, no more than ten minutes later, she was nowhere to be found. He said that he had looked for her for nearly an hour before calling the police. The time that he gave for her disappearance was half an hour *before* Toby had seen him with a little girl-talking to his man.

Toby had watched the rest of the news to see if there was going to be any update and then had turned the television off. Déjà vu. The news report had reminded Toby of when his niece had been abducted. In that abduction one of the members of his brother's satanic church had been on hand to give the police misleading information. Somebody like the clean-cut young man.

Toby cleaned up and then had driven back by the young man's house. Several police cars and a car with a local newspaper's name on the side were parked out front. Toby had driven around for a while to familiarize himself with the city, and then had circled back by the young man's house. This time all the cars had been gone, including the young man's.

It was approaching seven o'clock. Since, when he was at home, Dr. Milton usually ate dinner between seven-thirty and eight, Toby had driven back over to the Four Seasons. The young man's car had been parked in the parking lot.

Toby had parked his own car a few spaces away from the red Firebird, and then had entered the Four Seasons restaurant. The dining room was crowded, but he had spotted Dr. Milton, the young man and two other man seated at a table near the other end of the restaurant. Toby had taken a seat near the cash register and then had ordered a cup of coffee.

The two strangers were both in their mid-thirties and well-dressed. Dr. Milton and the young man had been drinking cocktails, but the other two had been having coffee. The two strangers had gotten up to leave within ten or fifteen minutes of Toby's arrival.

It looked like the young man was going to stay awhile, so Toby had hurriedly paid his check and was sitting in his car when the two strangers left the restaurant. They both had climbed into a new light green Ford sedan and headed toward downtown Colorado Springs. Toby had followed them to the Colorado Springs Police Department where they had parked in a reserved space. Toby had thoughtfully driven back to the Four Seasons. A member of his brother's satanic church had been a police lieutenant.

The young man's car was still in the parking lot. Toby wheeled into the space to the left of the car and killed his engine. He had already made up his mind. The "fire festival" -whatever that was-was tomorrow night and Toby had a feeling that that little girl was going to be the main attraction.

He had been sitting in his station wagon for about twenty minutes when he spotted the young man leaving the hotel. There had been a party of half a dozen people walking toward the hotel from the parking lot when the young man came out, but they were safely out of sight inside the hotel by the time the young man had reached his car.

Toby had slid over to the passenger side of his station wagon and, just before the young man had reached his car, Toby opened his door and casually got out. He had had a tire-iron, held out of sight, in his right hand. Toby had only left a couple of feet between the cars and he had smiled at the young man who was patiently waiting for him to get out of the way. Toby had squeezed past him and then had spun around, smacking the young man in the back of the head with the tire tool. The young man, dropping his keys, had pitched forward onto the back of his Firebird.

Ten minutes later, Toby was driving west toward the mountains with old Henry and a canvas bag full of grenades in the backseat, and the young man in the trunk.

Chapter 3

Toby had driven west on 24 for about thirty miles and then, at the Continental Divide, had driven north on a dirt road from Fluorescent. Finding a trail which wound into the trees about five miles out, he had taken it and then had parked two or three hundred yards from the road.

Gathering some firewood, Toby had made a small fire and then had pulled the young man out of the trunk. He had still been unconscious. Toby had bound his wrists behind his back with some duct tape, which he had had in his canvas bag, and pulling the young man's shoes and socks off, had then taped his legs together just above the ankles. Then, Toby had sat beside the campfire and waited until the young man regained consciousness.

"What happened? Where am I?" The young man tried to sit up.

Toby pushed him back down. *"Shut-up,"* he growled. He slowly got to his feet and brushed himself off, all the time glaring at the young man. Reaching down, he grabbed him by the ankles and dragged him over closer to the fire. *"I knocked you in the head and kidnapped you,"* Toby stated flatly. *"Like you people did to that little girl. Now, we're way out in the woods—where no one can hear your screams."*

Toby reached down and tossed another piece of wood on the fire. *"You're going to tell me everything you know about the little girl and the fire festival-or I'm going to fry your feet."*

"I told the police all I know, I swear. A man had her by the arm and they were arguing, but I thought it was a little girl and her dad."

Toby kicked the man's feet into the fire. The young man's agonized scream pierced the stillness of the forest. After two- or three-seconds Toby reached down and, grasping the man's pants legs, yanked his feet from the fire. The young man was sobbing. *"What method of sacrifice are they going to use on the girl?"* Toby asked.

By five o'clock the next morning, Toby had been satisfied that he had gotten all the relevant information that the young man had had. He had then knocked him unconscious again and, taping his mouth shut, had tossed him back into the trunk. Putting out the campfire, Toby, lost in thought, had then driven into Woodland Park for breakfast.

In the ten years that he had been killing satanists, Toby had run across quite a few kindred spirits. One of them had been an Air Force chaplain that he had contacted about eight years previously. The chaplain had been engaged in a legal battle with the Department of Defense over a revision in the *Chaplain's Handbook* which had accommodated members of the Church of Satan. Toby had merely written him a letter thanking him for trying to do the right thing and had offered to help in any way that he could.

The chaplain hadn't accepted any help, but he *had* answered his letter. Every Christmas and Easter since then, Toby had received a card from the chaplain. The chaplain had lost his suit with the Department of Defense and, soon after that, resigned his commission in the Air Force. For the past few years, the cards had been coming from the little town of Cascade, near Colorado Springs, where the chaplain was now a Baptist preacher.

Toby had had his name and telephone number in his wallet and after breakfast he had given him a call from a pay phone in the restaurant.

Toby had gotten straight to the point and, fortunately, the chaplain had had enough presence of mind not to ask any questions. Toby had explained that he was still investigating satanists and had stumbled into a child abduction. He had said that he was going to try a rescue, but some satanists would probably get hurt, consequently he wouldn't be able to take the child to the police afterwards.

The chaplain had told him how to drop off the child and, after saying that he would pray for him, had hung up.

Toby got a morning paper and sat back down for cup of coffee. It had been a little after seven by then, and it would be eight o'clock before Toby could make his next phone call.

Toby had wanted to do all that he could to keep the disappearance of the young man from upsetting the evening's "fire festival", so the last half hour of the interrogation had all related to personal information. The young man's name was Robert Mahon. He was a junior executive for an insurance company headquartered in downtown Colorado Springs. His office opened at eight o'clock, but Robert generally didn't arrive until nine.

At eight o'clock Toby had telephoned the insurance office claiming to be Robert's Uncle Larry. He had told the telephone receptionist that Robert's dad had had a massive heart attack and wasn't expected to live. The young man had told Toby that his parents lived in suburban Chicago, so Toby had told the receptionist that Robert's dad was en route to a Chicago hospital at that moment when the receptionist had told Toby that Robert usually didn't arrive at the office until nine, Toby had said that he had already tried to catch him at home. He told the receptionist that no one was at Robert's parent's house and that if he should continue to miss Robert at home, then she should tell him to call his Uncle Larry. He had told the receptionist that Robert had his telephone number.

That accomplished, Toby had spent the rest of the morning scouting out Rampart Range Road. Robert and a member of 'Id' were responsible for security, so Toby had been able to get precise information. He had easily located the trail that led to the site of the Black Mass, and then the spots where the guards were to be posted that night. Three of the road guards would be dropped off by the fourth, who would feign car trouble at the northernmost guard site. His vehicle, a station wagon, would be the only car on the road.

Once Toby had been satisfied that, under the circumstances, he was as prepared as he could get, he had located a secluded spot about six or seven miles north of the "fire festival" site where he could remain out of sight and get some sleep.

He had slept until three-thirty in the afternoon in the front seat of Robert's car, and immediately upon awakening had got out of the car to check the trunk. He hadn't heard a sound out of Robert since he had loaded him in the trunk that morning, and Toby was beginning to wonder if he was still alive.

Rigor mortis was already setting in. Apparently, Toby had hit him harder than he had intended. Pausing to think for a moment, Toby then had removed the tape from Roberts mouth, wrists and ankles and, tossing it into the woods, had wiped down the trunk area in an attempt to get rid of any possible fingerprints.

Next, he had driven to within a mile of the trail that led to the "fire festival" and, turning off the road, had driven Robert's car as far into the forest as he could. He had finally become stuck in a gully about two hundred yards off the road, where, after having finished his wipe-down of the car, he had left it. With the canvas bag strapped to his belt and old Henry in hand, he had then hiked back to the road and had begun making his way toward the fire festival.

By dusk, Toby had taken up a position near the parking area and had begun counting the arrivals. There had already been four people there-a guard near the parking area and three other people in a large clearing beyond the parking area.

The rest of the guests all arrived within thirty minutes of each other. Toby had counted a total of forty-two. They had all disrobed near their cars and had donned various colored robes before proceeding on to the other clearing. The last car to arrive had been a new, dark green Lincoln. Two men and two women had gotten out of the car, and after they had changed into their robes, one of the men had opened a rear door and had lifted out a little girl. The little girl had been unconscious and wrapped in a red blanket which they had tossed back into the car. The little girl had been naked and one of the women had made a remark which Toby couldn't hear but which had caused the other women to laugh raucously. Then, carrying the little girl, they had begun walking toward the other clearing.

Toby had thought about jumping them then, but he had lost sight of the security man and hadn't relocated him until they were already well on their way to the other clearing. It had gotten almost dark by then and Toby didn't have to worry so much about being seen. He carefully began working his way around the clearing.

The security guard, who had been smoking a cigarette near the path which led to the other clearing, hadn't heard Toby's approach until it was too late. When Toby had raised the sword, the tip of it had rustled an Aspen branch. The cigarette butt dropped out of the man's mouth as he swiveled his head in the direction of the sound. It was too late, though. Toby had already begun his swing. After smashing the dead man's radio, Toby, using Old Henry, had punctured the gas tanks of every car in the clearing. Then he had followed the path to the larger clearing.

He had arrived just as the child was being laid on a large wooden slab. A tall hooded figure in a white robe was standing at the foot of the slab. He was holding what looked like a small curved sickle of some sort in his left hand. The man had immediately began chanting as the girl was laid down. The four who Toby had followed from the parking area had quickly circled to the other side of a large bonfire. They took up positions with a large group of robed people who were standing slightly up from the base of a slope on the other side of the fire and began watching the white-robed figure between them and Toby.

In the meantime, Toby had unsnapped his canvas bag and had pulled out a grenade. He had been trying to decide whether to throw the grenade at the large group of people on the slope or at a smaller group closer to the altar, when Hermano had leaped from the tree-line above the satanists.

Toby and the tall hooded man at the altar had been the only ones to see Hermano's entrance, but when Hermano had roared out, "In the name of Jesus Christ," all heads had turned to look up the slope.

It had been a distraction of which Toby had instinctively taken advantage. Pulling the pin with his teeth, he had tossed the grenade at the nearer group and, in a crouch, had rushed the altar. Slowing down only enough to lop off the tall man's head, he had scooped up the girl and was almost back to the concealing shadows of the trees before the grenade exploded.

Toby paused at the tree-line long enough to toss another grenade, which he had hoped would serve as cover for the man at the top of the slope. Then he had raced back up the path. Passing the dead guard, he could smell the gasoline as he rushed through the parking area and ran up the trail toward the road. After a few seconds, when he had reached a slight bend of the trail, Toby had walked a short distance into the woods and carefully laid down the little girl. He had decided to wait at the bend for the guard that he had felt certain would come.

He had no sooner turned to walk back to the trail, when he heard a man, his voice coming from the vicinity of the trail, holler "*Freeze!*"

Toby, realizing that the command hadn't been directed at him, had quickly moved toward the voice. Leaving the trees, for the second time that evening he had unhesitating taken advantage of a distraction by Hermano.

Toby stood up and stretched his legs. He'd been waiting near the booby-trapped body for about fifteen minutes. He was beginning to wonder if the remaining three road guards had decided to walk, when he saw a flash of light on the treetops. A car was approaching from the direction of Rampart Range. Toby stepped off the trail and crouched behind a tree.

The station wagon slowly drove past Toby's position and stopped about ten yards short of where the dead guard lay. The front door on the passenger side and the rear door on the driver's side opened and two men, both holding Uzis, got out. As they cautiously approached the still figure on the trail, the driver's door opened, and the driver got out, leaving the lights on and the car running. A tall man, he leaned over the top of the door and peered at the corpse.

"Who is it?" He asked.

"Can't tell, he's laying on his stomach," both guards were standing over the dead man now, and the one who had answered the driver bent over and rolled the corpse over onto its back.

Toby heard the faint "ping" of the detaching grenade lever and instinctively ducked his head. The explosion engulfed the two guards with white death and knocked the driver onto his back near the rear of the wagon. Toby was out of the trees and on him before he could start getting to his feet. With a violent downward slash, Toby cleaved him from a point between his left shoulder and neck to a point near his midsection. Then Toby leaped into the station wagon and backed it up about twenty yards. Turning off the lights, he killed the engine.

After taking the ignition key and climbing out of the station wagon, he then began walking back toward the fire festival. Skirting the parking area, Toby noticed that the fire was less intense now than it had been a few minutes before.

The trees bordering the clearing were all Aspen and their newly budding leaves apparently hadn't offered much in the way of fuel for the fire. It was now confined to the burning hulks of metal that littered the clearing like a handful of charcoal briquettes tossed onto a smoldering campfire.

Toby paused at the path which led to the larger clearing and, switching the sword to his left hand, pulled out the Uzi.

The larger clearing looked like a battle-zone. Charred bodies were scattered about everywhere. Toby stood just inside the clearing, and for the first time in almost a week, smile.

As he surveyed the area, he noticed some movement near the tree line about twenty yards to his left. Cautiously, he walked over and found two badly burned men wearing the charred remains of white robes. They were both laying on their backs and began moaning as Toby approached.

Without a word, Toby calmly stood over them and unloaded half a dozen rounds into each.

Walking the tree line, he checked to make sure that there were no more survivors. Completing his circle, Toby walked over to where the tall Druid lay and, glancing around at the ground, stooped and picked up his head. He was curious to see if it was the girl's dad. Toby had only seen him from behind and he was about the same height as the man who Toby had seen at the mall.

Not recognizing the face, Toby carried the head over to the man's torso. Smiling again, he reached down and, taking the man's left hand, wrapped its fingers around the bloody beard. He carefully laid the hand and head down. Next, being careful not to leave fingerprints, he retrieved the sickle from beside the altar and, after dipping the blade in the dead man's blood, put the handle in his right hand.

Satisfied with the effect, Toby chuckled and turned to begin a head count of the bodies. They were all accounted for, none had escaped.

His business almost finished, Toby walked back up the path toward the parking area. He stopped where the dead guard lay and, wiping all the fingerprints off the Uzi put it in the dead man's hand. Then, holding the guard's finger on the trigger, Toby squeezed a few rounds into the air. Chuckling again, Toby circled the clearing and began walking back toward the guard's station- wagon.

Chapter 4

May 1 was a black day for the Hunt family. For Deirdre Hunt it began at 4:30 a.m. That's when the panic call from her dad had come in.

The Hunt family ranch was located in north-central Texas, about twenty miles west of Fort Worth. The house, at first glance an odd-looking potpourri of architecture, sat in the middle of five thousand acres of prime ranch land. On closer inspection, it became apparent that the house was actually a solid old two-story wood frame farmhouse onto which a sprawling modernistic east wing had been added. Since the east wing had been added after oil had been discovered on Hunt land, Deirdre's brother, Bill, jokingly called the clashing styles "pre-oil" and "post-oil". To the north, behind the the east wing, was an Olympic-size swimming pool and a little farther back-a helicopter pad, both of which were also "post-oil".

When the oil money had started flowing ten years earlier and the east wing had been added, Deirdre's mother had refused to move out of their upstairs bedroom in the old house. So, fourteen-year-old Deirdre, and Bill, who was then twelve, were given free run of the east wing.

The radio for communicating with her dad's helicopter was in the den of the east wing and Deirdre's room was closest to it. She had been the one who answered his call in the early morning hours of May 1.

When the radio buzzer had first gone off, Deirdre had rolled out of bed and, dressed in some of her brother's old pajamas, had dashed for the den. She paused at the entrance to the den and was trying to remember why she was up when the buzzer went off again. She raced across the den and, turning up the audio, grabbed the microphone.

"*This is Hunt 3, go ahead,*" she said.

"*Call the sheriff! I've flushed out some god-damned rustlers out here!*"

Deirdre heard what she thought were some gunshots and then her dad's voice was back on the air. "*Got the bastards--*" the transmission had gone dead in mid-sentence.

"*Dad!*" Deirdre waited, but there was no answer.

"*Dad, are you alright?*" Still, there was no answer. "*Hunt 1, this is Hunt 3, over. ---Hunt 1 this is Hunt 3,*" she repeated, her voice beginning to sound panicky. Deirdre dropped the microphone and ran for her brother Bill's room.

"*Bill!*" She threw his door open, flicked on the light, and rushed toward his bed. "*Bill, something happened to Dad!*" She reached down and shook him with both hands.

"*What! Who!*" Bill sat up in bed and tried to focus his eyes on his sister. Squinting in her direction, he threw off his covers and swung his feet off the bed. Wearing boxer shorts and a T-shirt, he grabbed his jeans and stumbled toward the door.

"*Where is he?*" He asked.

"*I don't know, he called on the radio, then it went dead,*" Deirdre followed her brother down the hall in the direction of the den. "*Let me get my bathrobe,*" she said, ducking into her room as Bill hurried on toward the radio.

"*Hunt 1, this is Hunt 4,*" Bill had his jeans on and was standing at the radio when Deirdre reentered the den. Fastening her robe, she paused to turn up the thermostat before walking over to join her brother.

"*Hunt 1, this is hunt 4, come in, over.*" Turning to Deirdre, Bill lowered the microphone and asked, "*What happene*d?"

"*Dad called and said that he had caught some rustlers. He said to call the sheriff.*"

Bill raised the microphone again, "*Hunt 1, this is hunt 4. Dad, are you alright? Over.*" He lowered the microphone.

"*Did he say where he was?*"

"*No, but I heard some gunshots and dad said that he had gotten somebody—that was the last thing I heard from him.*"

"*Crap! Did you call the sheriff?*"

"*Not yet.*"

Bill laid down the microphone and hurried back toward the door to the hallway. "*Get the sheriff out here, I'm gonna get dressed and take the pickup out toward the fish tank.*"

"*The fish tank?*" Deirdre, with the telephone directory opened, glanced up to look quizzically at her brother. She had been out on a date the night before and hadn't known that the whole family wasn't home until her father's emergency call a few minutes earlier.

"*Yeah. Oh, you weren't home.*" Bill paused in the doorway and looked back at his sister. "*Dad took the chopper out to the fish tank about sundown last night. He was going to camp and do some fishing. We've got half a dozen heifers that are about to calve up there and he kind of wanted to check on them, too.*"

"*The chopper! I get nervous every time he gets in that thing.*"

"*Yeah, I know-his favorite toy,*" Bill turned and walked hurriedly down the hall toward his room.

Sam Hunt had bought a helicopter and started taking flying lessons about five years earlier. He had taken to it "like a duck to water", as he would have put it, and the slightest excuse would send him running for the helipad.

It was common for him to fly to Jackson's general store, less than a mile away, for no more than a pack of cigarettes or a six- pack of beer. Bill had learned to fly, too, but neither Deirdre nor her mom would get in the thing.

Deirdre had always been afraid of it, but her mom had accompanied Sam on a lot of his flying excursions for the first couple of years. When he had landed on the lawn of the Courthouse Square in

Weatherford, though, she had climbed out of the helicopter and had refused to ever go near it again.

Deirdre was on the phone to the Sheriff's Department in Weatherford when Bill came back through. A grim look on his face, he was on his way to the built-in garage at the end of the east wing.

"*Bill,*" she held her hand over the mouthpiece.

He stopped and looked in her direction. He was carrying a lever action 3030 and a box of ammunition.

"*Be careful—and don't forget to turn on the radio.*" He nodded and walked on toward the garage.

Deirdre watched him leave. He was a grown man, now, and even bigger than her dad's six-foot frame, but she would always think of him as "little" brother.

The sheriff's deputy had promised to dispatch a car out to the ranch, so when Deirdre hung-up she hurried down the hall toward the old house. In the excitement she had completely forgotten about her mother, and she wanted to get her up before the police arrived.

After waking her mom, Deirdre had pinned up her long blond hair and had put on tight-fitting jeans and a white University of Texas sweatshirt. She was sitting on a couch in the den, sipping a cup of coffee with her mom when the doorbell finally rang. It had been almost half an hour since she had phoned the Sheriff's Department.

Dora Hunt got up and, carrying her coffee cup, hurried off toward the front door. Deirdre got up too and walked back over to the radio.

"*Hunt 4, this is Hunt 3, over,*" she took another sip of coffee.

After a few seconds, her brother's voice came back, "*Yeah, Dee.*"

"*I think the sheriff's department finally showed up, mom just went to the door. Anything new up there?*"

"*Naw, it's still too dark to see very much, though. Tell the deputy that Dad was definitely camping here. His bedroll's spread out and all the fishing gear is still here. Chopper's gone, though. Just send him on up.*"

"*OK, Hunt 4, and out.*" Deirdre laid down the microphone just as her mother, accompanied by two deputies, entered the den.

"Was that Billy?" Her mother asked.

"Yes, he said to send the deputies on up to the fishpond. Dad's gear, except for the helicopter, is up there."

After Deirdre had repeated the short conversation that she had had with her dad, the two deputies turned to go. One of the deputies was a stranger to Deirdre, but the other, a young man in his late twenties, hesitated near the hallway door. Looking back toward Deirdre's mom, he said, *"Don't worry, ma'am, we'll find him."*

"What took you so long?" Deirdre could barely control her rising anger. *"He could be hurt out there, somewhere."*

The older man stopped and looked at Deirdre. *"Sorry, ma'am. We've been real busy, tonight. Everything from vandalism to flying saucers. We just couldn't get out here any quicker. Sorry."* He turned and followed his partner down the hall.

"Do you know where the fishpond is?" She called out.

"Yes, ma'am," the younger man replied, *"I was out there with my dad and Mr. Hunt a couple of years ago."* Deirdre heard the hallway door into the old house slam. Apparently, the deputies were hurrying, now.

Slightly mollified, Deirdre turned to her mom, *"Do you know them?"* she asked.

"I think the young one is Frank Pierce's boy. I don't know the other one". Dora Hunt sat back on the couch and nervously brushed her hair back from her forehead. Still attractive, she was an older edition of Deirdre. Even though it was still cool in the room, she was perspiring profusely. *"I can't stand this waiting,"* she said.

Deirdre glanced out the patio doors, she could vaguely see the swimming pool and helipad now. *"It's starting to get light,"* she commented. *"We should find out something pretty soon."*

"Base, this is Hunt 4." Deirdre had turned the volume on the radio almost all the way up. The sudden noise caused them both to jump.

Deirdre walked over and picked up the microphone, *"This is Hunt 3, over."*

"Dee, we need to get an air search going out here. Did the deputy say anything about that? Over."

"No, and there were two of them. They're on their way out there now, over."

There was silence for a moment and then Bill's voice came back, *"Look, Dee, why don't you call Silas Cooper over at Early Bird and see if he'll fly his chopper out here? Over."*

"Will do, I'll get back with you. Out."

"Oh, Dee? There's a dead cow out here, about 100 yards from dad's campsite. It's, uh, well I'll tell you later. I need to check it out better in the light. Over and out."

Silas Cooper lived at Early Bird Airport, a small strip just inside Tarrant County, between Weatherford and Fort Worth. There were a few private planes and helicopters based there, but it served mainly as a fuel stop for small private planes and helicopters traveling into the Dallas-Fort Worth Metroplex. Silas had located and helped Sam Hunt arrange the purchase of Sam's helicopter and had given both Sam and Bill Hunt their flying lessons. A small wiry man in his late 60's, Silas was a bundle of energy who never seemed to sleep.

Deirdre apologized for calling him at such an early hour and quickly explained the situation to him.

"No problem, Miss Hunt. I'll fly right on out. And—you didn't wake me or anything. I had to handle an emergency repair around five. And don't worry, it might just be a radio malfunction. Your dad's a good pilot. I'll buzz the house on the way," he added.

Deirdre hung up the phone and walked back over to join her mother on the couch. Silas and Sam had become pretty good friends over the past few years and Silas had been out to the Hunt Ranch dozens of times.

"Silas said he'd buzz the house on his way out." With a sigh, she wearily leaned back into the couch. *"He said not to worry, Dad's A good pilot."* Leaving the deputies at the campsite, Bill and Silas, in Silas's helicopter, began crisscrossing the northern half of the Hunt

Ranch shortly after sunup. It took them about twenty minutes to spot the downed helicopter. Sitting upright, it was on a grassy hill about three hundred yards from Mustang Road, the eastern boundary of the Hunt Ranch.

Silas was on the radio calling for an ambulance as he maneuvered his own chopper to within twenty or thirty yards of the downed craft. He had no sooner touched the ground, then Bill was out and running toward his dad's still form, which could be seen slumped over the controls of the chopper.

"Dad!" Bill yanked the left door so hard that, breaking at the hinges, it came off in his hands. Flinging it aside, he reached in and pressed his fingers against his dad's neck, desperately trying to find a pulse.

"Oh, God. Oh, God. There's no pulse! Where'd all this blood come from?" Bill was looking at the left front of his dad's jean jacket, which was soaked in blood.

"Bullet holes," said Silas. Bill jerked around to see Silas bent over, looking at the broken door.

Silas straightened up and gently moved Bill to one side. Leaning over Sam, he carefully reached down and checked for a pulse. *"Sorry, kid. We're too late for him."* Grasping Sam's shoulders, he slowly pulled him back to an upright position. He then bent over him, closely inspecting the front of Sam's jacket.

"Yeah, bullet holes. Two of them. I'm surprised he got this thing down."

Forcing himself to remain calm, Bill stepped over to the helicopter door. He bent down, looking at the two holes just below the open window. He turned the door over, and two exit holes were apparent just above the door handle. *"Who would have wanted to kill Dad?"* he asked plaintively.

"Didn't Miss. Hunt say something about rustlers?"

"Yeah, and she said she thought she had heard some shots. And then

Dad had said, 'got the bastards', or something like that. Do you see his gun in there?"

Silas checked the passenger seat and the floorboards. *"Don't see one. What was he carrying?"*

"Probably his 357."

"Well, it's not in here."

Bill took a deep breath and let it out slowly. *"Would you run me back to the house? I better tell Mom and Dee."*

Dee sat on the couch in the den, vacantly staring out the patio door. Her eyes were red-rimmed, and she held a handkerchief with which she would occasionally dab at her eyes. Bill was sitting across the room at a desk near the radio. It had been an unseasonably hot day, but the late afternoon sun gave the pastureland behind the house a deceptively cool, serene look.

"You think Mom'll be alright?" Bill was bent over, unlacing his boots. He had just returned from the fish tank and his dad's Smith & Wesson .357 Magnum was laying on the desk near the radio.

"Yes, she's strong," Dee paused to dab at her eyes. *"Stronger than me. Aunt Una and Reverend Hall are with her. I think Doc Boyd gave her a sedative, he wanted to give me one, too."*

"Maybe you ought to get some sleep, Dee. Brother Hall said he'd handle any company." As if on cue, the doorbell rang again. Bill hadn't been home for more than fifteen minutes and already he had heard the doorbell ring half a dozen times. *"Dad was a popular guy,"* he said wistfully.

"Why, Bill?" She began sobbing again. *"Why would anybody kill Dad?"*

Setting his boots aside, Bill reached over and picked up his dad's gun. *"He got off five rounds—maybe he took somebody with him."*

Dee leaned forward and laid her handkerchief on the coffee table. Visibly trying to get control of herself, she brushed her forearm across her eyes and sat upright on the edge of the couch.

"Who?" She asked. *"There wasn't a sign of anything out there?"*

"Nothing but a dead bull. Dad's gun was between the bull and the campsite. He must have been holding it out the window—probably dropped it when he got hit." He paused, *"Something real strange about that bull."*

Dee leaned forward, *"there weren't supposed to be any bulls in that pasture, were there?"*

"Yeah, that's one of the things. But I mean the carcass, itself. Do you remember, years ago, when dad went to that conference in Albuquerque, New Mexico-about the cattle mutilations?"

Dee nodded, *"Vaguely, that was before the oil came in, wasn't it?"*

"Yeah, it was a couple of years before that. All over the southwest, dead cattle were being found with some of the body parts missing and all of the blood gone from the carcasses. There never was any sign of tracks and there never was any blood on the ground."

"Oh, yeah. Now I remember. Dad came back from the conference and threatened to stop paying his taxes. He said the government was trying to cover up something. They were blaming it on flying saucers or something," she paused. *"You know, when those deputies came by this morning, one of them said something about UFO reports."*

"Those were bullet holes in that door. Silas said he thought they were .223's, the size slug that an M-16 uses. Anyhow, what I was about to say-what was done to that bull was the same thing that had been done to those cattle back then. Left ear, left eye, and tongue were gone. Balls were gone, and it looked like somebody had cut out it's asshole. Real neat-and there wasn't any blood."

"How could anybody have done all that with Dad sitting a hundred yards away? Do you think it was done after they shot Dad?"

"No," setting down the gun, Bill got up and walked over to the patio door. He stood looking through the glass toward the helipad. *"No, I don't think so. I got out there pretty quick, and I didn't see anything."*

He turned around, *"You said something about the bull being in the wrong pasture. That's right, the only cattle that were supposed to be in the fish tank pasture where the heifers that were about to calve. That particular bull was supposed to be in that pasture beside it to the west. I checked the fence and there wasn't a break in it anywhere."*

"What did the deputies say?"

"The deputies," he said contemptuously. *"Who was that ass with Frank?"*

"Frank?"

"Frank Pierce Jr. His folks go to mom's church."

"Oh-yes. That's the one mom recognized. I've never seen the other one before. I don't think Mom has, either."

"Well, anyway, he acted like he was in charge. He said that that was the first time he had seen a cow brought down by wolves in these parts. Wolves!" He paused and managed to smile. *"I told him that it was also the first time I'd heard of wolves using a scalpel. He got real pissed. Made me leave. That's when I found Dad's gun, walking back to the pickup."* He glanced back over at the gun. *"I probably ought to tell 'em about it."*

Before Dee had a chance to comment, the phone rang. Bill quickly walked back to the desk and answered it.

"Hunt Ranch."

"Yeah." Bill frowned and then relaxed a little.

"Oh, hi Silas."

"Yeah, sure."

"To your place?"

"OK, yeah, I'll be right over."

"Bye," he hung up the phone. Sitting down, he began putting his boots back on.

"Was that Silas?" Dee asked.

Bill glanced up, *"Yeah, said he needed to talk to me right away."* He frowned as be began tying his laces.

"Did he say what it was about?"

"No. He sounded, uh, agitated or something."

Dee stood up and, still looking at her brother, shook her head, *"I can't believe how well you're holding up under all this."*

Bill sighed and got to his feet. *"You know what I'd like to do, Dee?*

*I'd like to walk back to the old house, go back to my old room, find my
old teddy bear, curl up and go to sleep."*

He reached over and picked up his dad's pistol. Flipping out the
cylinder, he took out the live cartridge and ejected the five empty shell
casings. He pulled open a drawer in the desk and, taking out a box
of .357 cartridges, began reloading.

"Do you think you'll need that thing?"

He looked up and smiled, *"My teddy bear can't fight worth a shit,"*
he said.

Chapter 5

"Herr Manticore. Herr Manticore". Each time the tall young man said the name he would stoop from the waist and gently shake the foot of Pierre Manticore. Then he would immediately resume a stance that looked like a soldier standing at attention. Pierre Manticore, laying on his back on the large canopy bed, cracked his eyes enough to see the blonde, crew-cut German once again stoop and reach out his hand.

"Enough!" Pierre kicked his foot so hard that the plush, red velvet comforter slipped half off the bed. *"What is it, Frans?"* Pierre sat up, inadvertently pulling the comforter the rest of the way off the young boy who slept by his side. The boy, dark skinned and nude, was curled into a fetal position.

The German's eyes never left Pierre Manticore. *"Herr Manticore, you have an urgent call from Washington-on the secure line."*

"The secure line?" That meant a trip downstairs to the radio shack. Groaning, Pierre struggled to swing his short, fat legs over the side of the bed. Naked and obese, he seemed to take pleasure in making the German feel uncomfortable as he waddled over to a low vanity. He picked up his bathrobe.

"The President probably lost his key to the men's room, again," he said.

"Pardon, Herr Manticore?"

"Never mind. I forgot, you have no sense---of humor."

"Yes. Herr Manticore."

"Ever screw a fat old man, Frans?"

The German blushed. Satisfied, Pierre slipped on his robe and walked back to the bed to cover the still sleeping boy. *"Well, let's get this over with,"* he said petulantly.

The last two days would have been exhausting even for a young man-and Pierre Manticore was many years past being a young man. Yesterday was the May Day celebration in Beijing, and the night before that, the annual Beltane sacrifice on the shores of the Black Sea.

The May Day festivities had been as pompous and boring as always, but the Beltane sacrifice had really been something special this year. Nine Afghan boys, all between the ages of eight and twelve had been sacrificed. Pierre had been given the honor of performing the first sacrifice, himself.

He had felt younger and more energetic on the night of Walpurgis. But after the flight to Moscow this morning and then the flight to Berlin, all he wanted to do now was sleep.

Frans accompanied him downstairs to the radio room, and then stood at attention outside as Pierre, still peeved, flung the door open and strode into the room. The two radio room personnel scurried out the door, closing it behind them.

He picked up the red phone, *"Manticore,"* he said.

"Mr. Manticore, we've got some problems here."

"Who am I talking to?" Pierre's voice had an edge to it.

"This is Harris, Mr. Manticore."

"Ah, yes, Harris. What's the problem, Senator? Did the NRA take a contract out on you?"

Senator Harris was quiet for a moment, *"We've either had a severe security breach or two of the principals in our corporation are warring."*

"Go on," Pierre set down by the phone.

"I don't have many details yet, sir. There was a joint I.D.and C.O.S. gathering last night. All participants were killed, forty some-odd of them."

"Killed? By whom?"

"*We don't know, sir. The bodies were just discovered a couple of hours ago, and, as I said, there were no survivors.*"

"*If they were warring, there should have been some survivors. Can you keep a lid on it?*"

"*I think so, sir. It was on government property. And what I meant was, there were no survivors of whom we are aware.*" Pierre sighed, "*After twenty-three years, you'd think we had all that shit behind us. Where was it?*"

"*Near Colorado Springs, sir.*"

"*I'll be there sometime late tomorrow, your time. Keep a lid on it, Harris.*"

"*I'll try, sir.*"

"*Do it, damn it!*" Pierre slammed the phone down. "*Jesus Christ,*" he muttered as he turned and walked back toward the door.

Chapter 6

"What do you make of it, Bob?" Chief Deputy Wally Bird had just shut the driver's door of the light green El Paso County Sheriff's car. Smoothing the crease in his tan, short-brimmed Stetson, he placed it on his head and joined undercover narcotics officer Bob Langly. Langly was squatting beside the nearest of four bodies, which lay motionless on the forest trail.

"Beats anything I've ever seen," Bob said, glancing up at Wally. *"What could have done something like that?"* He pointed at the long, deep gash, which ran almost the full length of the man's torso. *"That cut goes all the way through."*

"Chainsaw?" Wally stooped over slightly, looking at the cut. *"No, too neat. Those other three were burned. We haven't found this guy's arm yet."* He stood up, still looking at the man at his feet. *"I don't know who this guy was, but I think one of those others was Todd Johnson."*

Wally straightened up and glanced over at the other bodies. *"How can you tell?"* He asked.

"Hmmm? Oh, the one with his head chopped off--- the hair was burned off, but his face was recognizable. I'm pretty sure it was Todd." He took a deep breath and let it out slowly, *"If I hadn't had to work, I'd have been out here."* Wally glanced back at the late afternoon sun, *"Let's take a look at the rest of it, it'll be dark in an hour."*

Walking past the rest of the bodies, they continued on down the trail toward the parking area.

"I'm telling you, it's real spooky," Bob pulled a snub-nosed .38 from a shoulder holster and checked to make sure that it was loaded. Satisfied, he put it back in the holster and straightened his jean jacket. He pulled a two-way radio off his belt. *"Jerry, this is Bob. Wally and I are coming down."*

"10-4," the answer was almost immediate.

Bob glanced over at Wally as he clipped the radio back onto his belt. *"Jerry's really freaking out. He thinks two of those charred cinders down there are his mom and dad. We ought to send him home, he almost shot a magpie, earlier."*

"Sudden noise," he said in answer to the quizzical look that Wally had given him. *"He thinks there's a curse on the place,"* he paused. *"Maybe there is. Just wait 'til you see what's down here. Then you'll understand what I'm talking about."*

Wally walked a little slower as they approached the parking area. *"How many men have you got out here?"* he asked.

"Just Jerry and Red Grimes down here, Pat's back at Rampart Range. You saw him on the way in didn't you?" He looked at Wally.

Wally nodded, *"Yeah, he was parked southbound on the other side of the road."* They had come to the parking area and Wally stopped, surveying the burned-out cars.

"How many dead here?" He asked.

Before Bob had a chance to answer, a burst of static came from the radio. They both jumped. Bob snatched up the radio, *"Yeah, this is Bob."*

"Bob, this is Pat. A chocolate brown Continental and a Mercedes limo just turned onto the trail. They're coming your way." Bob looked questioningly at Wally.

"It's OK," Wally said to him. *"They're I.D., from Denver. I didn't expect 'em here this quick."* Then to the radio, he said, *"It's OK, Pat. They're expected."*

"10-4," came back.

Bob clipped the radio back on to his belt and began walking

around the edge of the clearing. *"As near as I can figure, there's between ten and fifteen bodies in the cars. There's also a dead guard on the other side of the clearing."*

Wally pulled a 9 mm Beretta from a shoulder-rig and, jacking a shell into the chamber, placed it in his right hip pocket. Straightening his jacket, he followed Bob around the edge of the blackened meadow.

"Keep an eye on those I.D. people," he said, glancing back up the trail. *"They were really pissed when I called them."*

Bob had stopped by the dead guard on the other side of the clearing. He looked back at Wally. *"How do we know **their** people didn't do this?"* he asked.

Wally stopped beside him. *"We don't,"* he paused. *"They had one or two high-level Druids here. I know for a fact that we had eight or ten high priests-important people. We lost a lot more than they did."*

"Another decapitation?" Wally was looking down at the dead guard.

"Yeah," Bob pointed to the Uzi, gripped tightly in the man's right hand. *"His weapon's been fired-I don't know at who–or what."*

"Or what?" Wally repeated, chuckling. *"You really are spooked."*

"Wait 'til you get a look at the big clearing. Maybe they summoned up something that they couldn't handle."

Wally glanced across the clearing, *"I think I just heard some car doors slam,"* he said. *"Let's get on down to the other clearing. They'll have the sun at their backs here."*

They hurried down the path to the larger clearing and as soon as they emerged, Wally motioned for Jerry and Red to join them.

"Listen," he said, *"some I.D. people have just arrived. They'll be down here in a few minutes."* He looked at Red, who was carrying an M-16, *"Red, get up that slope on the other side of the clearing. Act like you're checking out the terrain along the tree-line."*

Wally looked at Jerry and hesitated. Jerry looked wild-eyed and kept clicking the safety on and off on the 12-gauge riot-gun that he held at the ready. *"Are you OK, Jerry?"* he asked.

Jerry pursed his lips and didn't answer.

"Look, Jerry—don't lose it. We're not sure what happened here." Wally nodded at Red, who began climbing up the slope toward the tree-line. *"Why don't you help Red,"* he added.

"I'll tell you one god damn thing," spat Jerry, *"I've seen two guards with their heads chopped off and the only thing we've found that could have done that is in that dead Druid's hand,"* he snarled, pointing the shotgun in the direction of the altar.

"We don't know for sure!" Wally snapped. *"Get on over to the other side of the circle and act like you're checking out corpses. Don't blow it!"*

Jerry spun on his heel and angrily strode off in the direction of the slope.

"Come over here and look at this dead Druid," Bob called out. He was standing a few yards away, beside the altar.

Wally, watching Jerry walk away, shook his head and walked over to join Bob.

"Holy shit!" He exclaimed. He stopped abruptly and stared at the bizarre corpse, *"Holy shit!"*

"What do you make of that?" Asked Bob.

"Christ, I don't know. Looks like he cut off his own head."

"Jerry thinks he had all these people snuffed, and then whatever they had summoned snuffed him-- for revenge or something. He thinks I.D. did the general slaughter, throwing in some of their own people to make it look good-and then ran when they saw what happened to this guy." Bob looked questioningly at Wally.

"This place gives me the creeps," Wally tore his eyes away from the dead Druid and began inspecting the altar. *"Whatever happened here-I think the little girl got away."*

"Yeah, I know. There's not any blood on the altar, I've already looked," Bob was still looking at the Druid.

"No, I mean, I think somebody found her. Just before I left the Springs, some preacher from Cascade called and reported finding a naked little girl asleep in his church. Said she was seven or eight years old and had just woke up. She told him her name was Tracy Ulman."

"How'd she get down there?"

Wally shrugged, *"As far as I know, John and Nancy Ulman are laying out here somewhere,"* he nodded toward the unrecognizable mounds of burned flesh which littered the bonfire area and the base of the slope.

"Mr. Byrd!"

Wally turned around and looked back toward the path. *"Yeah, over here,"* he continued feigning an interest in the altar as he straightened up and casually put his hands in his hip pockets.

"Ah, yes. Mr. Byrd. Julian Wickerby, here." The distinguished looking middle-aged man with the British accent stepped into the clearing. He was followed by six other, more burly types, who were walking single file behind him. Except for Wickerby and the last man in line, they were all carrying Mac 10 machine guns. The last one, carrying an AK-47, stayed by the path. The others, except for one who remained with Wickerby, spread out and began inspecting the bodies.

Wickerby and his guard walked over to join Wally and Bob beside the altar. He stopped and looked at the dead Druid. *"You Americans do love your jokes, don't you?"* His voice had an icy edge.

His companion pointed at the head, *"It's Sir Henry!"* he exclaimed.

"Sir Henry?" repeated Wally. *"Henry Flynn?"*

"Yes, did you know him?" asked Wickerby. He was looking coldly at Wally.

"Met him at a party at the Broadmoor-a couple of months ago. He must have just shaved his head, seems to me he had a full head of hair, then."

"He wore a hairpiece. Quite the traditionalist-Henry. He was strongly opposed to this sort of mingling," he nodded in the direction of the charred corpses. *"He said you people couldn't be trusted."*

"Look," Wally shifted uncomfortably, *"we didn't have anything to do with this."*

"Mr. Wickerby! Look at this." Another of Wickerby's companions was standing over the bodies of the two Druids whom Toby had killed

with the Uzi. Wickerby, accompanied by his companion, Wally, and Bob walked over to join him.

"*What is it?*" Asked Wickerby.

"*These men were shot, Mr. Wickerby,*" he reached down and picked up a spent shell casing, "*same type of casing that was by that man in the other clearing.*"

Wickerby looked over at Wally, "*Have your people tampered with anything?*" he asked.

"*No,*" Wally was defensive, "*of course not. We were told to leave everything exactly as it was until the people from Washington got here.*"

"*We took the liberty of checking the guns of the man on the trail and the man in the other clearing.*" Wickerby paused. "*The only weapon which had been discharged was that of the man in the clearing-one of your men, I believe.*"

"*So?*" Wally still had his right hand in his hip pocket.

"*So. I'm not an expert on automatic weapons, but I feel confident in assuming that an Uzi holds more than nine rounds?*" Wally nodded. Bob, feeling uncomfortable at the threatening tone of Wickerby's voice, moved his right hand closer to the flap of his jacket.

"*We found only five shell casings on the ground near the body of that man and four unspent cartridges in the clip of his gun.*" He looked back at the ground near the bodies. "*There appear to be just enough shell casings here to finish filling his clip.*"

At that moment, Jerry, sounding hysterical, screamed out, "*Wally! God damn it! Wally!*" He was standing over one of the blackened corpses on the slope, looking down at it. "*Mom's rings! This is mom! Oh, God,*" he moaned.

"*Hey!*" The shout came from Red, who was still near the tree line at the top of the slope. He had found Hermano's trench, its cover still propped up with two sticks.

The sudden shout startled one of Wickerby's companions, a short, heavyset man standing near Jerry. He swiveled around and pointed his gun up the slope.

Jerry jerked his shotgun up and, at a range of about 10 feet, discharged it into the man's face. The clearing erupted into gunfire. Red dropped two of Wickerby's group who were midway up the slope, immediately-only to be cut down, himself, by the man stationed near the path.

The other of the strangers on the slope flattened behind some corpses and began firing at Jerry, who was racing across the circle toward the altar. Hit three times in the back, Jerry sprawled on his face about midway between the circle and the altar. He was dead before he hit the ground.

At the first sound of gunfire Wickerby's companion raised his Mac 10 and practically cut Bob in half with a long burst to the midsection.

Wally's Beretta was out and firing before Wickerby knew what was going on. In one quick movement, Wally dropped Wickerby with a shot in the chest and put three slugs into his companion before leaping over their bodies and diving into the trees behind them.

The man who had shot Jerry leaped up and sprinted over to his companion, who was still standing near the path. Reaching the cover of the trees, he turned and fired a few shots at the spot where Wally had entered the forest. The two Druids then raced up the path in the direction of the cars.

A few minutes later, Wally emerged from the forest and cautiously approached Bob, who was sprawled between Wickerby and his companion. He reached down and picked up Bob's radio.

"Pat, this is Wally. You still there?" He held the radio close to his mouth and spoke softly. His attention was on the clearing, ready to react to any sudden movement.

"Yeah, Wally. What's going on down there? Those two cars came out of there like bats out of Hell."

"They're gone?"

"Yeah, about a minute ago. Headed down toward the Springs. What happened?"

"I'll tell you in a few minutes," he paused, *"out."*

He tucked the radio into his jacket pocket and began checking the newly-fallen. Finding them all dead, he walked back over to the dead Druid who was laying by the altar.

Wally stood looking down at him for two or three minutes and then, shaking his head, began walking back toward his car. He sighed and cursed softly under his breath.

Chapter 7

Early Bird Airport was located just off Highway 80 about ten miles west of Fort Worth. It consisted of a single paved airstrip running north and south and a large ramshackle hangar that looked as if it had been built sometime prior to World War II. The hangar was situated at the northwest corner of the airstrip and served the dual purpose of hangar and home for Silas' two helicopters and himself. Years earlier, Silas had converted the south end of the hangar into a combination office and apartment and seemed content to live there-alone except for an aging German shepherd named Kraut.

Silas had two full-time employees-day workers-but they had both gotten off at six and except for the fuel truck and Silas's pickup, the parking lot was empty when Bill Hunt pulled in at sunset.

Leaving his pickup parked beside Silas's, near the office door, Bill got out and stretched. It had been a long and emotionally draining day and even though Bill was used to hard work, he felt a level of weariness that he had never before experienced.

"Billy, come on in. Kraut heard you pull up," Silas had opened the office door and was standing just inside holding Kraut with one hand and the office door with the other. Kraut was wagging his tail and trying to get past Silas. *"Let's go on back to the kitchen, the commuter-rush's over and I'm fixing to lock up the office."*

Squeezing past Silas, Bill paused to scratch Kraut's head and walked on back to the kitchen. It was situated between the office and the main hangar.

"Pull up a seat, Billy. I'll get us some coffee." Silas walked over to a modern kitchen sink and counter, which were flush against the east wall and, reaching into an overhead cabinet, pulled out a couple of cups. Bill stepped over to the center of the room and plopped down in a chair beside the table.

"You use anything?" Silas glanced back at Bill.

"Couple of spoons of sugar." Kraut had leaned his head on Bill's knee and was sitting beside his chair as Bill absently scratched behind the big shepherd's ears.

Silas set two cups on the table and, pulling out a chair opposite Bill, picked one back up and sipped. *"Just ripe,"* he said.

Bill forced a smile and picked up his cup. *"What's the problem, Silas?"* He asked.

Silas smiled. *"Just like your dad, straight to the point. That's good,"* he set down his cup. *"Look, Billy, I'm going to talk to you just like I would to your dad. You're the man of the house out there now and, it looks like your dad's killing might just be the beginning of some rough weather."*

"What happened?" Asked Bill. He straightened up and leaned his elbows on the table, staring expectantly at Silas.

"Well, a couple of things. I drove the pickup back out to y'all's ranch around lunchtime. You know, the pasture where the chopper was?" Bill nodded.

"Well, the chopper was still there, and I was going to see when I could pick it up-like you said. There was a couple of Sheriff's Department cars there and three or four other cars that I guess belonged to about half a dozen people in suits that were standing around. I don't know who they were, except for one of them. I'm pretty sure that he's a press aide for Congressman Burton."

"Burton! What's he got to do with this?"

Silas shrugged his shoulders, *"I don't know. Anyway, when I asked one of the Sheriff's deputies about picking up the chopper, he told me that* *they were going to have to haul it somewhere to run some tests. Said that* *they'd get ahold of your mom when they were through with it."*

"What kind of test?" Asked Bill. He took a quick sip of his coffee.

"He was kind of vague about that. Anyhow, I said,' Why don't you *just take the door, that's the only place where there was any bullet holes.'"* Silas paused to take a long drink of coffee. *"You know what he said?"*

"What?"

"He said,' What door?'."

"What door!" Bill exclaimed. *"Wasn't it there?"*

"I couldn't see it anywhere."

"What did you say?"

"Well, I started getting a bad feeling about the whole situation about *then, so I tried to kind of blow it off. I said something like,' I thought* *I'd seen a door laying around here somewhere', or something like that.* *Anyhow, they said they'd probably want to talk to me, later."*

"Was that it?" Bill asked.

"Out there, yeah. When I got back here, I started thinking about that *emergency repair that I'd done this morning."* He paused and frowned thoughtfully. *"It was somewhere around five o'clock. Kraut must have* *heard something because he woke me up barking at the office door. Well,* *I checked the office and then stepped out into the parking lot. It was still* *dark and I couldn't see anything past the parking lot-we got that flood* *light out there-but then Kraut takes off toward the south end of the* *landing strip.*

I was wearing pajamas and the pickup keys were in my coverall *pocket. So I grabbed the fuel-truck keys out of the office and drove up the* *strip after him."* Silas got up and, walking back over to the counter, poured himself another cup of coffee. *"Anyhow,"* he continued, sitting back down, *"when I got up to the other end of the strip, there was Kraut-* *barking at these two guys who were standing by an old Huey. It looked* *good, but it was pretty old. Had some sort of canvas contraption rigged* *up between the skids, snugged up to the belly of the chopper."* He paused, furrowing his brow. *"I parked almost nose to nose with the chopper-a little to one side. When I got out to put Kraut in the truck, I didn't notice any numbers on the chopper-- but I wasn't paying that much attention. Well, after I got Kraut out of the way I talked to this one guy in front of the chopper. The other one was out of sight-I figured he was working on it. The guy I talked to said they had a busted fuel line and had to set it down as quick as they could. He said that was the reason they didn't land by the hangar."* Silas paused, *"Want some more coffee?"*

Bill shook his head no, *"I still got half a cup,"* he said.

"Well, anyway, when I got back in the truck to go get a new fuel line, I could see numbers on the side of the helicopter. You get my meaning?" He asked. *"I think the guy who was out of sight was pulling some kind of covering off the numbers. Like I said, I was almost nose to nose with the chopper, so I couldn't make out what the numbers were, but when I came back with the fuel line, I parked beside the chopper to get a look. Well, I gave him the line and a few gallons of fuel, they paid cash. Then one of them said thanks, but they could handle it from there. When I got back in the truck I jotted down the number and went on back to the office.*

They flew out of here about six. It wasn't too long after that that your sister calls, so I didn't get around to checking out that number. At least not until just before I drove back to the ranch. The helicopter was registered to Central U.S. Avionics." He arched his eyebrow and looked at Bill meaningfully. *"That's one of the reasons I started getting a little spooked when I went back out there. See, Congressman Burton is the majority shareholder of that company."*

Bill leaned back in his seat, *"You think that chopper was out at the ranch last night?"* He asked.

"Just a minute," Silas said. *"I ain't finished."* He lifted his cup and drained the rest of his coffee. After setting his cup back on the table he got up and walked back over to the counter. Opening a drawer to the left of the sink, he took out a grimy, clear-plastic fuel hose. He brought it back to the table.

"This afternoon, I drove up to where those guys were parked last

night. This hose was laying on the ground up there." He laid it on the table in front of Bill.

Bill picked it up and began inspecting it. The hose was about an inch in diameter and 4 feet long. *"This looks like a bullet hole,"* he said, carefully inspecting a deep gash about a foot from one end of the hose.

*"That **is** a bullet hole. I seen plenty of them in Vietnam. Fairly large caliber."* He paused. *"I don't want to jump the gun or anything but a .357 would make about that size hole. You said your dad had a .357 with him, didn't you?"*

"Yeah. Oh, I found the gun. He had shot five times at something." Bill set the hose back down on the table.

"I can't figure how a rich guy like Burton could have anything to do with cattle rustling," Silas picked up the hose and, stepping back to the counter, tossed it back into the drawer. He grabbed a roll of paper towels and, pulling one off, began wiping his hands. He tossed the roll to Bill. *"A congressman rustling cattle. If it wasn't for your dad getting killed, it would almost be funny."* Silas walked back to the table and sat down. He looked at Bill for a minute. *"Listen, Billy, don't go flying off half-cocked. It ain't just cattle rustling, now. It's murder. I'll talk to the Sheriff's Department tomorrow-let them handle it."*

"I thought you had a bad feeling about them," Bill got up and put the paper towel roll back by the sink. Dropping the wadded towel into the trashcan beside the counter, he walked toward the door.

"Yeah. Well, I'll try to talk to the Sheriff, personal." He got up and followed Bill through the office to the parking lot. *"Just don't do anything until you know what's going on. If your dad was here he'd---"* his voice trailed off.

"Yeah, he'd what?" Bill managed a halfhearted smile as he opened the driver's door to his pickup. *"You know Dad, Silas. If he was in my spot he'd be at Central Avionics busting heads right now."* He sat down and shut the door. Rolling the window down he leaned his head out the window, *"Don't worry, Silas, I'll wait until after the funeral before I do anything."*

It was dark when Bill pulled out of Early Bird and headed down the dirt road that led back to Highway 80. He had hardly noticed the gray van that was parked across the road from the airport, and even if he had, he wouldn't have been able to see the two men who had leaned over in the seat as he passed.

They sat back up and watched his taillights disappeared down the road. The driver put a small portable two-way radio to his mouth. *"Jeff,"* he said softly.

"Yeah," the reply was almost immediate.

"He's coming. The deck's stacked. Over." He lowered the radio and looked back toward the airport parking lot. Silas was just walking back through the office door.

"10-4, out," came back on the radio.

The driver clicked off the radio, then laid it on the dash. He turned to the man on the passenger side. *"Let's use the side door,"* he said, *"a courtesy light comes on when you open the front ones."*

Bill pulled off Airport Road and sped back in toward Weatherford. He was in a hurry. It was almost 8 o'clock and Silas's coffee on an empty stomach had made him realize that he hadn't eaten since lunch. He glanced in the rearview mirror. *"Shit!"* he exclaimed softly. A Department of Public Safety patrol car was about twenty feet behind him, it's red lights flashing.

Bill pulled onto the shoulder and killed the engine. Dousing the headlights, he began rolling down his window.

"Get out of the truck, please," the highway patrolman was standing beside Bill's door.

"Sir?" Bill looked up, he was in the process of reaching into his hip pocket for his wallet.

"Get out of the truck, please," the officer stepped back from the door.

As Bill opened his door and climbed out, he noticed another officer standing behind and to the right of his pickup. "What's going on?" Bill asked.

"Turn around facing your truck and place your hands on the side of the bed." He frisked Bill as his partner walked up on the other side of the truck and shined his flashlight through the passenger window.

"What's that?" He asked, glancing over at Bill. Bill could see through the back window that the flashlight was focused on a round, flat snuff-box on the passenger side of the dash.

"Looks like a snuffbox," Bill answered. *"It's not mine."*

The patrolman opened the door and reached in, grabbing the snuffbox.

"You can turn around, now," the other officer said. *"Can I see your driver's license, please?"*

"Hey, Harry," the officer with the snuffbox walked around the front of the pickup and stood beside the other one. *"Take a look at this,"* he handed the snuffbox to the first officer.

"What's this, kid?" he asked, looking into the round open box. *"White tobacco?"*

Bill looked into the snuffbox. It was half full of a white powder. *"I don't know,"* he paused, *"like I said, it's not mine."*

"Is this your truck, kid?" The second officer asked.

"Yeah."

"Just step back to the squad car, please," the officer called Harry put Bill into the back seat of the highway patrol car and walked back to join the other one. They both then began a thorough search of Bill's truck.

After a couple of minutes, they returned to the patrol car-the first officer was carrying Sam Hunt's .357 Magnum. *"Read him his rights,"* he said, sliding into the driver's seat.

It had been almost twenty hours since Deirdre had been awakened by her dad's radio call, but sleep was the farthest thing from her mind. She had expected to hear from Bill hours ago and she was beginning to worry that he might have gotten into some sort of trouble. She had tried to call Silas at around eleven and had gotten no answer. It was fifteen after twelve, now, and she was toying with the idea of calling the Sheriff's Department when the phone rang.

She jumped off the couch and had reached the phone before the second ring. *"Hello",* She said.

"Dee."

"Bill! I was worried sick about you. Where are you?"

"You're not going to believe this," he said dryly.

"What's wrong?"

"I'm in the Tarrant County Jail."

"Jail? What happened?" Her knees felt weak as she sat down in the chair by the desk.

"I got busted for possession of cocaine," he said.

"What! Since when do you use that stuff! Oh, no!"

"I don't use that stuff," he said. *"I don't know where it came from, it was on the dash of the truck."*

She sighed. *"What do I need to do?"* She asked.

"You're not going to be able to do anything until tomorrow-uh-daylight, I mean. Get ahold of dad's lawyer and tell him what's going on. He'll know what to do-I hope."

"O.K., are you all right?"

"Yeah. Look, don't say anything to mom until you have to."

"OK. Lord, what next?" she moaned.

"Hang in there, Dee."

"Yeah, I'm all right. I'll talk to you tomorrow."

Chapter 8

Tuesday, the second day of May, turned out to be-if not as bleak a day for the Hunt family as had May first-at least as stressful.

Dee had finally managed to reach Roger Bowen, her dad's attorney, shortly before 9 a.m., and had put him to work on getting Billy out of jail. He had assured her that Billy should be home by lunch and had offered his condolences on the death of her dad.

"By the way, Miss Hunt," he had said. *"If you feel up to it, you might be interested to read an article in today's Dallas Morning News, regarding Sunday night's incident at the ranch,"* he paused, *"I believe it's on page three."*

After promising to pick up a Dallas Morning News, she had hung up and walked over to join her mom and Reverend Hall in the kitchen of the "old" house.

"Dora, I know it's a lot easier to preach patience at a time like this than it is to practice it, but it isn't going to matter to Sam," he paused, leaning across a table to gaze intently into her mother's eyes. *"He's home now, Dora. He isn't concerned about the body he used to travel around in."*

Deirdre poured herself a cup of coffee and joined them at the table. *"More trouble?"* She asked.

Her mom, dressed in jeans and a western shirt, sighed and looked at her daughter. She forced a smile. *"You look pretty today, dear. In spite of it all,"* she added.

"Sure, Mom. *This bathrobe does a lot for me.*" She took a sip of coffee. "*Just wait 'til I brush my hair—then I'll really be a knockout,*" she said flatly. "*What were y'all talking about when I walked in?*" She asked.

"*The Sheriffs Department,*" her mother answered. "*They said they have to hang on to your dad's-body-for a while longer to run some kind of test. I don't have any idea what to tell people about the funeral.*" She put another spoon of sugar in her coffee and began idly stirring it.

"*Have you got ahold of Uncle Dave?*" Dee asked, looking at her mom.

"*Dora gave me a list of people to call last night,*" Reverend Hall answered. "*I tried to call your Uncle Dave first, but the person who answered the phone said he no longer lived there.*" He paused, then added, "*he said that he could probably get a message to him, though.*"

"*Is he still living in Denver?*" Deirdre glanced at the pastor.

"*Apparently. Actually, the man I talked to was kind of tightlipped about giving out any information.*" Tasting his coffee, he set the cup down and reached for the sugar bowl. "*I seem to have made this a little stronger than I intended,*" he said. After adding a spoon of sugar to his coffee he turned back to Deirdre and pursed his lips, a habit that Deirdre always found mildly irritating. "*Does he still belong to that motorcycle gang?*" he asked.

Deirdre shifted uncomfortably, the topic of her Uncle Dave had always been a sore point with the Hunt family. He was her dad's younger—and only—brother, but Sam Hunt had made it clear that Uncle Dave wasn't welcome at the ranch. Two years earlier, her dad had literally kicked Uncle Dave off the ranch.

"*He doesn't belong to a gang,*" she replied defensively, "*he just has some friends that do.*"

"*Please, let's not get into that,*" her mother looked up from her coffee. "*Not now.*"

"*Yes, yes, you're right, of course,*" Reverend Hall reached across the table and patted Dora's hand. "*This should be a time of forgiving, a time for healing old wounds, not--*"

"There isn't anything to forgive!" Deirdre stood up so abruptly that her chair tipped over, crashing to the floor. *"He didn't do anything, it was those people who were with him."* Sobbing, she spun around and rushed from the room.

"Goodness. I'm terribly sorry. I didn't intend--"

"It's all right Brother Hall," Dora interrupted. *"It's just the strain."* She sipped her coffee. *"What she said was right, though,"* Dora said. *"Dave really didn't do anything wrong. Those men who were with him were on their way to New Orleans. Dave was trying to get rid of them as soon as they'd had a chance to rest. He just wasn't doing it quick enough to suit Sam."* Dora glanced at the door, *"She'll be back in a few minutes to apologize,"* she said.

Deirdre was back in ten minutes, looking much fresher than when she had had left. She had changed into light yellow sweat pants with a short-sleeve matching sweatshirt and white jogging shoes. She was still brushing her hair as she walked into the kitchen. Setting her purse on the table, she looked sheepishly at her mom and Reverend Hall.

"I'm sorry about the scene I made a while ago," she said. *"I'm just really on edge, today."*

"Me and my big mouth," apologized Reverend Hall.

"We're all under a lot of pressure," interjected Dora, smiling up at her daughter. *"Where are you off to?"* She asked.

"Oh, I thought I'd get out of the house for a while. Do you mind if I use dad's car-mine's got some kind of fuel problem?"

"No, not at all, dear. The keys should be in the top drawer of the desk," she paused, *"in the den."*

"OK, thanks Mom." Deirdre leaned over and kissed her on the cheek. *"See you later, Reverend Hall."* Picking up her purse she turned toward the door.

"Oh, Dee?"

"What, Mom," Deirdre stopped and turned around.

"Is Billy here? I haven't seen him all morning."

"Oh. Well, he's out somewhere. He should be back around lunch,

though. I'll be back in a little bit," she smiled and hurried on through the door.

Dora sighed and leaned back in her chair. *"She's hiding something,"* she said.

As soon as Deirdre had backed her dad's white Lincoln Continental out of the garage, she picked up his mobile phone and called Roger Bowen's office.

Mr. Bowen wasn't in, but she left word with his secretary that all calls should be made to her dad's mobile phone to avoid alarming her mom. That finished, she pulled a small address book from her purse and flipped over to a phone number that her Uncle Dave had given her about four months earlier.

The Hunt Ranch had two separate telephone lines. The phone located in the den was listed under Hunt Ranch, while the phone in the old house was listed under Sam Hunt's name. Uncle Dave, knowing that only Deirdre and Bill were likely to answer the ranch phone, had called on that line shortly after Christmas.

He had just wanted to check in and find out how the family was doing, but before he had hung up he had given Deirdre the phone number of a girlfriend who he had said usually knew where he was.

She called the number and leaned back in the seat. She hadn't really thought about what she was going to say. Her dad, Dave's brother, being dead was bad enough, but things seemed to be getting worse. The way that Bill had talked last night made it seem like something very sinister and frightening was going on. And she had a sick feeling in the pit of her stomach that it was just starting.

Uncle Dave, for all his faults, could remain steadfast and cool even when things seemed to be falling apart around him. She remembered *that* from his quiet, rational conduct, while her dad stood screaming in his face, two years earlier.

"Come on, Uncle Dave," the phone had rung three times, and she was almost ready to cry, again. She didn't know what she would tell him, something like *"Uncle Dave, Dad is dead and somebody got Billy*

thrown in jail. Please come down here before something else happens." The phone kept ringing. Or, more to the point, *"Uncle Dave, somebody's trying to wipe out our family, and I'm scared, please come home."*

After ten rings, Deirdre hung up the phone. Shifting the transmission into drive, she sped off down the driveway. She forced herself to slow down as she approached Mustang Road.

"Come on, Deirdre. Get ahold of yourself," she mumbled to herself. She knew Jackson's Store wouldn't have a Dallas Morning News, so she turned south to drive down to the truck stop on Highway 80.

It was about 10 o'clock when she got there, so the parking lot was relatively empty. She parked near the door and, grabbing a Dallas Morning News from the rack, went inside.

Sitting at a small booth near the registers, she opened the paper to page three. That sick feeling in her stomach came back. *"Saucer Sighting Near Weatherford",* was the only article on the page.

After ordering a cup of coffee, she read through the article. Three different people had reported sighting a UFO in various locations north of Weatherford in the early morning hours of May 1.

It was described as a round, metallic, saucer-like object about 50 feet in diameter with blinking white lights. The article went on to say that a mutilated cow, like those so common in the mid-70s, had been found near one of the sightings. The cow, a bull belonging to the Hunt ranch, the article said, wasn't the worst of the tragedies in the wake of the flying saucer. Sam Hunt, owner of the Hunt Ranch, had apparently sighted the object himself, and in his excitement had accidentally crashed his helicopter, not far from the mutilated bull. Deirdre laid the paper down.

"Damn," she said. She almost felt faint.

She had been sitting in the truck stop for about ten minutes when two elderly women came in and took the booth behind her. What appeared to be the oldest woman, walking slowly with the help of a cane, took the seat immediately behind Deirdre. Her companion, a stout, sixtyish woman with dyed red hair took the seat across from her.

"Isn't it a pity?" Deirdre overheard the red-haired woman say.

"Yes. Yes, it truly is," the older woman agreed. *"I really don't know what she can do, now."*

"No. I guess she's all alone."

Deirdre could feel the older woman shift in her seat.

"Miss, could we have some coffee, please?" Apparently turning back to the red-haired woman, she continued, *"She used to have a brother,"* she paused, *"but he's gone now, too."*

"Well," the redheaded woman replied, *"it truly is a shame and all, but you know what they say,"* she paused. *"People always end up getting what they deserve. After all, what do we really know about her personal life? She might have done all kinds of things that we don't even know about."*

"Yes, that's true. But--"

Deirdre got up to leave so quickly that her purse spilled, upside down, onto the floor. Hastily scooping the contents back into her purse, Deirdre hurried to the door.

"Ma'am!"

Deirdre turned around.

"Your ticket." The waitress was holding Deirdre's ticket up and walking toward the register.

"Oh, I'm sorry," Deirdre said. She stepped back to the register and, opening her purse, pulled out a five-dollar bill and laid it on the counter. Not bothering to collect her change, she walked on out the door.

The gray-haired woman twisted around and watched the door close. Turning back around, she smiled impishly at her companion and winked.

The car phone began buzzing as Deirdre unlocked the driver's door. She quickly scooted behind the steering wheel and picked up the phone. *"Hello,"* she said.

"Miss. Hunt?"

"Yes."

"Roger Bowen. I'm down at the Tarrant County Jail." He paused, *"it doesn't look like I'm going to be able to get Bill out today."*

"What's wrong?" Deirdre asked, her heart sinking.

"I'm not sure. There's something going on that they're not telling me about, but I don't have the vaguest idea what it is. I'll keep trying, of course. Don't worry, we will get this straightened out."

"Well, thanks Roger. I guess I'd better tell Mom."

"Yes, I'd advise that. She's stronger than you think."

"Yeah. Well, call me if anything happens. Oh--will they let me visit Bill?"

"Yes. Just get there before five."

"Thanks, Roger." She hung up the phone. Deirdre drove back toward the ranch, dreading the talk with her mom. Just as she was about to turn into the driveway, though, she remembered a couple of things that she had intended to pick up while she was out. Passing the driveway, she drove a little farther down Mustang Road and pulled into Jackson's Store.

An old red Chevrolet pickup with a long whip-like CB antenna on the rear was parked out front. A man with long black hair, who appeared to be in his early twenties, was sitting in the driver's seat. He whistled flirtatiously as she walked by.

Tom Jackson was just inside the door restocking a soft drink machine.

"Hi, Tom," she said, walking toward the rear of the store to pick up a loaf of bread.

"Hi, Dee, I'm sorry to hear about your dad."

"Thanks, Tom," she reached for the last loaf of wheat bread.

"Hey, bitch! I was going to get that bread." Deirdre paused and glanced to her left. A tall, red-haired girl, looking no more than eighteen or nineteen years old, was standing there with her hands on her hips.

"Sorry," Dee said, quickly pulling her hand back.

"Sorry!" The girl spat out. *"You rich bitches are all alike. Think*

everything belongs to you." She grabbed the loaf of bread and walked back to the counter.

Deirdre waited until the girl had paid and walked out the door before, she approached the counter.

"*Kids seem to be getting worse every year,*" Tom complained. "*Did you need some bread?*"

"*I think I've lost my appetite, Tom. I'll take some aspirin, though.*"

After paying, she walked out to find the red pickup still parked out front. The girl Dee had just encountered in the store was sitting in the passenger seat. Trying not to look at them, Dee walked back to the Lincoln and reached for the door.

"*Hey!*"

Dee looked up as the man in the pickup opened his door and stood on the running board, facing her. His fly was opened, and he had his penis in his hand. "*How would you like to screw?*" He asked as the red-haired girl giggled beside him.

Dee dropped her aspirin as she fumbled for the door. Not pausing to retrieve it, she crammed the key in the ignition, started the car and spun out of the parking lot.

It took longer to get control of her emotions this time than it had earlier that morning. After returning to the ranch, she had locked her bedroom door and lay sobbing on her bed until she had fallen asleep.

She awoke to the sound of someone pounding on her bedroom door.

"*Dee! Dee, are you, all right?*" Her mother's voice, though louder than usual, was calm and evenly modulated.

"*Yes, Mom. Just a minute.*"

She let her mom in, and in a rush told her all about Bill's arrest, Mr. Bowen's comment about something more going on than a routine cocaine bust and ended by telling her about the Dallas Morning News newspaper article. By the time she finished, Dora's continued calm demeanor began to have a calming effect on her daughter.

"*That flying saucer article explains the phone call I got earlier,*" Dora said. She continued, "some man called a couple of hours ago and asked if he could come out and look at the mutilated cow. Said he was a reporter for a magazine called UFO Update." She sighed, *"that's all we need on top of everything else--a circus in the north pasture."* Dee smiled and followed her mother into the old house.

Her mother glanced at the wall clock as she poured a cup of coffee for herself and Deirdre, who had taken a seat at the kitchen table. *"It's one o'clock now, we'll have to get in and see Bill pretty quick."* She paused, *"I'm afraid I've got some more bad news,"* she said, looking at her daughter.

Dee looked up and furrowed her brow-waiting.

"Silas got killed," her mother said, setting the cups on the table. Sitting opposite Deirdre, she continued, *"according to the twelve o'clock news. He was killed in an armed robbery out at Early Bird sometime last night. One of his employees found him this morning."*

Dee couldn't stifle the short intake of breath. *"Silas! Bill was out there last night."* She looked down at her coffee cup. *"Mom, I've got this terrible feeling that something--"* she paused, looking for the right word, *"evil--is going on here."*

The rest of the day, except for the late afternoon trip to the Tarrant County Jail, was pretty uneventful. Bill, reflecting on his mother's strength of character, had remained calm when told of Silas's death. He had told Dee to "hang in there" and had urged her to keep trying to contact Uncle Dave.

Deirdre had remained at home all day Wednesday, and as far as she knew the situation remained pretty much the same.

On Thursday, the Sheriff's Department told them that they could pick up Sam's body the following day, so Dora made plans to have the funeral on Saturday.

Since Tuesday, Deirdre had continued trying to contact her Uncle Dave every few hours. She finally reached him late Thursday night.

She talked to him for forty-five minutes and related everything that had been happening—including the old women's conversation at the truck stop and the incident at Jackson's Store.

He had told her to remain at home as much as possible, and he would try to be in Weatherford by Saturday.

Chapter 9

The Colorado Rockies are beautiful in the mid to late spring. In early May there may be an occasional dusting of snow, which serves as a reminder that these are, after all, mountains. But, other than that, an abundant resurgence of life is the primary theme. The trees begin budding amid wildflowers and lush sturdy grass that climb the mountainsides where snow drifts lay a few weeks before.

The spot where Hermano had chosen to pitch camp was an exceptionally picturesque and tranquil site a few miles out of Cripple Creek. There was a panoramic view of mountain peaks to the west that was breathtaking, even after four days of familiarity. The view was, in fact, so majestic that Hermano had spent much of his time sitting with his back against an old spruce, gazing off into a wilderness area that had, so far, escaped the poison touch of man.

On Thursday, the fourth day of his hermitage, Hermano was no closer to reconciling himself with the new direction his ministry had taken than he had been on Sunday night.

He had been quietly gathering information on the Church of Satan for ten years, and he had known that someday he would be called on to use his knowledge in a more aggressive manner.

But now that that time was upon him, he wasn't sure how to proceed.

The carnage that he had witnessed Sunday night had left him with a feeling of horror. Not horror at the slaughter of the satanists, but horror at the realization that he took pleasure in recalling it.

"Love your enemies," Christ had said, and, *"Turn the other cheek."*

*"But they're not **my** enemies! They're **your** enemies!"* Hermano had yelled at the mountain tops. *"You loved David! It's **his** kingdom that's to be reestablished!"* He said, *'But do not I hate them, O Lord, who hate You? I hate them with **perfect** hatred; I—Count—Them. --**My**--Enemies.'"*

Hermano had searched the Scriptures, looking for some kind of guidance—some kind of justification for what he had witnessed Sunday night. In his heart, he could see the necessity for it.

"They murder children!" He had pleaded. *"They want their **souls**!"* He had added.

Finally, on Thursday afternoon, he found the passage for which he had been searching. He read from John 18:36, "Jesus answered, My kingdom is not of this world. If My kingdom were of this world, My servants would fight, so that I should not be delivered to the Jews; but now My kingdom is not from here."

At the time that Jesus spoke, Hermano thought to himself, the only people who were anti-Christ were Jews, but now there is a huge, secret organization of anti-Christs, an organization of hereditary Jews <u>and</u> Gentiles. Actually, more Gentiles than Jews.

Hermano glanced back at the distant mountain peaks. A huge dark cloud was rolling in from the west. After four days of clear skies and picturesque serenity, the timing of the approaching storm didn't escape Hermano.

He looked up. *"Have I offended You?"* He asked aloud.

Distant thunder was his answer.

In fifteen minutes the storm was upon him. He just had time to get all his gear back into the Jeep before the first flakes began falling, but once they had started it was less than a minute before he found himself in the middle of a bizarre electrical blizzard.

He couldn't see the lightning, but at times the thunder was deafening as a thick wet blanket of snow began to cover the campsite.

When, after thirty minutes, the storm gave no indication of letting up, Hermano began to get concerned about getting back to the road. The Jeep handled snow well—within reason—but this storm was proving to be **most** unreasonable.

After forty minutes, he slowly and carefully began driving back toward the Cripple Creek-Florescent highway. The Jeep proved as dependable as always, and half an hour later he was sitting in the Cripple Creek Café sipping coffee and gazing out the window.

He believed that God sent signs. And he had no doubt that this peculiar spring storm was intended as a sign. But was it a sign that he had wandered into a forbidden area? Or was it God's way of effectively terminating Hermano's seclusion? It had certainly done **that**.

The snow was still falling. Hermano figured that there was at least five inches already on the ground and the storm didn't show any signs of letting up.

By seven o'clock Hermano began to get concerned about getting stuck in Cripple Creek. The road from Highway 24 to Cripple Creek was a good road, but it wasn't unusual for Cripple Creek to get snowed-in for days at a time in a winter storm.

At 7:30, he carefully began making his way back to 24. The drive was slow, but uneventful, and by nine o'clock he was eating a late supper in The Brazenhead Restaurant in Woodland Park.

He hadn't really decided where he was going to go from there. He had originally planned on spending about two weeks at his retreat. But now, due to circumstances beyond his control, those plans would obviously have to be altered.

He looked out the window at the gently falling snow. There was no longer any thunder and Woodland Park hadn't gotten nearly as much snow as had Cripple Creek. He estimated about three inches on the ground as he looked out at the parking lot— vacant except for his Jeep.

The restaurant closed at ten, so he would have to make some sort of plans, he realized. He motioned to the waitress for another cup of coffee. He wanted to talk to the preacher of that little church in Cascade, where he had left the girl, but—he looked at his watch—it was already after nine and he didn't know who the preacher was or where he lived.

He leaned back in his chair and gratefully took a sip of fresh coffee. Tomorrow morning would be a much better time to try and locate that pastor. But that meant that he would have to find a place to sleep tonight.

Cascade was only about 10 miles away, midway between Woodland Park and Colorado Springs. But since it was in the middle of Ute Pass, there weren't very many places where Hermano could pull over for the night. About three miles west of Cascade, though, he pulled off 24 and drove into the little town of Green Mountain Falls.

It was no longer snowing by the time Hermano nosed into a little roadside park beside the tiny business district. Fountain Creek meandered through the park and actually went under part of the business district before flowing into a pond that served as an ice-skating rink in the winter months. From the pond, the creek continued its course on down Ute Pass and through Manitou Springs, a suburb of Colorado Springs.

Despite the winter storm that Hermano had just experienced, the spring-thaw was well underway and Hermano could hear the gentle rushing of Fountain Creek as he killed the engine, wrapped himself in a blanket, and began trying to make himself comfortable for the night. The businesses had long since closed and there was little traffic. Within twenty minutes Hermano was sound asleep.

Friday morning dawned as clear and crisp has had the four mornings of Hermano's seclusion. By nine o'clock he had eaten breakfast and was turning into the parking lot of the church in Cascade. A small Datsun pickup was parked near the side door, so after leaving his Jeep beside it, Hermano walked around to the front and entered the church through the main entrance.

"Hello," Hermano called out. *"Anybody home?"*

"Be right with you," the voice came from an office located behind and to the right of the pulpit.

A couple of minutes later, a short middle-aged man with gray hair and rosy cheeks bounced through the door. Without a pause, he rushed over to Hermano and held out his hand. *"Chaplain Harris,"* he said. *"Or Pastor Harris, or Brother Harris or,"* he paused, *"even 'hey-you' will get my attention."* He smiled.

Hermano couldn't help but smile back. *"My name's Hermano,"* he replied, shaking the man's hand.

"'Brother', hmmm? Sounds like your parents were either Christian or confused," he laughed. *"No offense, my parents must have had delusions of grandeur when they named me Peter."* He looked around him and, smiling, said, *"This ain't exactly the Vatican, but I call it home."* He looked back at Hermano. *"What can I do for you?"* he asked.

Hermano stepped over to the pew where he had laid the little girl on Sunday night. He patted it. *"I delivered a package here a few days ago,"* he said. *"I'm trying to locate the person who sent it."*

The smile left Chaplin Harris's face. *"You know,"* he said, *"I begin each morning by praying and randomly opening the Bible for a verse to meditate on throughout the day. Listen to today's verse."* He pulled a small Bible from his jacket pocket and, quickly thumbing through it, began to read; *"Behold, I have created the blacksmith, who blows the coals in the fire, who brings forth an instrument for his work; and I have created the spoiler to destroy."* He closed the Bible and put it back in his pocket.

"That's from Isaiah *54:16,"* he added. *"Let's step outside and take in some of this mountain air,"* he said, walking past Hermano and through the front door.

Hermano followed him to a park bench, located near the corner of the church by the parking lot. He sat down beside Chaplain Harris, whose gaze was fixed on a spot down the dirt road near 24.

"See that green car?" Chaplain Harris asked.

Hermano followed his gaze and saw a light green late-model Ford parked near the intersection, facing away from the church. *"Yes"*, he replied.

"It's been down there since Monday -- day and night. There's always one or two people sitting in it." Chaplain Harris turned to face Hermano, *"This person who sent the, uh, package—by what name did this person call you?"*

Hermano thought for a moment. *"Preacher"*, he replied.

Chaplain Harris smiled. *"Sorry, he told me to ask that. He called early Monday morning and said you'd probably be back. I'm supposed to take your address and he'll get in touch with you."*

"Oh," Hermano thought for a minute. *"My address."* Hermano hadn't seen his parents in over a year, but on the spur of the moment, he gave Chaplain Harris their phone number and address which was in the country, a few miles south of Fort Worth, Texas.

"I wish there was some way of getting out of here without going past that green car, but I'm afraid that that's the only way out," Chaplain Harris said as Hermano climbed back into the Jeep.

Hermano shut the door and shrugged his shoulders, *"Que sera-sera,"* he said. Chaplain Harris smiled. *"How true,"* he said. *"God be with you, Brother"*.

Hermano returned his smile. *"And you, Peter."*

Hermano tried to avoid looking at the green Ford as he approached the intersection. He was careful to come to a complete stop before he turned right to follow 24 on down to Colorado Springs.

The two men in the green Ford craned their necks to get a look at Hermano's license plate as he went by. *"Did you get that?"* The driver turned to the man in the passenger seat.

"Yeah, Colorado Springs prefix. Probably a local." He wrote for a moment in his notepad. Then, putting it away, he threw his left arm back over the seat and leaned against the door. He continued watching the church.

Hermano's mind had been made up for him, he was going to Texas. But first, that unmarked police car had made him curious about the official reports on Sunday night's carnage. He hadn't read a newspaper in a week and he had no idea how the slaughter of such a large number of satanists would be reported. He had a feeling that they were all dead. According to Peter, the huge swordsman—or the "spoiler", as Peter seemed to think of him—was still alive and well. That meant that many, if not all, of the satanists weren't.

He was in a little bit of a hurry to get to the address he had given Peter, but he felt he could spare the time to satisfy his curiosity. He decided to drive over to the El Paso County Public Library and read the last week's issues of the Colorado Springs Gazette.

The newspapers hadn't as yet been put on microfilm, so he obtained the small stack of five newspapers and found a vacant desk.

There wasn't anything in the Monday paper, but he hadn't really expected that the news would have broken early enough to make the Monday edition. The Tuesday Gazette had a small front-page article about the recovery of the kidnapped child, but nothing about the fate of her abductors.

The article about the child stated that she had apparently wondered, naked, into a church in Cascade and was found there late Sunday night by the pastor. The Sheriff's Department, according to the article, hadn't been able to determine where she had been or who had taken her. It went on to mention that, now, her father couldn't be found.

In the Wednesday edition there was an article about a commuter aircraft which had crashed in Pike National Forest, killing all 38 people on board. The crash was supposed to have occurred early Monday morning. And, also, in the Wednesday edition, there was a report that the father of the kidnapped child, along with five others, had died in a fiery automobile accident near Woodland Park.

In all the newspapers, the only deaths relating to Rampart Range Road was a Thursday front-page report. It stated that three Sheriff's deputies and five foreign nationals had died in a head-on collision about ten miles north on Rampart Range.

"*Damn,*" Hermano mumbled. Nothing. They had covered the whole thing up. He shook his head and picked up the stack of papers. The power of the organization that he was opposing was almost beyond belief. And he was just one man. He sighed. Well, perhaps that was about to change.

Gripping the steering wheel low with both hands, Hermano took his foot off the accelerator and, placing it on the floorboard beside the other, straightened his legs as much as possible. He sat back down and arched his back, trying to suppress a yawn. It was almost two in the morning and Hermano had been driving for six hours. He had had supper with an old acquaintance in Pueblo and was now on his way to Amarillo, Texas, through the "Panhandle".

It was a chilly night, but he rolled down the window and leaned his head back against the doorpost. The cold air seemed to revive him a bit, but after a couple of minutes he rolled the window back up.

"*Burr,*" he said softly. He settled back in the seat and was once more deep in thought. Last week's turn of events was still all that he could think about. He could see the necessity for what he had witnessed, but there was just no way that he could justify it.

"*God,*" he said aloud. "*You know my mind. You know what's troubling me, now. Please. Give me some kind of sign. Some kind of guidance.*"

He waited. Finally, leaning forward, he tore his eyes off the road long enough to look up at the sky. It was a clear, moonless night and the stars looked cold and far away.

Hermano leaned back and looked at the road. There didn't seem to be anything in front of him but an endless expanse of night. He sighed and reached forward to twist the radio dial.

"*God,*" he said, "*I'm going to put the station indicator all the way to the left. Then I'm going to turn on the radio and begin moving the indicator to the right. On the third station that I can hear clearly, I'm going to stop and begin listening for Your message.*" He paused, "*I know that You can do anything*", he added. Hermano turned the radio on. Slowly, he turned the dial to the right. When he found his third station, he turned up the volume and leaned back again.

*"I don't have to tell you—we are **there**,"* The man's voice was raspy and sounded like that of an older man. His tone, though, conveyed excitement as he said a little louder, *"Yes, we're there!"*

"The Lord Jesus said that when his Gospel of the Kingdom was preached throughout the world, for a witness to all nations, then the end would come. And I'm telling you brothers and sisters—we're there!

If you doubt that the Gospel has been preached throughout the world for a witness to all nations—then you tell me where it hasn't been preached. And I'll tell you, 'bull'! And I'll also tell you that if you believe that—then why aren't <u>you</u> there preaching?

No, brothers and sisters, it <u>has</u> been preached throughout the world for a witness to all nations. We all are—by Jesus Christ's own definition—in the end-time."

Hermano leaned forward, he turned the volume up a little more.

"And what are the things that happen in the end-time?" the voice asked. *"Wars and rumors of wars, earthquakes, famine, people quaking for fear of the things coming on the earth. All that—yes. But how about the individual things? Brothers and sisters let me tell you. This is a world-wide ministry you're listening to. The message that you're listening to tonight is being broadcast live—via satellite—all over the world. And tonight, as our Lord said, 'in your hearing', I'm going to take it upon myself to fulfill prophecy.*

*Since the Gospel of the Kingdom **has** been preached throughout the world for a witness to all nations. And since Jesus said that where-ever two or more are gathered together in His name, then there is He among them,"* he paused, then continued, *"taken together, since the Great Commission <u>has</u> been fulfilled, that means that His Spirit has been manifested in every nation of the world.*

Darkness flees from Light, brothers and sisters. Therefore—here it comes--", his voice got deep, and even, *"the kingdoms of this world have become the Kingdoms of our Lord and of His Christ, and He shall reign, for ever and ever!"*

The prerequisite! Hermano thought, as he swerved over to the shoulder of the road and stopped. He remembered what he'd read on the mountain. *"If my Kingdom were of this world, **then** would My servants fight---".* Hermano's tears were coming so profusely that he could no longer see to drive, so he turned off the ignition and got out of the Jeep.

Looking up at the clear cloudless sky, he shouted *"Thanks! Thanks, Lord!"* Then, leaning back against the left front fender, he said, *"but I'm so small. And Your enemies-**our**-enemies—are so,"* he paused, searching for the right word, *"so formidable."*

The thought that came to his mind was so clear and concise that it was as if an audible voice had said, *"Not by might, nor by power, but by **My** Spirit."* The resulting emotional surge was so sudden and intense that Hermano began sobbing.

He was only about five miles northwest of Dalhart in the far northern part of the Texas Panhandle, and the spot where he had pulled over seemed as good a place to sleep as any. He could drive into Dalhart for breakfast in the morning and still be home before supper. Exhausted, he climbed back into the jeep and, laying across the steering wheel, was soon sound asleep.

Chapter 10

It was almost noon when Hermano pulled off the road in front of the hitchhiker. He was on Highway 287, about 40 miles south of Amarillo. The hitchhiker, wearing a brown parka, jeans and cowboy boots, jogged the fifty feet to the Jeep, opened the passenger door and slid in.

"Thanks," the man said. He was a husky six-foot two with blond hair cut short and a short-cropped blond beard. There were creases around his eyes and a sprinkling of gray in his beard, but his athletic physique belied his apparent middle-age

"Going far?" Hermano asked as he pulled back onto the highway.

"Too far to get there by one o'clock," the man said with a sigh. He looked over at Hermano, *"do you know what time it is?"* he asked.

Hermano suppressed an urge to say, *"the end-time,"* and glanced at his watch. *"Ten minutes until twelve,"* Hermano replied.

"Crap!" The man unzipped his parka and, reaching inside, asked, *"Do you mind if I smoke?"*

"No, go ahead."

Lighting a cigarette, the man leaned back in the seat. *"Oh, my name's Dave Hunt,"* he said, offering his hand. Hermano smiled and shook it. "Hermano," he said.

"I was supposed to be in Weatherford-Texas-by one o'clock," Dave paused, *"my brother's funeral,"* he added.

"Oh," Hermano glanced at him. *"Sorry."* There was a long silence.

"We weren't very close," Dave said, *"not in the last few years."* There was another long silence.

"I got the weirdest phone call Thursday night," Dave said. *"My niece-even though my brother and me are on the outs, I try to keep in touch with my niece and nephew. Anyway, on Thursday night my niece calls-I live in Denver-and says that my brother Sam got killed. She said-and these were her exact words-'something evil is going on here'."* He paused, *"she said that Sam got killed when he caught some people mutilating a cow--out at the ranch."*

Hermano glanced at him. *"Mutilating?"* He asked.

"Yeah, you know, removing sex organs, eyes and ass. She said she thought they drained the blood, too." He paused, *"You know anything about that stuff? It happened quite a bit in the late 70s."*

"Yeah," Hermano answered, *"I know quite a bit about it. 'Something evil' was the right choice of words."*

"Anyway, she said that the guy that was with my nephew when they found the body got killed the next day. Then she said that my nephew got framed—or set up—for a cocaine bust on that same day, too." He paused, and then added, *"she said that weird people are harassing her."*

"The Church of Satan," Hermano said, looking around at him.

Dave sighed. *"That's what I figured,"* he said.

Hermano looked back at the road. *"What are you going to do?"* he asked.

"I don't know. I'll have to wait until I get there and play it by ear. I would have already been there, but my scooter-- a Harley 74 —broke down in Amarillo last night. I left it at a filling station."

There was another long silence as Dave vacantly gazed out the passenger window. Sighing, he looked over at Hermano, *"Sam pretty much took over running the ranch when Dad died-that was in '68. The Vietnam war was going full throttle by then, I was a wild-ass kid, 18 years old. Sam was already married and—anyhow,"* he paused, *"to make a long story short, I joined the Marine Corps and Sam stayed home and ran the ranch. Hell! I didn't care. The ranch was half mine and I-when*

I even thought about it-knew that Sam would do a good job of keeping it together.

*It kind of ate at Sam, though. You know, his kid brother went off to war and he stayed home with the women. I **really** didn't think of it that way, but I think he thought I did. So, when I got orders to 'Nam in '69 he quit writing. I mean, for a year in 'Nam I wrote letters that he never answered. Then, just before my tour was up, I got captured-up by the D.M.Z..*

That was in '70. I was listed as MIA, so Sam and Dora figured I was dead. Well, I guess Sam's conscience got him, because from then-on he was Sam the Super-Patriot. You know, with those bumper stickers that say 'America: Love It or Leave It'?"

Dave stretched and continued, *"Hell, I was gung-ho. I left home in '68. But when I came back in '73 ---. Well, either '73 or '75 –take your pick. I came back in '73, but the government stuck me in a psychiatric hospital until '75. They said that I had—what did they call it? --acquired stress syndrome or something like that, A.S.S.--which is what they took me for –an ass.*

Anyway, when I came back, I pretty much washed my hands of this country. Or, at least, of whatever it is that runs it. See, when I was captured, I was taken into North Vietnam. But I only was In North Vietnam until 1971. In the last part of '71, I was taken to East Germany. Taken by the Soviets and guarded by the Soviets—but in East Germany." He looked at Hermano.

"They picked my brain. I mean, picked it for every insignificant detail that you can imagine. Hell, I was only a lance corporal—I didn't have any military secrets. But they didn't care about military secrets—they wanted to know what I wore to the senior prom." He paused, *"you know what sticks in my mind most about that whole thing?"* He looked at Hermano.

Hermano glanced at him and looked back at the road. *"What?"* He asked.

"The cage they kept me in. No, actually, the grating on the floor

of the cage. It was steel grating with little holes drilled all in it—cock-roach doors—and on the end of each 2-foot-wide strip of grating, it had stamped,' Roth-Unicorn: made in U.S.A." Dave laughed bitterly.

"I still have nightmares about that. But that's not why my own government ended up sending me to the hospital. See, after a while, I got to figuring that the Soviets weren't never going to let me out of there alive. You know, they weren't supposed to be holding American prisoners. Were they going to let me loose, so I could talk about it? Shit no! I figured they were going to waste my ass.

So I started getting real serious about making a break. And you know, after two years of shit-luck, all of a sudden things really started to click—my way.

*A German psychiatrist got real careless—I'd always been easy to handle, before—and I made my break. It's a long story, but I got into West Germany. And like a big dumb-ass, I went straight to a military base—an **American** military base. I should have gone to the newspapers.*

Anyhow, they stuck me in a military hospital, shot me up with something, and I woke up in Da-Nang, South Vietnam.

The doctors said that I was found wandering around in the D.M.Z.. They wanted to know what P.O.W. Camp that I escaped from. When I told them, they said that I was having some kind of delusions. Had dreamed-up the whole thing. Then they de-briefed me—for the next two years." He looked at Hermano.

"They didn't treat me or anything, just stuck me in a mental hospital for two years. When they finally let me go, some ass-hole of a major says, 'if you go shooting off your mouth about that East Germany thing, we'll simply point out that we had to hospitalize you for two years because of your psychotic delusions.'

"Psychotic delusions!" He paused. *"All this will probably get dredged up when I start looking for satanists' heads to bust,"* he chuckled. *"They'll say, he's having more of those psychotic delusions."*

Dave looked over at Hermano. *"I hope you don't mind me ranting about all this stuff. Since Deirdre called, it's about all I've thought about."*

Hermano had been quietly and attentively listening to Dave's story. He looked over at his passenger. *"Dave, I've been investigating the dark corners of this country for ten years. What you're saying doesn't come as a surprise,"* he paused, *"I believe your story."*

Dave smiled his thanks. *"Well, Sam didn't,"* he said. *"When I got home, I started shooting off my mouth to anybody who'd listen. Newspapers. You know-they'd interview me because I was a POW.*

They wouldn't print anything before checking with the government, though. And the government said just what the Major said they'd say. 'Poor Dave, those years in a North Vietnamese POW camp really pushed him off the deep-end.'

It ended up the newspapers didn't print anything, and Sam blew his stack. He figured I was a dangerous subversive-and a lunatic to boot.

Well, I had to get out of Weatherford. So I bought a Harley-Davidson and split. And that's what I been doing ever since, still got the same Harley." He sighed.

"Money hadn't been any problem. He might be cantankerous, but Sam **is** *honest. At the beginning of every year he deposits 15% of the profits into my savings account in Weatherford. I have some of the money transferred to a checking account in Denver-so I don't ever have to worry about cash. I've got about five hundred on me, now."*

He looked at Hermano. *"I don't know how big a hurry you're in to get where ever it is you're going-but I'll give you $500 to run me to Weatherford."*

Hermano smiled. *"I'll do it for free,"* he said. "It's not far out of my way." He looked at Dave. *"I'd like to help,"* he said. *"Seriously. You see, I'm a kind of minister-not the kind that has a church. But the kind that has a mission, -- to do all that I can to fight the Church of Satan. If it's the Church of Satan that you're going to be confronting in Weatherford, then I could be real handy to have around."* He paused, thinking.

"Why don't you see what you can find out this weekend and give me a call Monday," Hermano said *"I'll give you my folks telephone num-ber, before I drop you off."* He glanced at Dave. *"I need a job. Does the*

ranch hire workers? Without your dad and nephew there, maybe they're shorthanded."

"That's a good idea," Dave said, *"I'll check with Dora."*

"I can just be an acquaintance from Colorado that needs a job," added Hermano. *"I'd kind of like to keep a low profile-at least at first. I could probably find out more that way."*

At 5:30, after giving Dave his parent's telephone number, Hermano pulled over and stopped on the shoulder of Mustang Road, about a half-mile north of Jackson's Store. Dave had asked him to stop there, so that he could walk home through the pastures.

"If we're going to be secretive about this, we might as well do it right," Dave had said.

"Say, Dave," Hermano said, leaning across this seat and speaking through the open passenger window. *"If it's the Church of Satan, they're a lot more sophisticated than you might think. When you call me, call from a pay phone."*

Dave waved and, climbing over a barbed wire fence, started off across the north pasture.

It had been an emotionally exhausting day for Deirdre. The funeral had been at one o'clock, but they hadn't left the graveyard until after three. She, her mother, and Aunt Una had gone from the cemetery to Reverend Hall's house where they had remained until supper. Deirdre had driven on home just before six, leaving her mother and Aunt Una to follow later in Aunt Una's car.

Deirdre looked out the plate glass windows of the sliding patio doors and was surprised to see that it was almost dark. She hurriedly got up off the couch and walked over to a panel of electric light switches, near the garage door. She flicked on the garage lights, the driveway light, the front porch light, and for good measure, the pool and helipad lights. She hadn't felt comfortable after dark at the ranch since her dad's death. For the past few nights she had turned on every outside light at the ranch as soon as the sun went down.

She turned from the light panel and started walking back across the room to the couch. About midway there she happened to glance out the patio windows and stopped abruptly. A man was walking across the helipad.

At first she panicked and started to race for her car. She had taken two or three quick steps toward the garage door when she regained control of herself. No! She wasn't going to be run from our own home. She dashed over to the desk and opened the bottom left drawer. Pulling out a black snub-nosed .38, she opened the cylinder to make sure that it was loaded, snapped it shut, and walked over to the patio door. The man had crossed the helipad and was almost to the deck of the swimming pool.

"Hold it right there, mister!" She slid the patio door open with such force that it crashed against the door frame. She stepped through the door with her right arm extended, the gun cocked and pointing at the stranger.

"Don't shoot, Little Lady," drawled Uncle Dave's imitation of John Wayne. *"It's the cavalry."*

"Uncle Dave!" Deirdre lowered her arm and rushed across the patio. *"I was afraid that something had happened to you."* She hugged him tightly for a couple of seconds and stepped back. *"And where is your motorcycle?"* She asked.

"Broke down in Amarillo. I had to thumb it on in. Where's your mom?" he asked, looking beyond her toward the patio door.

"Oh, she and Aunt Una are still over at Reverend Hall's. We ate supper over there. Come on in," she said, turning and walking back toward the den.

Chapter 11

The Vail social calendar always went into a tailspin when Pierre Manticore was in town. The competition for one of his coveted dinner invitations-and the lengths to which his would-be guests would go to-to obtain one -were legend in Vail society.

Pierre's parties always began at 11:30 on Sunday morning and usually didn't break up until sometime Monday morning. There, Vail locals and seasonals could expect to rub shoulders with a balanced mixture of movie stars, politicians and industrialists. You could tell the difference, it was said, by the condition of their drinks. The movie star's drink was always full, the politician's drink was always empty, and the industrialist's ice was always melted.

The invitation competition for today's party had been even more cut-throat than usual. Word hadn't gotten around that there was even *going* to be a party until mention had been made of it in the Thursday **Rocky Mountain News**. Pierre's secretary hadn't been seen without a phone in his hand from then until late Saturday, when all calls were forwarded to an answering service.

By four o'clock Sunday afternoon, Pierre's party was in full swing. There was a croquet tournament on the front lawn, a poetry reading in the library, and a popular rock band in the ballroom.

Laughter and gaiety were the theme of the party. The only frowns to be seen were on the faces of the people occasionally glimpsed descending the stairs from Pierre Manticore's third-floor office. Pierre hadn't been seen all afternoon and the only assurance that he was really there was the presence of his Arab "boy". He had been a constant spectator at the croquet tournament since shortly after one.

The people seen leaving Manticore's office could also have testified of his presence. But like well-dressed errand-boys, they always left the premises as soon as they had descended the stairs.

Pierre popped another chocolate covered cherry into his mouth and frowned. Whenever he became angry, he always resorted to sweets, and the angrier he got-the richer the sweets.

"Mr. Manticore, Wally Byrd is here to see you," Pierre looked up to see Jon, his personal secretary, standing in the doorway between his office and the waiting area.

"Send him in," Pierre answered.

Hat in hand, Chief Deputy Wally Byrd quietly entered Pierre's office.

"Sit down, WallyBird," Pierre said, waving his hand toward an easy chair that was pulled up in front of his desk. Deputy Byrd sat erectly on the edge of his chair.

"Now, WallyBird, tell me—in your own words—why you decided to shoot our friends." Pierre popped another chocolate covered cherry into his mouth. Wally cleared his throat.

"I, uh, I didn't see what started the shooting." He paused. *"One of my men found a dugout that someone had apparently used as a hiding place. When he called out to tell me about it, all hell broke loose. Those I.D. people started it."* Wally stared down at his hat--balanced precariously on his knees. He absently began smoothing the hat's crease.

"WallyBird, WallyBird. Tsk, tsk, tsk." Pierre's eyes belied the lightness of his tone as he stared across the table at Deputy Byrd. *"You've made a bad situation worse, WallyBird. Now, what's this about a dugout?"*

Wally glanced up and, meeting Pierre's cold stare, quickly looked back down at his hat.

"*Somebody had dug a trench near the tree line,*" he paused, "*On a slope overlooking the fire festival.*"

"*Who?*" Asked Pierre.

"*We don't know.*" He meekly looked up at Pierre. "*It was covered with a new sheet of plywood that had been camouflaged on top. We figure somebody had dug it to spy on the festival.*"

"*You figure!*" Pierre spat out. "*What do you **know**?*"

Wally shifted uncomfortably. "*We found the lumberyard that sold the sheet of plywood,*" he offered, "*and we got a description of the man who bought it. The salesman said he looked like an Indian, about 6 foot tall.*"

"*That's it?*" Asked Pierre. Obviously irritated, he popped another chocolate covered cherry into his mouth.

"*The salesman didn't get a look at his car,*" Wally looked back down and began lightly dusting the brim of his hat.

"*Leave that god damned hat alone and look at me when I'm talking to you!*" Pierre had stood up and was glaring down at Deputy Byrd. "*So that is it! Listen you two-bit constable. You find out who was in that dugout-or I'm going to see that **you** get put in a dugout. 6 feet under! Get my meaning?*"

"*Yes, sir.*" Deputy Byrd's voice was weak, and he was beginning to feel faint.

"*I don't believe that old man could have chopped off somebody's head with that sickle—much less his own.*" Pierre paused, sitting back down. "*Somebody else was involved out there-and I want to find out who-now! Get out of here.*"

"*Yes, sir.*" Wally got up and quickly left the room.

Deputy Byrd was in such a hurry to leave the Manticore château that he didn't notice the big man working on the station wagon near the driveway entrance. Toby looked up and, seeing Deputy Byrd turn east toward Denver, quickly closed the hood. He slid into the driver's seat, started the engine, and pulled onto the highway, trailing about half a mile behind.

Toby, well concealed, had witnessed the shoot-out at the fire-festival site on Monday afternoon, and, having obtained Byrd's license plate number, had located him by the next morning. Deputy Byrd had been a man living in constant fear, and Toby had found it impossible to get inside his residence to plant a bug. He had been following him as well as he could since Tuesday morning, but until today that had proved to be a waste of time. After six long and frustrating days, though, today's trip to Vail had finally been the payoff.

Toby didn't know who lived in the Château which had just been visited by Byrd, but whoever it was, Toby felt certain, was clearly superior to Byrd. Byrd's quick visit and hasty departure certainly appeared to be the actions of an underling making a report. Toby only wanted one thing from Byrd now-the envelope he had seen him present to the gate guard to gain admittance.

As he drove, Toby reached under the front seat and pulled out a sawed-off double barreled 12 gauge, which he laid on the passenger seat beside him. Killing Byrd would be simple but taking the time to stop and search him for that envelope could prove risky. The Sunday afternoon rush of traffic from the mountains back to Denver was well under way and Toby's primary hope in getting both Byrd and the envelope was that Byrd would stick to the pattern that he had been setting all week.

In the six days that Toby had followed him, Byrd had never gone to and come back from a destination by the same route. Driving from Colorado Springs to Vail, he had taken 25 north to Denver and then 70 west, both heavily congested freeways. But going back, he could cut several miles off his trip by going southeast on 9. Nine intersected 70 at Frisco, about twenty-five miles east of Vail, and was far less congested than either 70 or 25.

Deputy Byrd stopped to eat dinner at a truck stop in Frisco, and then, much to Toby's satisfaction, took a right onto Highway 9.

The sun was about to go down and Deputy Byrd was driving well within the speed limit. When they were four miles southeast of 70,

Toby sped up and passed. He wanted that envelope, so he couldn't run the risk of Byrd driving off a cliff after he had been shot. Toby wanted to get out ahead and locate a fairly level, or at least heavily wooded, stretch of highway while it was still light.

Toby was past Breckenridge in ten or fifteen minutes, but it was another twenty minutes after that before he located a suitable stretch of highway. Satisfied with his ambush site, Toby pulled over onto the shoulder to make a U-turn. On the roadside sign in front of him it said "Fairplay: City Limits".

Smiling, Toby turned around and drove back a couple of miles to wait for his envelope.

"Sticky wicket," quipped one of the croquet finalists as the crowd roared its approval. The pretty young red-headed finalist had just missed on her third attempt to get her ball through the first wicket.

Towering over the rest of the crowd, Toby's short-cropped black and gray hair made him look more like a misplaced Marine Corps drill instructor than a croquet enthusiast. Smiling when the rest of the crowd laughed, Toby didn't know and couldn't have cared less what was going on.

His eyes were fixed on the wide oaken front door of the Manticore château. Two people had entered the château through that door in the twenty minutes that he had been standing with the crowd. A large man had answered the door so quickly each time that Toby had no doubt that he was standing or sitting just inside.

He had already checked out the ballroom and the library, which, except for a couple of restrooms, were the only rooms in the house accessible to the average guest. Toby had stood in the ballroom long enough to watch one or two carefully screened guests ascend the stairs which hugged the inner wall. When asked, another guest had responded that they had been summoned for an audience with Pierre *"Audience"* was the word he had used. Toby had frowned and walked back outside.

Toby already knew that the château belonged to Pierre Manticore.

He had learned that from the desk clerk at the Ramada Inn, about a mile from Manticore's driveway.

After Toby had blown Deputy Byrd off the road and had obtained his invitation, he had driven back to Vail and checked into the motel nearest the château. It was eight o'clock then, and it was now—Toby looked at his watch-- 9:30.

This was beginning to look as if it was going to be a next to impossible task. There were four entrances into the Château; a side door into the library, folding double-doors into the ballroom, the locked entrance to an underground garage, and the front door. Except for the outer door, the only other door in the library opened into the ballroom. So that left the ballroom and the front door as the only entrances into the non-public part of the house. All the inner doors in the ballroom were locked, the only way out was up the stairs or out the folding doors.

Toby looked away from the front door and began a more careful inspection of the ground. He had brought a small listening device (a "bug" about the size and shape of a quarter) and a "booster" with him. Although he didn't have any idea where or how he was going to plant the bug, he decided that he may as well go ahead and plant the booster. The "bug", with a range of about 400 yards, would be useless anyway without the booster, which could increase the range to about 3 miles. The booster, though, about the size of a cigarette pack, wasn't so easy to conceal.

Studying the copse of trees on the other side of the croquet field, he decided to try planting the booster over there. If the bug was planted in the house, then, from the copse of trees the booster would be within range. It would relay the bug's signal on to Toby's motel room.

He walked around the well-lit croquet field and paused at the edge of the trees to make sure that he wasn't being watched.

Satisfied, he bent over as if to tie his shoes and, in a crouch, moved sideways into the woods. He straightened when he was out of sight of the croquet field and began searching for a likely spot to plant his booster.

It took about five minutes to locate the seven-foot stump of a tree, which had apparently been sheared by a lightning strike. Reaching up and feeling the top of it he was happy to discover a three-inch-deep hollow in the center of the stump.

Sitting upright, the booster was a perfect fit. That accomplished, Toby quietly made his way back to the croquet field. Stepping out of the trees, Toby was confronted by a dark-skinned Arab boy who looked to be about 11 or 12 years old. The boy, dressed in sneakers and jeans was wearing a sable coat, which Toby guessed would sell for at least $10,000.

"You are supposed to use the restrooms in the house," the boy said.

"I didn't think I'd make it," Toby laughed.

The boy smiled, *"I did the same myself, a while ago."*

"Your folks here?" Asked Toby.

The smile left the boy's face, *"No, they are--,"* he hesitated, *"not here."*

They were both quiet while they looked out at the croquet field. After a few minutes, the boy looked back up at Toby.

"Are you a soldier?" He asked.

"No, I --uh-- I used to be a football player."

"My dad's a soldier," the boy said. *"A mujahedin,"* he paused. *"In Afghanistan."*

"Oh. Those are very brave men," Toby replied. *"How did you get over here?"*

"My master brought me." The boy quickly looked back at the croquet game.

"Your---Master?" Toby studied the boy more closely.

"Pierre Manticore. This is his house."

"Oh." Toby tried not to show the excitement he was feeling. Toby's size and physical appearance were deceptive. Though he appeared to

be a huge, dull, bear of a man, his mind was sharp and extraordinarily quick. And he was an opportunist.

"*I don't believe that I've seen Pierre all evening,*" he said.

"*He's in the upstairs study,*" the boy said. "*He's had meetings all day.*"

"*Oh.*" Toby looked back out at the field and then glanced back at the boy. "*That's a nice coat,*" he said.

"*Thanks. One of my master's friends sent it to me.*" The boy smiled up at Toby. "*People that want to see my master often send me gifts.*"

Toby smiled. "*There's so many people who want to see Pierre, you must get to open presents almost every day.*"

"*Almost,*" the boy agreed. They both looked back out at the playing field.

"*Well,*" Toby said, "*if you're from Afghanistan, then you must be a Muslim. I have a lot of friends who are Muslims.*"

"*Yes,*" the boy said with a frown. He stuffed his hands as far into his coat pockets as he could. "*I could recite fifty surahs from the Koran before I was seven years old.*" He paused, "*my parents sold me when I was seven. There wasn't enough food.*"

"*Seven? That's pretty young to leave home.*" Toby glanced back at the field. He looked relaxed, but his mind was racing. "*Is Pierre a Muslim?*" He asked.

The boy gave a short, bitter laugh. "*No,*" he said. "*He gets mad if I mention Allah—God.*"

"*Well, maybe you're the way that God will reach Pierre.*" Toby smiled down at the boy.

The boy, shifting uncomfortably, looked back up at Toby, "*The master treats me like—like a prince,*" he said. "*But once, when he caught me praying, he had me whipped.*" He looked back at the playing field. "*He really doesn't like me to talk about God.*"

"*Oh,*" Toby paused, "*well, if you care about him, there are ways to change that.*" He paused again, "*Have you tried the 'Eye of Allah'?*" he asked.

"*The what?*" The boy looked back at Toby, "*The eye of Allah? I've never heard of that.*"

"*Well, it's actually called the 'Hidden Eye of Allah'. It's the Koran.*" Toby paused, "*when I was traveling in the Mideast an Imam in Mecca told me about it. You take the Koran and conceal it in the work area of the unbeliever who you love. God will take it from there,*" he paused again. "*With Pierre, you should---hmmm--does he have a lot of books in his upstairs study?*"

"*Yes,*" the boy said, looking at Toby with renewed interest. "*He has tall bookshelves with lots of books.*"

"*Then you should take your Koran and sneak it onto the bookshelves. With all the other books, it probably wouldn't be noticed.*"

The boy looked crestfallen. "*I don't have a Koran,*" he said plaintively. "*I don't go anywhere without master and he would never let me buy a Koran.*"

"*Do you open your own gifts that come in the mail?*" Toby asked, trying not to show his relief.

"*Yes.*"

"*Well, maybe I can help you then.*"

Chapter 12

"Hermano! Hermano, telephone." Hermano put down his book and glanced at the back door of his parents' white wood-frame farmhouse. His mom was standing in the doorway, smiling over toward the tree-shaded picnic table where Hermano had been reading all afternoon.

"I think maybe it's that call you've been waiting for," she said, brushing her long hair back from her forehead. The smile-lines in her otherwise smooth reddish-brown face and the gray streaks in her black hair were the only indications of her advancing age. Hermano hadn't been able to come home many times in the past few years, but every time he had, his mom's energy and her enthusiastic approach to even the most menial tasks had amazed him.

"Supper'll be ready in about an hour," she added, turning to go back into the kitchen.

Hermano got up and jogged to the door, going through the kitchen to take the call in the living room.

"Yes?" He said.

"Hermano, this is David—you gave me a ride a couple of days ago."

"Yeah, I was hoping you'd call," Hermano sat down on a wooden kitchen chair, parked against the wall and under the wall-phone. *"How have you found things at the ranch?"*

"Worse than I thought. I just finished talking with Bill—he's still in jail."

"Where are you, now?"

"Pay-phone. Across the street from the County Jail. Can we get to-gether somewhere this evening? Fairly early, because I don't like leaving the women alone out there. Their preacher's eating supper there tonight, so he'll probably be around till about ten or so."

"Well, I can be in Fort Worth in thirty or forty minutes."

"Great! Let's see, do you know where Northeast Mall is?"

"Yes, I haven't been there in a few years, though."

"OK, uh, Melbourne Street borders the mall on the east side. There's a Pablo's Mexican Food Restaurant on Melbourne, across the parking lot from the mall. Can you be there by about six o'clock?"

"I'll try," Hermano said. *"See you then."* He hung up the phone.

"Say, Mom," he called out.

"Don't say it, I heard," drifted in from the kitchen. *"Your dad's going to be grouchy all evening."*

"Sorry, Mom. Tell Dad I'm sorry, but—well, it's my work. He'll understand."

The drive to northeast Fort Worth took Hermano forty minutes and, by his watch, it was exactly 6 o'clock when he pulled into Pablo's parking lot.

He had no idea what David might be driving, so, not knowing whether he was already there or not, he decided to go on in.

"Hermano, over here." David was standing just inside the door, looking apprehensively toward the mall through a front window.

"I just got here, myself," he said, turning around to shake hands. *"I wasn't sure you were serious about all this until I called—I still wasn't sure you'd show up. Thanks,"* he said, leading Hermano into the dining area. *"I hope you like Mexican food—I'm buying."* They took a two-man table on the far side of the restaurant.

"Well, like I told you on the phone," he began, scooting his chair close to the table and leaning over it on his elbows, *"this is more serious than I thought."* He paused. *"Have you ever heard of Congressman Jim Burton?"* He asked.

"Yes," answered Hermano.

"*Well, it looks like he might have something to do with all this.*" He went on to relay Bill's story of all that had happened on May Day, including what Silas had told Bill about Central US Avionic's helicopter.

"*And then Silas tells Bill that one of the people at the spot where Sam's helicopter came down was one of Burton's aides.*" David leaned back in his seat. "*Well, what do you think?*" he asked.

Hermano sighed. "*The Church of Satan cuts through all the social barriers,*" he said wryly. "*I think they blundered—pretty badly. And I think that they're trying to keep a bad situation from getting worse.*" He paused. "*I think your family's in considerable danger,*" he added as he leaned back in his chair to allow the waitress to set down their food. After she had left, Hermano looked across the table to find David intently studying him.

"*Why do you want to get involved in all this?*" David asked.

Hermano thought for a minute. Then he asked, "*What are your religious convictions?*"

"*My religious convictions? Well---I believe in the existence of God.*" David paused, "*I guess I'm not all that religious, though.*"

Hermano sighed, "*No offense, but this might be a good time to get your act together. The people—or organization—that you're up against **are** religious. With a distinctly negative slant, though. I'm religious, too—but diametrically opposed to them. I guess you could say that I'm a kind of minister,*" he went on. "*But instead of feeling that I have a calling to preach, I have a calling to do all that I can to oppose and destroy the Church of Satan.*"

Dave leaned back in his chair with a look of mock surprise on his face. "*Destroy!*" He exclaimed.

"*What do you think they intend to do to your family?*" Hermano raised his eyebrows.

"*No, I mean, we're two guys, and what we're talking about is a big, powerful organization. I was thinking more along the lines of—survival.*"

"*Survival? Look, David, these people are already beaten. They just need to have it pointed out to them—or rammed down their throats.*

*God really **does** exist. He really does care what's going on. And He really **can** do something about it."* Hermano paused. *"He often works through people, people who have surrendered themselves to Him.*

Just think. Driving—or hitchhiking—from Denver to Weatherford—what are the odds of you running into somebody like me?"

Dave chuckled. *"You've got a point, there."* He leaned forward, *"Just so you understand -- that this could get real messy before it's over."*

"I think I can promise you that," Hermano said.

"Well—cowboy—you know where you dropped me off on Mustang Road? The bunkhouse, where you go to apply for a job, is three or four hundred yards north of there. We passed it just before you dropped me off. I'll be there from about three o'clock until about five o'clock tomorrow afternoon."

Tuesday passed without incident. Hermano was "hired" by the Hunt Ranch by four 0'clock in the afternoon and he spent the rest of the daylight hours touring the ranch with Dave. Dora and Deirdre had been in Fort Worth visiting Bill, so Hermano hadn't had a chance to meet them before Dave had dropped him off at the bunkhouse at around 6:30 p.m. It had, by then, been too late to eat supper with the other half dozen cowhands, so Dave had handed him $10 and told him to drive into Weatherford to eat.

"Meals and a bunk go with the job," Dave had said.

After supper Hermano had returned to the bunkhouse, which was actually a sturdy old three-bedroom farmhouse surrounded with corrals, outbuildings and farm machinery and, after locating a pillow and blanket, had turned in for the night. Being odd-man-out, with two men to a bedroom, Hermano had cheerfully volunteered to sleep on the living room couch.

Breakfast in the bunkhouse kitchen had been served at 6:00 a.m. And by seven o'clock Dave had arrived to assign daily chores. Hermano had been assigned the job of tightening up the slack in some barbed wire fence on Mustang Road, between the bunkhouse and Jackson's Store.

"Try and stay close to Jackson's Store to see who stops there," Dave had said. *"If that old red pickup with the whip antenna stops, call me from the bunkhouse. Deirdre saw it there once since that guy exposed himself to her, but that was Monday—when I was in Fort Worth."* Handing Hermano the keys to one of the ranch pickups, Dave had then left for the ranch house, promising to get back in touch around noon.

The fence on Mustang Road was already tight, so until ten o'clock Hermano spent the better part of his time just trying to look busy.

A few minutes after ten, hearing a car door slam, Hermano looked toward Jackson's Store to see a light blue Volkswagen parked near the entrance. A young, attractive woman with long blond hair tied back in a pigtail, was just walking through the door. Hermano had seen that VW parked beside the ranch house the day before, when he had had his tour with Dave. And since the woman fit Deirdre's description, he walked back to the pickup to feign getting a drink of water so that he could keep an eye on the front of the store.

Hermano had no sooner opened the door of the ranch pickup, when an old red pickup truck with a whip antenna roared past. Gravel flying, it slid into a parking spot beside the VW. A young man with long black hair, and his slightly taller red-headed female companion, quickly got out and hurried into the store.

Hermano climbed on into the pickup and quickly drove the two hundred yards to the store. After parking slightly behind and to the right of the red pickup, Hermano killed the engine and paused for a moment to study the three-inch by three-inch sticker that was on the lower right side of the pickup rear window. It was a black pentagram on a light green background—the words "drive safely" were printed just below the pentagram.

Hermano opened the door and slid out. Shutting the door, he stepped around behind the red pickup and looked at the license plate. Then, hearing the man's voice raised in conversation inside the store, Hermano decided to chance getting a look at the CB radio. Circling around the pickup, he opened the driver's door and leaned inside—the radio was set to channel six. He quietly shut the door and, walking back around the pick-up, proceeded on to the store's front door.

"Listen, chick, you might as well accept the fact that some dark, lonely night I'm going to get the chance. I'll find out then, if that blond hair is real." Dee, looking panic-stricken, was leaning against the counter near the cash register. The black-haired man leered as he leaned in so close behind her that she couldn't turn around without brushing against him. The sales clerk and the red-haired girl weren't anywhere to be seen.

"Who owns that red pickup?" Hermano called out as he walked through the front door.

"I do, why?" The black-haired man turned around as Hermano walked over toward where he and Deirdre were standing. Deirdre quickly slid out from between him and the counter.

"What's that star on the back-window sticker mean?" asked Hermano, stopping a couple of feet in front of the man. Hermano, at 6 feet and 180 pounds was roughly the same size as the man, but Hermano's solid, rugged look made him appear larger. Hermano's mouth was smiling, but his eyes were coldly staring into the eyes of the black-haired man. The man looked away.

"Hell, I don't know. It's just a star," he started to turn back around to Deirdre, but Hermano continued.

"I think it's called the pentagram, isn't it?"

"Looks like you know more about it than I do," the man said, glancing back at Hermano.

"I doubt that," said Hermano coldly. *"You know, a few months back, I saw a TV special about satanism, and they showed stars just like yours on it. Are you a satanist?"*

"No, man. Look, it's just a safe driving sticker." Deirdre had moved a few feet farther down the counter and the black-haired man started to turn in her direction.

Hermano quickly stepped up to the counter between the man and

Deirdre and, turning to the man, who was obviously getting angry, he said, *"Well, that's good---that you're not a satanist, I mean. There are supposed to be some in this area. Cowardly, repulsive creatures—I doubt they'd **admit** to being satanists."* Hermano smiled and added, *"the scum."*

"Can I help you folks?" The teenaged girl, apparently the sales clerk, was returning from the back of the store with the tall redheaded girl. *"Sorry we took so long. Never did find what she was looking for."*

"What's that?" asked Hermano. He winked at the black-haired man, *"Safety stickers?"*

Red-faced, the black-haired man whirled to look at his companion. *"Come on, Holly. Let's split."* He headed toward the door with the redheaded girl, looking confused, following behind.

After they had walked out, Hermano turned and smiled at the sales clerk. *"This lady was in front of me,"* he said, nodding toward Deirdre.

"Go ahead," Deirdre said, smiling at Hermano, *"I kind of like having you go out before me."* She glanced at the door.

Hermano picked up a small package of mints and, paying for them, stepped back from the register. He glanced at Deirdre.

"I'll wait around outside until you leave," he said. Turning, he walked toward the door.

"Thanks," Deirdre called out.

A couple of minutes later, Deirdre came out the front door of the store and was relieved to see that the red pickup was gone. Hermano was standing with his back against the driver's door of the ranch truck.

"Say, isn't that a Hunt Ranch truck?" Deirdre asked as she walked over to her car.

"Yeah. I just started working there, today," Hermano said, smiling at Deirdre.

"Well, you're sure earning your keep," she said. She looked over the top of the VW at Hermano as she opened her door. *"I'm Deirdre Hunt. I guess my uncle must have hired you."*

"*Yeah, Dave. He took me on a tour of the ranch, yesterday. He said that y'all were gone to Fort Worth or something.*" He opened the door of the truck. "*Nice meeting you,*" he called out. "*Oh, by the way, I'm Hermano.*"

"*Thanks again, Hermano.*"

Hermano sat in the truck and watched her until she pulled into the ranch driveway. Then he started the pick-up and drove back to the spot where he had been working.

In less than ten minutes, Dave, driving another Hunt Ranch pickup, came sliding to a halt beside Hermano's truck. Dave jumped out and hurriedly walked around the truck to join Hermano near the fence.

"*Dee told me what happened,*" he said. "*A low profile, hmmm? Why didn't you call?*"

"*There wasn't enough time, they pulled up right after Deirdre.*" Hermano paused, "*I recognized her VW from yesterday's tour,*" he added.

"*Well, shit! I wanted to get ahold of them.*" Dave looked back toward Jackson's Store.

"*And get yourself thrown in jail? Don't do them any favors.*" Hermano handed Dave a small piece of paper.

"*Here's their license plate number. Let's find out where they live. Why don't you use the bunkhouse telephone to call the Department of Motor Vehicles—in Austin. Just ask for 'Identification' and then find out who owns the truck and where they live.*"

Dave smiled. "*Great!*" he exclaimed, taking the paper.

"*Oh, and Dave—I know they're pretty outdated, but can you get me a CB radio for the truck? That red truck has one, and I checked it out before I went into the store. They were set on channel six.*"

Dave was walking back toward his truck, "*Sure thing,*" he said. "*We've still got a couple of them in the hall closet at the bunkhouse. See you in a few minutes.*" He spun out, heading for the bunkhouse.

In half an hour, Dave was back with two CB radios, some wire, and two clip-on antennas. Together they installed the radios in some brackets which had already been attached for that purpose under the dash of each pick up. Then, running antenna wire to the tops of the passenger doors, they attached the clip-on antennas.

"Why don't you keep tuned in to channel six, and I'll run on over to Mineral Wells," Dave said as he climbed into his pickup. The address of Alvin Speers, the registered owner of the red pickup, had been a street address in Mineral Wells.

"Dave," Hermano said quickly. He was standing by the opened driver's door of his truck. *"Right now, this is the only address we've got on probable members. I know you really want to get that guy, but why not wait until we've accumulated a little more information?"*

Dave sat behind the wheel of his pickup and, frowning, looked at Hermano. He sighed, *"Yeah, you're right. I'll just check out the residence,"* he reached for the ignition.

"Say, Dave. You wouldn't drive by there in a Hunt Ranch truck, would you?" Hermano was smiling.

Dave paused with his hand on the key. He looked back at Hermano *"Smart-ass,"* he said, grinning. *"I'll have my scooter back tomorrow. Two of the hands are going to drive up to Amarillo and get it after lunch."* He leaned back in the seat. *"Speaking of lunch, why don't you follow me up to the house. We can eat and talk strategy. Dee wants to meet you, anyway."*

Dee, carrying a tray stacked with sandwiches, a large bowl of potato chips, and three tall glasses of tea, slid the patio door open with her bare foot and then stepped out onto the patio.

"Can one of you guys shut the door?" She asked, walking toward the round covered patio table, where Dave and Hermano were seated.

"Sure," Hermano jumped up and walked past her to slide the door shut. When he got back to the table a paper plate and glass of tea were set at his place.

"Dig in," Deirdre said as he sat down.

"Here's what we want you to do, Dee," Dave said, talking around a mouthful of sandwich. He chewed thoughtfully for a few seconds, *"after lunch, I'm going to go over to the bunkhouse and get some paint I'll put Hermano to painting the driveway gate, down at Mustang Road. He'll have the pickup parked behind him with the CB turned on You just drive out to Mustang Road and turn toward Weatherford—drive a half-mile or so, turn around, and come back to the house."*

He took a long drink of iced tea. *"Then I'll drive to the store, come back to the house for a few minutes, get the Lincoln and drive into Weatherford."* He set the glass down. *"Is there a CB in the Lincoln?"* He asked, looking at Dee.

"Yes," she answered, *"and a mobile phone."*

Dave quickly ate the rest of his sandwich, finished his tea and stood up. *"I want to talk to Dora for a few minutes before we go. Is she in the old house?"* he asked, looking at Deirdre.

She had just taken a bite of sandwich and motioned for him to wait a minute. Dave impatiently busied himself lighting a cigarette.

"Yes, she's in the kitchen. Reverend Hall's with her. Mom was fixing them some lunch when I was in there," answered Deirdre.

"Reverend Hall. That guy ought to move in over here." grumbled Dave. Looking at Hermano, he said, *"I'll motion to you when I'm leaving."* He stepped around the table and walked toward the door.

Deirdre couldn't wait for him to get out of earshot. As soon as he had walked into the den, she looked at Hermano.

"I drove up Mustang Road, yesterday---way past our property." She paused. *"I don't think I've ever seen our fence looking better. Especially that stretch that Dave said he had had you working on."*

Not knowing what to say, Hermano took a quick bite of sandwich and smiled, motioning for Deirdre to wait a minute.

"Yeah, think up something good," Deirdre laughed.

Hermano took a drink of tea. *"A new employee doesn't question his boss's orders,"* he finally said.

"Come on," she said. *"You're not some vague acquaintance of Dave's that just happened to be coming from Colorado at the same time as him."*

"Well, I was real low on funds and Dave wanted somebody else here that he was relatively sure wasn't part of whatever is going on." Hermano took another bite of sandwich.

"You're not going to talk, are you?" Deirdre faked a pout and took a bite of her sandwich.

Hermano smiled.

"How is your brother?" He asked, changing the subject.

"Oh, he's OK. Our attorney still hasn't been able to get him out of jail, though." Deirdre stared out at the swimming pool. *"You know, usually the pool isn't filled until mid-May. Bill talked Daddy into filling it early this year, though."* She paused, *"He hasn't even been able to swim in it, yet."*

They talked for a few more minutes, mainly about the ranch and, having finished lunch, Deirdre began gathering up the paper plates. They both turned toward the patio door when they heard it open. *"I'm heading to the bunkhouse now,"* Dave called out. *"Hermano, I'll meet you down at the gate in fifteen or twenty minutes."*

"I'll be right on down," Hermano answered.

"Just what exactly are we doing?" Asked Deirdre after Dave had disappeared back into the den.

"Well, that red pickup pulled up to the store no more than a minute after you did. We're going to try and find out if someone is watching your driveway.

I got a look at the CB in the red pickup. We're tuned-in to the channel he was set on. We'll see if anything is broadcast on that channel when you're driving in and out."

"Oh. Well, I'll see you in a few minutes."

Chapter 13

Half an hour later, Hermano looked up from where he was painting the gate and smiled at Deirdre as she drove past in her VW. She returned his smile and, turning to the right on Mustang Road, sped off in the direction of Weatherford.

Hermano heard the CB crackle. A female voice said, *"C.-B-2"*. A couple of seconds later somebody keyed their microphone but didn't say anything.

Less than five minutes had passed when Deirdre came back up Mustang Road and wheeled into the driveway to stop beside Hermano. They both looked toward the CB when the female voice immediately came back.

"C-B-3," it said. The message was followed shortly by the static of a keyed microphone.

Hermano looked at Deirdre. *"Recognize the voice?"* He asked.

She shook her head. *"I don't think so,"*. She said.

"Whoever it is, has to be able to see us from where-ever they're at. Why don't you get out of your car and walk over here, act like you're looking at my work. Face toward the road and—without being obvious—check out each direction. See if you can spot any structure that we can be watched from." He paused thoughtfully as she got out of the car. *"That woman sounded pretty young, I didn't hear that redhead—Holly—talk, but could that have been her?"*

Deirdre walked over to stand aside where Hermano was painting. *"I don't think so,"* she said, casually looking up Mustang Road.

Hermano pointed to the parts of the fence that he had already painted and said, *"The only structures that I've noticed within sight of the gate are Jackson's Store and those two houses that are setback in the trees across Mustang Road, about 100 yards to the south."*

"Those would be Mr. Jackson's houses."

"Mr. Jackson from the store?"

"Yes. He owns the store and lives in the larger of those two houses. His son and daughter-in-law live in the nearer house. I've met her a few times—that could have been her voice."

"OK. Why don't you take on off back to the house and let Dave make his run."

Ten minutes later, Dave came flying down the drive in Deirdre's VW. He tooted the horn once as he slid onto Mustang Road and headed north toward Jackson's Store.

The female voice crackled over the CB, *"C-D-1"*, it said, to be followed by the keyed mic.

When Dave pulled into Jackson's Store, also visible from the two houses, the voice said, *"C-D-4"*.

On Dave's return Hermano heard, *"C-D-3."*

Half an hour after Dave's return to the ranch, Hermano looked up from his painting to see Dave coming back down the drive in Sam's Lincoln. He stopped and, leaning across the seat, spoke out the open passenger window.

"What do you think, Hermano?"

"Did you hear her?"

"Yeah, loud and clear. Somebody else did too."

"The keyed mic?"

"Yeah. So, what do you think?"

"Maybe one of those two houses across the road and to the south."

"Old-man Jackson's? Yeah, maybe. Dee says he's got a daughter-in-law about the right age for the voice."

"I think I've figured out a way to check it out. It might work," Hermano said. He continued, *"If we got something big and long—like the ranch's tractor-trailer rig—parked on the other side of the road and a few yards south, the view of the driveway would be blocked from those houses,"* he paused. *"You could get some of the hands to load up the trailer with cattle and have the truck out there in three or four hours. I could get in the pasture to the south and watch those houses and listen to the radio while Dee drives in and out."*

"Great. I'll call Dee on the car phone and have her get some hands together." He started to straighten back up in the seat but, remembering something, leaned back out the window. *"There are some binoculars up in the den."* He straightened up and drove out of the driveway turning south.

"A-D-2," the female voice reported.

Hermano finished painting the gate shortly after three o'clock and, after returning the paint and supplies to the bunkhouse, drove up to the ranch house. Leaving the pickup parked in front of the old house, he rang the front doorbell.

"Hi," Deirdre said, opening the door. *"Dave said you'd be by—for some binoculars or something."* She opened the door wide and stepped back, *"Come on in,"* she said.

She led Hermano back toward the kitchen. *"I want you to meet mom,"* she said. *"She and Reverend Hall are having their eighth or ninth cup of coffee. He's—uh,"* she smiled back at Hermano, *"persistent."*

"I really don't see anything in the Scriptures that denies the possibility of extra-terrestrial life. After all, Jesus said he had sheep to call that were not of this fold." Reverend Hall, hands clasped between his knees, was leaning forward over the table, gazing intently at Dora. Dora smiled.

"That may be so, Brother Hall, but these sheep don't seem to think anything of slaughtering other people's cattle." She turned around and smiled at Dee and Hermano.

"Brother Hall's decided that little green men mutilated that cow—and

that Sam was accidentally killed when he got too close to their spaceship."
She got up and introduced herself to Hermano.

"Sit down and I'll get you some coffee," she said.

*"I didn't say that that's what happened, I just said that the idea isn't
so far-fetched."* Piqued, brother Hall took a quick drink of coffee.

Sitting down, Hermano smiled and leaned forward. *"Pardon me,"*
he said, looking at Reverend Hall. *"Were you talking about the' One
Shepherd-- one flock,' part of the Gospel according to John?"*

"Yes. You seem to know your Scriptures," answered Reverend Hall,
looking closely at Hermano.

*"I always kind of thought that the flock that Jesus was talking about
was the descendants of Ishmael,"* Hermano said, still smiling.

"You mean Moslems?" Reverend Hall sat up more erectly in his
chair. *"Not hardly."* He then looked back at Dora. *"After all,"* he
continued as if Hermano had never spoken, *"there were several reported UFO sightings on the night of—Sam's misfortune."* He paused
a moment. *"The Sheriff's Department though, seems convinced that it
was wolves."*

Deirdre had listened to all that she could stand. *"Dad called them
rustlers. And after the gunshots, he said that he had got 'em. I don't think
he would have called flying saucers, or wolves for that matter--' rustlers'".*

There was a long silence.

*"In 1978 or 1979, there was a big conference of ranchers and law en-
forcement officers in Albuquerque, New Mexico,"* interjected Hermano.
*"The purpose of the conference was to compare notes on all the cattle
mutilations that were going on back then."* Hermano took a sip of his
coffee and continued, *"They didn't arrive at any unanimous conclu-
sions—except the conclusion that the government seemed to be trying to
cover it all up. There was a lot of talk about **helicopter** sightings at the
mutilation sites, though."*

Reverend Hall began staring at Hermano, again.

"Let's go, Hermano," said Deirdre as she pushed her chair back
and stood up.

"Aren't you going to drink your coffee, dear?" Asked her mom.

"Dave had an errand that he wanted Hermano to run for him," explained Deirdre. *"I probably ought to get him on it before Dave gets back."*

Hermano dutifully followed her toward the door. *"Nice meeting you,"* he said, smiling at Dora as he walked out of the kitchen.

"I know I shouldn't feel this way," Deirdre said over her shoulder as she entered the den, *"but I just can't stand that man I can't even decide why."* She walked over to the desk and took a large pair of binoculars out of the bottom drawer. She handed them to Hermano.

"Lupe and Floyd said they'd have the truck parked out there in--," she looked at her watch, *"half-an-hour. They're going to walk up to the house and then I'll run to Jackson's and back."* She paused. *"How long should they leave the truck there?"*

"As soon as you return from Jackson's they can move it. Can I just leave through the patio door?"

"Sure," she said, walking him to the door. *"Drop by the house afterward, will you? Just come around and knock on the patio door."*

Hermano smiled. *"OK,"* he said. *"See you then."*

Hermano drove through the pasture south of the house until he got some trees between himself and Jackson's houses. The trees were thirty or forty yards west of Mustang Road, on Hunt property. Hermano felt confident that he had remained unseen as he positioned himself in a dry creek bed that ran north and south through the trees.

Fifteen minutes later, he saw the Hunt Ranch's semi drive up north-bound on Mustang Road and park twenty or thirty yards south of the Hunt Ranch driveway. Two men got out of the truck and walked toward the ranch entrance.

Within five minutes Hermano saw a green Chevrolet four-door back out of the garage of the northernmost house, the house occupied by Jackson's son and daughter-in-law. The car, with a clip-on CB antenna of the type being used by Dave and Hermano, slowly rolled down the driveway to a spot five yards short of where their driveway intersected Mustang Road.

Hermano trained binoculars on the car and focused the lens. A young black-haired woman, trying to sit as low in the seat as possible, appeared to be focusing her own binoculars on the Hunt driveway.

Ten minutes later, Dee, in her VW, came down the ranch driveway and turned left to head toward Jackson's Store. Hermano watched the black-haired woman bring a microphone to her mouth.

"C-B-1." Her voice came from the CB in Hermano's truck.

Hermano watched as the black-haired woman dutifully reported Dee's trip to Jackson's Store and her return to the ranch, each report being followed by the sound of a keyed microphone.

A couple of minutes after Dee's return to the ranch house, Hermano saw the two ranch hands walking down the driveway to return to the truck.

Hermano brought the binoculars back up when he noticed a Parker County Sheriff's Department patrol car approaching from the south. A slender, middle-aged man was driving, and a younger, dark-haired man was in the passenger seat.

The patrol car slowed down as it passed the parked semi and then sped up and whipped into the Hunt driveway. The Sheriff's deputies had driven about thirty yards up the driveway when they stopped to talk to the two ranch hands.

From his gestures, the middle-aged deputy appeared to be lecturing the cowboys. This went on for a couple of minutes and then the patrol car backed down the driveway and headed back toward Weatherford. The cowboys jogged to the truck, scrambled into the cab, and sped off up Mustang Road.

"Hello, Lupe?" Deirdre, phone in hand, was sitting on the corner of the desk in the den. Hermano seated on a chair beside her, was leaning over the desk writing on a sheet of paper. *"Lupe, when y'all left the house a while ago, what did those deputies want?"* She listened

a moment. *"Oh, did he say why?"* She glanced around at Hermano who had finished writing and was now looking intently at the paper.

"Yeah, I know. Lots of times." She listened for a moment. *"Why don't the two of you just go back to whatever Dave had you doing. -- yeah, bye."* She hung up the phone and scooted off the desk.

"What's that?" She asked, looking over Hermano's shoulder at the paper.

"It's a list of the Jackson woman's messages and what they meant. Real simple code—but good enough, considering that anyone happening to hear one of her transmissions wouldn't have any way of knowing the meaning of it."

"See," he said, pointing to the last transmission. *"The VW is 'C', you're 'B', and returning to the ranch—or, at least, turning into the driveway of the ranch— is '3'. So, the transmission is ' C-B-3'. Simple. Dave's 'D', turning left out of the driveway is '1', turning right-- '2', and so on. First vehicle, then person, then movement or destination."* He paused a second.

"What did Lupe say?" He asked.

"He said that the older deputy chewed him out for parking on the shoulder of the road—said he was impeding traffic or something. They park it like that all the time up by the bunkhouse—no one's ever complained before." She thought for a moment.

"It sounded like the two deputies who came out to the house the day Dad was—killed." She said. *"The younger one, and his folks, go to mom's church."*

"How about the older one?" Asked Hermano.

"I guess he's new—at least, I've never seen him before last week." She paused.

"I think I'll go to church with Mom, Sunday, and try to talk with that younger guy. Want to go?" She asked, smiling at Hermano.

"I'd like that, thanks," Hermano returned her smile and stood up. *"Well, it's time for me to knock off. When's Dave supposed to be back?"* He asked.

"He said he'd be home for supper," answered Deirdre, following Hermano to the patio door. *"Do you want me to have him call you?"*

"No, that sheet of paper on the desk explains the radio transmissions. Tell him that that woman at Jackson's house is definitely the lookout." He paused for a moment. *"I've got some business that I've got to take care of tonight and tomorrow morning, so tell him that I'll probably be back out here sometime around lunch. Try to stick around the house—for safety's sake,"* added Hermano as he slid open the door and stepped out onto the patio.

"I'm beginning to feel like a hermit," complained Deirdre as she followed Hermano out onto the patio, sliding the door shut behind her. *"I'll walk you to the truck,"* she said.

The downtown Fort Worth offices of the Tarrant County Sheriff's Department were crowded and busy on Thursday morning. Hermano, dressed in cream-colored slacks and a white turtleneck, had to wait almost an hour before he could get in to see Chief Jailor Tom McHenry.

Deputy McHenry, a bald, nearly obese man in his mid-50s, looked up from his desk as Hermano introduced himself. Then, noncommittally, he went back to his paperwork.

"I'm doing a story—in the form of a report—on the influence of the organized Church of Satan, and its ability to adversely affect the life of the average citizen. So, with your permission, I'd like to get some pictures—tomorrow afternoon—of Bill Hunt. It would help if I could get some shots with bars in the background."

Deputy McHenry looked up from his report. *"What the hell are you talking about?"* He asked. *"Bill Hunt?"* He reached over and opened the bottom drawer of a filing cabinet that sat facing his chair on his right. He quickly pulled out a file with 'Bill Hunt' written across the top. He opened it and studied the top sheet. *"Says he was arrested for possession of cocaine and carrying a concealed weapon."* He looked up at Hermano and shrugged his shoulders, *"What so mysterious about that?"*

Hermano smiled, *"What it should say is, 'After Bill Hunt's dad caught members of the Church of Satan dumping a mutilated cow on his property, and then pursued them—he was murdered. Then his family, to keep them preoccupied with other problems, was attacked by means of the organization's many contacts and considerable influence.'"* Hermano paused, still smiling, *"that's what my article will say—among other things. It would help if I could get those pictures tomorrow afternoon."*

"Who'd you say you work for?" Asked Deputy McHenry as he closed Bill's file.

"I'm freelance—but I'm published, so I shouldn't have any problems selling it."

"Freelance hmmm? Well—call me tomorrow after lunch, and I'll see what I can do."

Hermano thanked him and headed for the door. As soon as he was gone, Deputy McHenry picked up the telephone.

Chapter 14

Toby, dressed only in his underpants and a T-shirt, sat back down on his bed and leaned against the two pillows which he had stacked against the headboard. His motel room was spacious, with comfortable furnishings, but it was beginning to get cluttered and untidy after two days without maid service. He sipped his coffee and listened to the low static coming from an electronic device that was about the size and shape of a large portable radio, a "boom box". The device, sitting on the dresser, was attached by two wires to an adjacent reel-to-reel tape recorder.

The voice-activated tape recorder hadn't come on in the day and a half that Toby had been listening. *"You dumb-ass,"* he muttered to himself. *"What a hair-brained scheme."* He chuckled and took another sip of coffee. It was Thursday afternoon and Toby hadn't left his room since Tuesday night. He sighed and stretched his legs.

Monday morning, he had driven into Denver and had spent most of the day visiting bookstores. He had been shopping for two copies of the Qur'an, one for the boy, whose name had turned out to be Ali, and one for the "Eye of Allah".

There hadn't been any problem finding a Qur'an-- in Arabic and English-- for the boy but finding one the right width for the "Eye of Allah" had proven more difficult. That Qur'an had had to be a particular minimum width, and Toby had visited five bookstores before he had found it.

Returning to his motel room that evening, Toby had carefully inserted the quarter-sized listening device between the spine of the book, and it's thin red-leather binding—his "Eye of Allah" was ready for action.

The device had tested out perfectly and the next morning, after wrapping both books together and then addressing them to Ali at the Manticore château, he had mailed them from the Vail post office.

"Nuts," he muttered. They should have gotten the package yesterday. He should have heard something by now, unless one of a multitude of things that could have gone wrong **had** gone wrong. He looked at the clock. Suppertime and he was almost out of groceries.

He didn't have to be in the motel room to record -- the voice-activated recorder would do that automatically. He had wanted to be present at the first reception to check his equipment, though. He looked at the clock again, then, with a disappointed sigh, he rolled out of bed and began putting on his pants.

Toby finished his dinner shortly after eight o'clock and stopped off at a bar called The Seven Veils for a couple of beers before returning to the motel.

He sat at the bar and thoughtfully drank his beer as he tried to decide where to go from here. It looked as though his attempt to bug Manticore's office had been a bust and he really hadn't made any plans beyond Vail.

He'd spent a lot of time the last couple of days thinking about that crazy preacher who he had encountered at the fire festival. He smiled as he remembered Hermano's interruption of the ceremony.

Toby figured that he owed that preacher on two scores. If the ghostly apparition hadn't jumped out when he did, Toby doubted that he could have pulled off the rescue of that little girl. And if the preacher hadn't followed Toby up that trail toward Rampart Range, Toby's encounter with that first road guard might not have worked out so favorably.

He finished his beer and motioned to the bartender for another. If his bug didn't pay off by tomorrow, he decided, he would drive back toward Colorado Springs and see if that preacher had ever contacted Chaplain Harris.

"Manticore---"

Toby was instantly alert. He had heard the name mentioned in a conversation between two men seated at a table near the bar.

"---*like to have gone,*" one of the men was saying, "*but I had to be in New York early Monday morning.*"

"*Did you get an invitation for this Sunday?*" The other man asked. "*I thought he had left town.*"

"*He did. He flew back in this afternoon, though. I---*"

Toby got up, laid a five-dollar bill on the bar and hurried out the door.

Driving slightly above the speed limit, Toby was back at the motel in about ten minutes. Key in hand, he bounded up the stairs two at a time to his second-floor landing. He was just reaching for the doorknob when he froze. He could hear a voice inside his room talking in a steady even tone. It was a high-pitched voice and at first Toby thought that it must be a woman. He reached under his coat and pulled out an army Colt .45 automatic. Releasing the safety, he pulled the hammer back.

As he again reached for the door he realized that the voice was that of a young boy—reading. "Ali!" He exclaimed. Quickly unlocking the door, he put the gun away and stepped in.

The voice was coming from the tape monitor. It was Ali reading from the Qur'an. "*Those who dispute about the signs of God without any authority bestowed on them, --there is nothing in their breasts but the quest of greatness, which they shall never attain to. Seek refuge then in God. It is He who hears and sees all things.*"

"*Alright! All right!*" Toby exclaimed. He walked over to the tape recorder, made sure that it was running smoothly, and then, turning the monitor volume down slightly, sat on the edge of his bed. Smiling, he listened to Ali's child-like voice.

"I hope you read the note, kid," Toby said aloud.

When he had mailed the Qur'an, he had included a short note which read: "The large one has been blessed for the Eye of Allah—the smaller one is for you."

"Don't forget which is which, kid." Toby couldn't stop smiling as he leaned back and made himself more comfortable.

The boy had read until shortly after eleven. After that, Toby had listened to over an hour of mysterious rustling sounds. Then, for the rest of the night there had been nothing but the low monotonous sound of static.

The next morning, Toby awoke to the sound of a ringing telephone. Rolling out of bed, he stumbled toward his room phone, which was sitting on the dresser beside the tape recorder. He snatched up the phone before the second ring. *"Yeah?"* he growled. There was only a dial tone.

"R-r-r-ing." Toby looked at the phone for a second before realizing that the sound of a ringing telephone was coming over the tape-monitor.

It rang one more time before a man's voice said, *"Manticore residence."*

There was a pause, and then, *"Mr. Manticore won't be taking calls until 10 o'clock. If you leave your name and a message, I'll leave it here on his desk."*

Another pause and, *"As you wish. Yes, goodbye."*

Toby heard the sound of the phone being hung up, retreating footsteps, and then the sound of a door being shut.

Toby was ecstatic. He slammed his fist down on the dresser. *"All right! You did it, kid!"*

Smiling, wide awake now, he began to busy himself brewing a pot of coffee. The ramifications of his good fortune were just beginning to soak in. After ten years of going after lower and middle level satanists, because of the selfless actions of the little boy, he was now tied into a main artery, if not the juggler, of organized satanism.

"*Thank you, Allah!*" He stopped. The smile faded from his face. He had intended to say 'Ali'. Thoughtfully, the coffee brewing, he walked into the restroom and began washing out his cup.

Chapter 15

Hermano had spent a little longer than he had intended at the Tarrant County Courthouse on Thursday, and it was after noon before he had gotten back to his parents' house. He had quickly changed back into his jeans, boots, and work shirt and was on his way out the door when his mom had grabbed him by the arm.

"Your dad's in the kitchen," she had said, *"hoping you'll have lunch with him."*

"Well---", Hermano had said thoughtfully, remembering that he had told Deirdre that he would be back by lunch.

"You haven't done much more than say 'hi' to your dad since you've been back," his mother went on persistently, still holding his arm.

Hermano had smiled. *"You're right, Mom."* He turned and patted the hand which was still gripping his arm, *"I guess I'm not in that big of a hurry."*

As it turned out, it was almost 3:30 p.m. when Hermano turned his Jeep Wagoneer into the driveway of the Hunt Ranch. As he approached the ranch house he saw a Parker County Sheriff's Department patrol car parked in the drive, near the front door.

Frowning, he veered off to the right as he approached the house and parked near the garage. He climbed out of the Jeep and walked around to the front door. Just as he was reaching for the doorbell, the door opened, and Dora ushered two sheriff's deputies out onto the front porch.

"*Hermano! Hi. Deirdre has your chore assignment,*" said Dora, and she stepped back from the door. "*Just go on through the house, she's back in the den.*" Dora turned to the deputies, "*One of our hands,*" she commented, as Hermano smiled and squeezed past her.

Hermano walked into the den and saw Deirdre standing at the patio door, looking out toward the pool.

"*Hi*", said Hermano, "*everything all right?*"

Startled, Deirdre had jumped slightly and turned around. "*Hermano! I'm sure glad you're back.*" She turned and looked back at the pool. "*Come here and look at this.*"

Hermano walked over to join her at the door. He looked out at the pool. The swimming pool water was rust-colored, and a dead cow was floating on its side near the center.

"*That's blood in the water,*" she said matter-of-factly. "*The deputies think that someone led the cow onto the deck on the other side of the pool, cut its throat, and pushed it into the pool. I didn't notice it until I opened the drapes—after lunch. The deputies think it happened last night.*" She paused. "*I'm surprised I didn't hear anything.*"

"*It might be better that you didn't,*" said Hermano. "*Where's Dave?*"

"*We haven't heard from him since he left yesterday afternoon. A couple of the hands brought his motorcycle by last night and I had them put it in the garage.*" She turned around and walked over to the desk.

"*By the way,*" she said, "*he told mom about you. That you're an expert on the Church of Satan.*" She picked up a coffee pot. "*Fresh pot, want a cup?*" She asked.

"*Yeah, thanks.*" Hermano walked over and took a seat on the couch. "*That—in the pool—is plain old terrorism.*" He paused, "*I wish I knew what's happened to Dave.*"

"*Well, we started trying to call him—on the car phone—late last night, and tried again a couple of times today,*" she said, handing him a full cup and then sitting down beside him on the couch.

"*No answer?*"

"*No. He could just be out of range, though.*" She took a sip from her cup and set it on the coffee table. *"I tried the local hospital and the jail this morning, but they didn't have him."*

"What jail?" Asked Hermano.

"The one here in Weatherford. I didn't try Fort Worth, yet."

"Is Mineral Wells in this county?" asked Hermano.

"No, it's in Palo Pinto County. Why?"

"Maybe you'd better try their jail," suggested Hermano. *"That red pickup—the one that the guy who's been harassing you drives—is registered in Mineral Wells."*

"Oh," Deirdre got up and walked back to the desk. She picked up the phone. *"I hope not,"* she said as she began dialing directory assistance.

"Palo Pinto, please," she said into the receiver.

After obtaining the number for the Palo Pinto County Jail, she disconnected from the operator and began dialing. *"Hello,"* she said. *"Do you have a man named David Hunt in jail over there?"* She looked at Hermano and raised her eyebrows. *"What did he do?"*

Setting his cup down, Hermano stood up and walked over to stand beside Deirdre.

"Well, how can I go about getting him out?" Frowning, she listened for a few seconds. *"Monday! Why so long?"* She shook her head. *"OK, thanks."* She hung up the phone and looked at Hermano.

"Dave was arrested last night near Possum Kingdom Lake—for assault and battery." She sighed. *"He can't get out of jail until he sees the judge—on Monday."*

"Monday," Hermano repeated, walking back to the patio door and looking out at the pool. *"Whatever happened might have had something to do with this,"* he nodded toward the pool. *"At least his arrest might have made them feel confident about coming so close to the house."* He walked back to the couch and sat down.

"Did they say who he assaulted?" He asked.

"No." The sound of a tractor engine caused them both to look in the direction of the patio.

"I told Lupe to get a tractor and bring a couple of the hands up to help him get the cow out of the pool," said Deirdre, still looking at the patio door.

"How close—or, rather, how reliable are the hands you've got work-ing for you?" Asked Hermano.

"Well," Dee said, walking back toward the couch, *"I wouldn't ask any of them to risk their lives for me. We have a dozen hands, six in the bunkhouse and six more that live off the ranch."* She sat down. *"Two of the ones that live off the ranch have given me notice that they'll be leaving after next week."* She paused a moment. *"I don't know what the situation will be after that cow in the pool. They all seem to be freaked out."*

Hermano shifted uncomfortably. *"Look, I don't mean to sound presumptuous or anything. But, do you mind if I move my stuff up to the house?"* He paused, *"I could sleep on the couch or something."*

Deirdre's face brightened. *"Would you?"* She asked. *"That wouldn't be presumptuous—I'd really appreciate it."*

Hermano smiled, *"Why don't you ask your mom?"*

"She won't mind," said Deirdre. She stood up and walked toward the hallway. *"I'll ask her, though. Be right back."* She disappeared up the hall.

There were three bedrooms in the east wing of the house; Deirdre's, Bill's, and the master bedroom. The master bedroom, because of Dora's refusal to leave the old house, had remained unoccupied ever since the east wing had been built. Dora had insisted that Hermano sleep there.

"Sleep on the couch!" She had exclaimed. *"With three extra bedrooms in the house? You tell him to stay in the master bedroom. And—Deirdre, I don't know whether you've noticed that he's a good-looking man, but--"*

"Mom!" Deirdre smiled. *"I've noticed—but I don't think he could care less. He's a real nice guy, but he's real serious minded."* She laughed. *"I don't think he's even noticed that I'm a woman."*

"Umm—hmm, sure," her mom smiled. *"Well, Dee, you just remem-ber that you're a lady."*

Hermano had gone to get his gear from the bunkhouse while Deirdre tidied up the master bedroom, and he was settled into his new lodgings by six o'clock. Dora had supper ready by 6:30 and she and Deirdre had both insisted that Hermano join them.

"What exactly do you do about satanists?" Asked Dora. They had finished their meal a couple of minutes before and as Deirdre cleared the table, Dora sat across from Hermano, politely—but intently— studying his face.

"To tell you the truth—I've been investigating satanists for ten years, but I've only recently come to the realization that something had to be done about them." He paused. *"I guess—deep down—I realized that sooner or later something--"* he paused again, *"unpleasant would have to be done."*

"What?" Persisted Dora. She had begun idly stirring her tea.

Hermano was obviously uncomfortable. *"They worship Satan,"* he said. *"the father of lies. Do you take them to court? Lying under oath successfully would be—to them—a commendable thing. And there are so many of them, now. In court, you run the risk of one or both of the opposing attorneys being satanists; you run the risk of the judge or one of the appeals judges being a satanist, and you run the risk of one or more of the jurors being a satanist.*

A few satanists have gone to trial. But when they do, their cases get dragged on and on and on until, frequently, it's finally whittled down to nothing.

And if you did send a few to jail, just think of this. They're obligated to recruit, and they believe that recruiting increases their own power. You might send one satanist in and have ten that he's recruited come out—before he does." Hermano took a drink of his tea.

"And if you don't do something--" he took a deep breath and let it out slowly, *"well, they murder children. It's normal for criminals to mur-der other adults—but this is an altogether different thing. They murder for the sake of murder, it's a religious obligation—and children are easy targets. The longer you wait to deal with them—it's like a cancer—the*

longer you wait, the bigger and more serious it gets. It gets bigger, because they all strive to recruit. It gets worse, because the more they recruit-- the more people there are who are obligated to do evil deeds."

"*They have to be killed,*" said Dora.

Hermano took a long look at her and sighed again. He nodded, "*They <u>have</u> to be killed,*" he stated.

Chapter 16

Toby opened the broiler section of the oven and checked his steak. Almost done. His mouth was watering. It had been so long since he had eaten anything but restaurant food, that he could hardly wait to cut into that steak. He looked at the clock--- seven o'clock.

He'd missed a lot of Manticore's office conversation today—but he could listen to most of it, on tape, later in the evening. The only hour of conversation that he had actually lost, had been from twelve to one p.m., that's when he had transferred his receiver and recorder from the motel room to the one-bedroom cottage that he had rented.

That morning, after realizing that his off-the-wall scheme had been successful, Toby had begun seeking more secure and private lodgings. Since ski season was over, there had been a wide range of condos and cottages available for summer rentals. The cottage that he had decided to rent had been a little more than a half mile on the other side of Manticore's driveway entrance. So, by one o'clock on Friday afternoon, Toby had set himself up in the comfortable little furnished cabin, which had come with all bills paid.

After hooking up the receiver and recorder, he had made a quick trip to the store and had spent the rest of the afternoon listening to the obnoxious Mr. Manticore.

Toby walked out of the little kitchen and sat down in a comfortable chair near the desk which held his receiver and recorder. The voices coming over the monitor were merely those of Manticore and his secretary, Jon-going over preparations for Sunday's party.

Toby figured that this was an indication that the weekly business was coming to an end. Frowning, he got up and walked back into the kitchen.

He had just finished supper when he heard a name mentioned on the monitor that sent him hurrying back into the living room. The name that had excited Toby was that of Congressman Jim Burton.

"Where is he?" Asked the voice that Toby recognized as Manticore's.

"Downstairs, sir.", the voice was Jon's. *"He says that it's of the utmost urgency."*

"Anything that requires creative thought is always an emergency with these bureaucrats. Send him on up."

A few minutes later, Toby heard another voice that sounded excited and out of breath. *"Mr. Manticore. I'm sorry to visit unannounced like this, but I felt certain that you'd want this information delivered personally—and immediately. I flew straight up from Dallas as soon as I had all of it."*

"Yes, yes," Manticore said impatiently. *"Now, what is it that is of the 'utmost urgency'?"*

"Listen to this tape –and then I'll explain."

Toby listened to what sounded like a briefcase being opened. A few seconds later, he heard a new voice which he assumed was on Burton's tape.

"And, if you don't do something," the voice said, *"well, they murder children. It's normal for criminals to murder other adults—but this is an altogether different thing. They murder for the sake of murder—and children are easy targets. The longer you wait—it's like a cancer—the longer you wait, the bigger and more serious it gets. It gets bigger, because they all strive to recruit. It gets worse because the more they recruit, the more people there are who are obligated to do evil deeds."*

"They have to be killed," a woman's voice said.

"They have to be killed," the first voice agreed.

Toby, leaning forward in the easy chair, heard a click as Burton's tape was shut off.

"You bothered me for this?" Manticore sounded irritated. *"We're way beyond the possibility of being <u>hindered</u>—much less stopped. Who cares what a couple of nobodies think. If he <u>really</u> understood—he would know that we've already won."*

Toby could hear Manticore sigh, his voice became more conciliatory. *"If the man really bothers you—put a surveillance team on him. Grind him into the ground."*

"That's not all, Mr. Manticore," Congressman Burton said. *"That conversation was taped last night at a ranch house near Weatherford, Texas. Our people—uh—a small group in Weatherford, has had the house under surveillance for a week or two. They placed the bug that picked up that conversation in the kitchen of the ranch house. They've been having some problems with the family that lives there—the Hunts.*

A small problem, nothing serious, but since the Sheriff is one of our people, I sent my trouble-shooter over to work as a deputy and kind of keep me informed. Well, my trouble-shooter got the license plate number of the man who you just heard on that tape. When he called it in last night, I fed it into the computer. The computer kicked back an alert which said to contact Colorado Springs."

"Colorado Springs?" Manticore sounded more interested.

"Yes, it turns out that that license number was recorded at a church in Cascade. The church where that little girl was found on May 1. Hazelwood, the man I contacted in Colorado Springs, asked for a description of the man at the ranch and hung up. He called me back in about half an hour and said that that was the man you were looking for—something about buying a piece of plywood."

"He bought the plywood?" *"---and he was seen at the church?"* Manticore sounded excited. *"Good work, Burton! You did well in coming to me with this."*

"I thought you'd appreciate it. I assumed that Hazelwood would have contacted you about it by now."

"He should have. OK, where exactly is Weatherford, Texas?"

Toby listened as Congressman Burton gave Manticore directions to Weatherford and the Hunt Ranch, and then a brief description of the Hunt family. After they had talked for a few more minutes, Manticore had suggested that they have dinner. The voices got fainter until they were finally cut off by the slamming of a door.

Toby stood up and began pacing. He didn't understand the meaning of the "plywood" part of the conversation, but that man who they were talking about had to have been that black-faced guy that had jumped out at the Fire-Festival. The man that Toby had called "Preacher".

He's really fixing to get it, thought Toby. And he doesn't even know it's coming. The Hunt Ranch was bugged so Toby couldn't even telephone a warning without tipping his hand about Manticore's own bug.

"Damn!" Toby exclaimed, plopping back down in the easy chair. He'd have to drive to Texas; he wasn't going to let them get that preacher with some kind of sucker punch. Toby's mind was racing, he would have to cover himself here as well as he could in a short space of time and then take off. He jumped up and hurried out the door to the station wagon.

"Hello, Peter Harris here."

"Chaplain Harris? Do you recognize my voice?" Toby was standing in a phone booth at a Vail service station.

"Yes, I think so."

"I'd really like to have that counseling session, now. Can we meet at the place we agreed on? As soon as possible," Toby added.

"I can be there in an hour."

"Thanks. Talk to you then." Toby hung up.

When Toby had called Chaplain Harris on the morning of May first to find out if the girl had been delivered safely, he had told him that if the "preacher" came by to get his address. Toby had also told him that, quite probably, within a few days his phone would be bugged, and he would be watched. To avoid having to say anything of importance over the telephone the next time he called, Toby had devised a plan whereby he could talk to Chaplain Harris on a "safe" phone.

Toby had given him the name of a 24-hour restaurant in Colorado Springs. He had told him that when he called again he would ask for a counseling session, and Chaplain Harris should then drive to that restaurant. Toby would telephone him again at the restaurant.

Chaplain Harris had said an hour, so after Toby had hung up the telephone, he drove to a grocery store and stocked up on a week's supply of food and ran it back by his cottage. By the time he had put the food away the hour was up and he drove back to the pay phone.

"Peter Harris, please. He should be sitting at the counter." Toby waited while the waitress paged Chaplain Harris.

"Just a minute, sir. He just walked in the door," she said, and then laid the phone down. A few seconds later, he heard Peter Harris's voice.

"This is Peter Harris," he said, sounding out of breath.

"Chaplain Harris, this is Toby."

"Ah, I'm glad to know that you're still alive. I have that man's name and address," he paused, *"and telephone number."*

"Good. Thanks, Chaplain. Look, I'm sorry to get you involved in this, but—I need your help again. It concerns saving the life of that man that delivered the little girl."

"I'd be happy—no, thankful—if you'd let me help."

"Were talking about a major inconvenience," Toby said. *"It'll take several days and would involve traveling—tonight."*

"Tonight?"

"I have to start as soon as possible, or it'll be too late." He could hear Chaplain Harris sigh.

"OK," Chaplain Harris said. *"My life's been too soft, lately, anyway."*

"Do you know if you're being followed?" Asked Toby.

"I think so. An unsavory type came in here right behind me. He's watching me, now."

"OK. Do you know where the Penrose Hotel is—on Highway 70, in Denver?"

"Yes."

"Can you be there in two hours?"

"It's nine o'clock, now. Yes, I think I can be there by eleven."

"Not <u>by</u> eleven —<u>at</u> eleven. As exact as you can make it. Park in the parking lot in front of the hotel. Walk through the hotel lobby and take the hallway on your right. Walk to where the hall T's, turn to the right. Just after you turn the corner, you'll see two elevators on your right. Only one of them has 'parking garage' on it. Take that one to the garage." Toby paused. *"I'll be parked near the elevator door in the garage—at exactly 11 o'clock."*

"OK, but I need to warn you. I've only got about fifteen or twenty dollars on me."

"You're covered. See you at eleven."

"Wait. I almost feel like I know you, but we've never actually met. What do you look like?"

"I'm—uh-- big. You'll know me."

Toby looked at his watch. Two minutes past eleven. He leaned back in the driver's seat and looked through the open window at the elevator. He had forgotten about this being Friday night—the parking garage was busy, and he wondered how long he would be able to sit there without some attendant running him off.

The elevator door opened. A short gray-haired man got out alone and stopped, looking directly at Toby.

"You really <u>are</u> big, aren't you?" He smiled and ran around to the passenger door. *"Toby, I presume,"* he said, sliding into the seat and shutting the door.

"Glad to meet you," said Toby as he tromped the accelerator and

sped up the ramp and out of the garage. *"Duck down—just in case,"* he said as they circled the hotel to get back onto 70.

After they were a couple of miles from the hotel, Toby turned to his smiling partner. Toby grinned and said, *"Sorry about all this cloak and dagger stuff, but it's the best I could do on the spur of the moment. I stayed in that hotel for a week about a year ago and I remembered the layout."*

Chaplain Harris swung his left arm over the back of the seat and looked out the rear window. *"Seems to have worked,"* he said. *"A white van followed me from Colorado Springs—no sign of anybody behind us now, though."* He looked back at Toby. *"Well, what have I gotten myself into?"* he asked.

"Actually, it's more like baby-sitting than anything else. I need someone I can trust to sit with a receiver and tape recorder." He smiled and glanced at Chaplain Harris. *"I've tapped the office of one of the top satanists in the world."*

Toby went on to summarize his situation in Vail—omitting the part about his execution of Deputy Byrd.

"A listening device in the binding of a Qur'an—planted by a child! Marvelous!" Chaplain Harris looked at Toby appreciatively. *"That was incredibly ingenious."*

Toby laughed, *"It was a hair-brained scheme, and the kind of luck I could use in Vegas,"* he replied.

"Toby," Chaplain Harris was studying his companion, *"when you're serving God—there is no longer any such thing as luck."*

They arrived back at Toby's darkened cottage shortly before one a.m.. As Toby unlocked the door, he could hear the sound of a child crying—coming from inside. Realizing that it must be the monitor, he opened the door and turned on the light. Chaplain Harris followed him in.

"Who's that crying?" He asked, looking at the monitor.

"Must be Ali," replied Toby as he turned down the monitor. He rewound the tape a few feet. *"Let's find out what made him start crying."*

He adjusted the controls on the tape recorder and began replaying the tape. They could hear the boy's voice, reading from the Qur'an.

"O man! What has seduced thee from thy Lord most beneficent? Him who created thee. Fashioned thee in due proportion and gave thee a just bias. In whatever form He wills, does He put thee together.

Nay! But ye do reject right and judgment! But verily, over you are appointed Angels," Ali began sobbing, *"to protect you---"*

After that, there was only the sound of the child's crying. Chaplain Harris looked at Toby. *"There's no such thing as coincidence,"* he said.

Toby sighed and began readjusting the tape recorder. He turned the monitor back up—the child's sobbing had tapered off and he could now be heard turning the pages of a book. Toby turned to Chaplain Harris.

"What can I do?" He asked defensively. *"Even if the boy would leave, there's a couple of dozen guards around that château. I'm not kiddin'—Manticore's better protected than the President."* Toby pulled out his wallet and, opening it, took out a slip of paper and laid it on the desk. *"This is the telephone number of the pay phone at that Vickers service station we passed just before getting here. I'll call you at that phone on Monday evening. Say-- nine o'clock, your time."*

Toby took out a pen. *"Now, what's the name, address, and telephone number of that preacher—uh—Hermano?"*

He wrote the information down on a sheet of paper and put it back in his wallet.

"I've got two retirement checks waiting for me in Dallas," Toby said as he pulled a small stack of $20 bills from his wallet. *"I'll leave half of this here—there's food in the cabinets and refrigerator."* He laid several twenty-dollar bills on the desk and put his wallet back in his pocket. *"Well, that---"* he began.

"Ali!" The man's voice blurted from the monitor. Toby and Peter both jumped.

"What are you doing?" The voice asked.

Toby looked at Chaplain Harris. *"Manticore,"* he said.

"I—I--," the child's voice stammered, *"I just wanted a quiet place to read."*

"You're not ever supposed to come up here. Let me see that!" Manticore sounded angry.

"It—it was a gift, Master," the boy said.

"A Qur'an! Who gave you this?" There was the sound of a slap. *"Who gave it to you?"*

The boy began sobbing. *"It came in the mail,"* he sobbed.

"I won't have books like this around you!" The sound of tearing paper could be heard over the monitor. *"Where are you going!?"* Manticore shouted. There was the sound of a door being slammed.

Chaplain Harris looked at Toby. *"Isn't there anything that can be done?"* He asked.

Toby shook his head. For the next few minutes he busied himself preparing for his trip. After loading his clothes, guns, and sword, he came back into the cottage to see Chaplain Harris, bent over the monitor.

"Listen," Chaplain Harris whispered. Toby walked over and joined him.

"What did you let him leave for?" Manticore sounded angry again.

Chaplain Harris looked at Toby. *"He's on the phone to his gate guard,"* he whispered. *"The guard just called in."*

"No, stay there," Manticore said. *"I'll take care of it."*

There was a short pause, and then Manticore's voice came back. *"Jon,"* he said, *"Ali's just run out the front gate heading for the highway. Go get him for me."* There was a pause, then, *"I don't care what you have to do, just get him."*

Toby looked at Chaplain Harris. Chaplain Harris smiled and gave Toby a thumbs-up sign.

"Take care," Toby said as he wheeled around and dashed through the front door.

"Good luck," called Chaplain Harris.

"No such thing as luck," came back as the car door slammed shut.

Toby drove east on 70 and slowed to fifteen or twenty mph as he neared Manticore's driveway. The driveway was about a hundred yards long, so he figured that Ali had probably reached the highway by now.

He spotted the boy walking east on the right side of I-70. He was about fifty yards past the driveway and slowed his run to a fast walk as Toby drove up beside him. Toby reached across the seat and rolled down the passenger window. *"Ali! It's me, the guy that sent you the Qur'an."*

Ali stopped and peered through the window. *"You,"* he said. *"How---,"* he quickly straightened up and looked behind him.

A car had just pulled out of Manticore's driveway and, driving on the shoulder, was coming up behind Toby's station wagon.

"Get in kid! Don't let them get you back." The boy looked undecided as he looked at Toby and then back at the approaching car.

"Ali!" The car had come to a stop about five yards behind Toby. A tall man was getting out on the driver's side. *"Mr.. Manticore sent me to bring you back,"* he said.

"I'm not going back! He tore up the Qur'an!"

"Ali! Get in this car right now!" The man shouted.

He shut his door and started walking between his and Toby's cars.

With a loud screech Toby shifted into reverse and floor-boarded his accelerator. Jon didn't have a chance. Before he realized what was happening, he was crushed between Toby's station wagon and his own car.

Toby pulled forward a few yards and, looking up and down the highway to make sure that there wasn't any late-night traffic, got out of his car and walked back to Jon.

Jon, still alive, lay moaning in front of his blue Mercedes. Toby pulled out his colt .45 automatic and fired a round, point-blank, into the side of Jon's head. He calmly put the gun away and, after checking to make sure none of his tail lights were broken, walked back to his door.

"*Let's get out of here,*" he said, looking across the roof at Ali who, horrified, was staring at the still body of Jon.

"*Come on,*" Toby looked up and down the highway. "*The cops will be here any minute.*"

Ali looked at Toby. "*You killed him,*" he said.

"*Ali,*" Toby motioned with his right arm toward Manticore's château, "*these men are enemies of God.*" Ali still didn't move.

"*Ali,*" Toby sighed, his voice became softer, "*God sent me to take you away from them.*"

Ali looked at him for a moment longer, opened the passenger door and climbed in. As Toby got back behind the wheel, Ali solemnly looked across the seat at him.

"*Are you an angel?*" He asked.

Chapter 17

"You sure are in a good mood today, Mom," said Dee as she helped set the table for breakfast.

"Sunday breakfast just wasn't the same last week without Bill here," answered Dora, smiling at her daughter. *"Are they up?"*

"Yes, they were talking in the den when I got up. I think Bill really likes Hermano."

"I think Bill isn't the only one," teased her mom.

"I admit it," smiled Dee. *"He's kind of-- one-of-a-kind."* She paused. *"I think that's why Bill likes him, too. He—Bill—said that Hermano was the first 100 percent Christian he'd met that didn't seem wimpy."* She laughed.

Dora picked up a stack of toast and carried it to the table. She smiled at her daughter. *"How's the romance coming?"* She asked.

"Great!" Deirdre fluttered her eyelids. *"We touched hands last night."*

Dora laughed. *"I guess he _is_ a hundred percent,"* she said. *"You'd better call them before this gets cold."*

"What? No grits?!" Exclaimed Bill as he and Hermano walked into the kitchen. *"What's breakfast without grits?"*

"Jailbird," teased Dee as she set down a platter of scrambled eggs.

Bill sighed as he sat down. *"Ah, home sweet home,"* he said. *"I still can't believe that they dropped all the charges."*

"I don't know what happened," said Dora, *"and neither does Roger.*

I called his office Friday morning and he didn't offer any hope of getting you out for the weekend. Then I called him back after you got home Friday afternoon, and he didn't even know you were out."

"Let's not look a gift horse in the mouth," said Dee, she sat down across from Hermano. *"Don't forget,"* she said, looking at Hermano, *"church today."*

Hermano smiled. *"As long as I can wear jeans and a sport shirt,"* he said.

"We're country folks," said Dora. *"Deirdre, would you say grace?"*

"Grace? Wow, this is the Hunt Ranch isn't it?" teased Bill.

"We're going through some changes," said Dee. *"Hermano- was-here,"* she quipped and smiled across the table. *"Why Hermano, are you blushing?"*

"The grace, Dee. I'm starved," laughed her mom.

Church services began at eleven. The Hunts, with Hermano, took seats near the rear of the church shortly before the hour.

"I wish Uncle Dave was with us," said Dee, as she sat down between Hermano and Bill.

"Dave?" Whispered her mom. *"I don't think he's ever gone to church—at least not since I've known him."*

Deirdre looked at her mom, seated to her left on the other side of Bill. *"The night before he got thrown in jail, I caught him reading the family Bible. Can you believe it? Uncle Dave?"*

"Goodness. I guess the Hunts really are going through some changes."

The topic of Reverend Hall's sermon that week was forgiveness.

"He did away with the idea of 'an eye for an eye'," said Reverend Hall, leaning across the podium and holding an opened Bible in both hands. He was looking at the Hunts. *"Love your enemies, pray for those who abuse you,"* he said. *"Turn the other cheek!"* He looked straight at Hermano.

A hard gust of wind blew the side door open. It crashed against the wall, giving the whole congregation a start. Reverend Hall jumped so violently that his Bible fell off the front of the podium and landed with a loud slap on the floor between him and the congregation. --- He didn't look in the direction of the Hunts for the rest of the sermon.

The service was over shortly after twelve. As Hermano and Deirdre were walking toward Hermano's jeep, Deputy Pierce, out of uniform, approached them.

"Miss Hunt?" he called out.

"Please, just call me Deirdre—or Dee." Dee and Hermano stopped and waited for him to catch up with them.

"Thanks," he said, stopping in front of them. *"I'm Frank."*

"I hope so," quipped Dee, smiling.

Frank returned her smile, *"Yeah, I'm fixing to be that kind of 'Frank', too."*

"I'm Hermano," interrupted Hermano, offering his hand. Frank shook it.

"Listen—uh—Deirdre," he stammered, *"I've been trying to figure out a way to talk to y'all for days. Can we meet somewhere this afternoon—uh—out of the county?"*

"Out of the county? Fort Worth?"

"That'd be fine," he replied, looking around nervously.

"Well, how about Kip's Restaurant on Camp Bowie? Around four o'clock?"

"Good, I'll be there," he replied.

"Hermano will be with me," added Dee.

Frank hesitated, gnawing his lower lip. *"Well, OK. I'll see you then."*

Mustang Road was the only road which actually bordered the Hunt Ranch. However, on the other side of the ranch Meadowlark Road came in from the west and made a 90° curve to the north, touching the northwest corner of the Hunt property. There was no gate at that location, but there was a detachable section of fence, ten yards in length, which had been rigged up some twelve years earlier for oil drilling equipment.

Deirdre had remembered the make-shift gate when Hermano had asked about a way to leave the ranch without being observed. It had meant driving diagonally across the ranch in Hermano's jeep and had taken an extra hour, but by four o'clock Hermano and Deirdre were having coffee at Kip's in Fort Worth.

Frank Pierce, still wearing civilian clothes and looking nervous, walked into the restaurant at 4:15.

"Let's sit farther away from the door," he said, walking past them and taking the booth farthest from the front door. Without comment, Dee and Hermano got up and, taking their coffee cups, went back to join him.

Frank ordered a glass of iced tea and after the waitress had walked off he looked at Deirdre. *"Did--uh--did you take any kind of precautions to see that you weren't followed?"* He asked.

Dee looked at Hermano, who was sitting beside her.

"We weren't followed," said Hermano.

"Oh, good. I should have cautioned ya'll about that earlier." He glanced at Hermano and looked back at Dee. *"Did you notice that Reverend Hall was watching us when we talked after church?"*

"No," she replied, *"what difference does it make? What's this all about, Frank?"*

"Well," he paused, thinking. *"I'll start with the morning your dad was killed. You remember when Hutch, the guy that I was with, said that we were late because of flying saucer reports and other stuff? Well, that wasn't true. We were late because Sheriff Blocker made me wait at the office until Hutch arrived."* He paused. *"I don't know who this Hutch is. That morning was the first time I'd ever seen him—or heard of him. He came into the office dressed in one of our uniforms, though. Sheriff Blocker*

*said that I should go with him—because I know the county real well—
but that I should act like he was just another deputy. Sheriff Blocker said
that he was some sort of special investigator, working for the state."*

"Is Sheriff Blocker usually in the office that early?" asked Hermano.

*"No, that's another thing. He usually doesn't come in 'til around nine
o'clock, but that morning he came in about five minutes before the call
from the ranch."* The waitress set down his glass of tea and he waited
until she had left before continuing.

"The next strange thing," he said, *"was when Silas came out to see
about picking up your dad's helicopter."*

"The missing door with bullet holes," said Hermano.

"You knew about that?" He asked, studying Hermano more closely.

"Bill talked to Silas, just before Silas was murdered," Hermano
replied.

*"Oh. Well, there wasn't any door to be seen when Hutch and I got
out there. But Sheriff Blocker was already there."* He took a drink of his
tea. *"Anyway, when Silas left, Hutch turns to some guy in a suit and says
'Did you hear that?'. And then the guy says, 'We'll take care of it.' I don't
think they knew I was listening—at least I hope not. The next thing I
heard about Silas was that he was dead."* Frank sighed and continued.

*"Hutch carries this beeper around with him—you know, the kind
that signals you when you got a phone call? It's fancier than anything the
county issues. Anyway, whenever it beeps, Hutch heads straight for a pay
phone. The first couple of times, I saw him take a piece of paper out of
his jacket pocket like he was calling a number that was on it. I guess he
learned the number, because after the first couple of times he didn't pull
it out anymore.*

*Well, he left his jacket in the car one time—after he had gotten a
beep, --and I fished around for that piece of paper while he was making
his call. I memorized the number on the paper and then put it back before
he returned."*

"Do you know whose number it was?" Frank raised his eyebrows
and looked at Dee.

"Sheriff Blocker's?" She suggested.

"No—this'll blow your mind. Reverend Hall's."

"Reverend Hall's!" exclaimed Dee.

"Shhh," Frank looked around nervously. *"I checked it out. It's Reverend Hall's home phone."*

"Reverend Hall," repeated Dee, *"I can hardly believe it."*

"I can," interjected Hermano. *"Tell me, when you and—Hutch— drove out to the ranch to run off that truck that was parked on the shoulder of the road, had Hutch just gotten one of his beeps?"*

Frank thought for a moment. *"Yeah, and then he made his call. We drove straight on out after that."* He paused again, *"Just who exactly are you?"* He asked, looking at Hermano.

"Hermano is an expert on the Church of Satan," offered Dee. *"He's helping us."*

"The Church of Satan," repeated Frank. *"You know, that's the first thing I thought of when I saw that cow by the fish tank. Wolves!"* He said contemptuously. *"You think they're behind all this? The Church of Satan, I mean?"* He asked, looking at Hermano.

"No doubt," Hermano said. *"Why did you suspect the Church of Satan when you saw the cow?"* He asked.

"I went to a seminar on satanic crimes a while back. Right after all those bodies were dug up in Matamoras, Mexico. You know," he added thoughtfully, *"the Mexican head of Interpol was supposed to be in the group responsible for that."*

"Interpol?" asked Dee.

"International Police," explained Hermano. He looked back at Frank who was quietly studying his glass of tea. *"It goes a lot higher than him,"* said Hermano.

"Huh?" Frank snapped up his head and looked at Hermano.

"Your Sheriff—it goes a lot higher than him."

"How did you know what I was thinking?"

Chapter 18

"Senor? Senorita?"

The little boy's voice had come from the shadows, from the direction of the helipad. It was eight o'clock and for the past hour Dee and Hermano had been sitting at the poolside table watching the water level in the swimming pool slowly rise.

Using the same circuitous route they had used in leaving the ranch, they had returned an hour earlier and had found Bill filling the pool. He had drained and scrubbed it the day before, and apparently had begun filling it while Dee and Hermano were in Fort Worth. Bill and Dora had gone into the house a few minutes earlier.

"Yes?" Answered Dee, standing up to peer into the darkness. The swimming pool deck lights were on, but they had neglected to turn on the helipad lights.

The little boy stepped forward out of the shadows. He was dark-skinned and wore baggy trousers and a work-shirt that was a couple of sizes too large. Dee assumed that he was one of the ranch hands' children.

"Do your folks know that you're out here?" She asked.

The boy didn't answer but walked onto the deck and stopped beside the table. He looked at Hermano, who was still sitting on the opposite side of the table.

"Are you Hermano?" He asked.

"Yes," answered Hermano.

"*I—uh,*" the boy shuffled his feet uncomfortably, "*I'm supposed to ask you to come and talk to the—uh—to someone.*"

"*Where?*" Asked Hermano.

"*You're just supposed to come with me,*" replied the boy. "*He said you were a friend.*"

"*He?*" Asked Hermano, standing up. "*Who sent you?*"

"*The—uh—I think he's an angel,*" answered the boy.

"*Oh,*" said Hermano, smiling as he stood up, "*then we don't want to keep him waiting, do we?*" He stepped around the table and followed the boy into the shadows.

They had walked almost a hundred yards to the northwest of the house when the boy stopped. "*We're being followed,*" he said, looking back toward the house.

"*It's the woman,*" a man's voice had come from a few yards to Hermano's left. "*She's carrying a rifle.*"

"*That's Deirdre,*" Hermano said quickly, "*she's probably concerned for my safety.*"

"*She should be—so am I. Preacher.*"

"*You!*" Exclaimed Hermano. "*Just a minute, I'll ask her to go back to the house.*" Hermano walked back toward the deck lights and, after a few minutes, returned.

"*Are you still here?*" He asked.

"*Yeah,*" answered Toby.

"*She refused to go back. She's sitting down back there, waiting.*"

"*Sounds like my kind of woman,*" laughed Toby. "*I'm glad to finally meet you, Hermano.*" The big man stepped out of the darkness and shook Hermano's hand. "*My name's Toby.*"

"*How did you find out where I was?*" Asked Hermano after he and Toby had sat down cross-legged near the spot where they had shook hands.

"*From the Church of Satan. I managed to get a bug into one of their control centers.*" He paused and smiled, "*You're at the top of their shit-list.*" He laughed.

"I'm almost jealous."

"What did they say about me?" Asked Hermano.

"Well—they got your license number when you visited Chaplain Harris. Then they got it again, here. Sorry, but they're blaming what happened off Rampart Range on you." He paused. *"They said something about a piece of plywood—that you had 'bought the plywood', or something like that. What does that mean?"*

"Oh," Hermano was quiet for a moment. *"I had been watching that Beltane celebration from a dugout. The dugout was covered with a piece of plywood—camouflaged,"* he added. *"I had just bought the plywood in Colorado Springs the day before."*

"Ah, yeah, that must be it. What I overheard was somebody giving a report. The guy giving the report was Congressman Burton—so that shows you how high the shit is going to be falling from."

"You must have really tapped into an important spot," commented Hermano.

"Yeah, and speaking of that, you and a woman had a conversation about it being necessary to kill the members of the Church of Satan. Whatever room you had that conversation in is definitely bugged. I overheard a recording of your conversation. Maybe other rooms are bugged, too. I don't know."

"The kitchen," said Hermano. They were quiet for a moment.

"What's going on out here, anyway?" Asked Toby.

Hermano began with when he had picked up Dave hitchhiking and brought Toby up to date. *"Bill said that Silas had recognized one of the people at the site where Sam's helicopter had come down, an aide to Congressman Burton. Also, a helicopter that Silas had helped repair that morning, with a bullet hole through the fuel line, belonged to a company owned by Burton."*

"So," Toby said, thoughtfully, *"that phony preacher must have planted the bug."*

"Probably," agreed Hermano.

"Preacher—uh, Hermano—are we in agreement that these satanists have to be killed?"

"Yes, we're in agreement. But not just these—all of them."

"Good. Can we count on these people—the Hunts?"

"Yes. The woman I was talking with—on that recording—was Dora Hunt, the girl who's sitting back there's mother." He paused, *"Who's the little boy? He isn't a Mexican."*

Toby laughed. *"Did he screw up on his 'senor and senorita'? I made him practice it half a dozen times before I sent him to the house."* He chuckled. *"He's an Afghan—a mujahedin, now. I snatched him from the head honcho satanist in Vail. He's a good boy. I told him I'd try to get him back to his people."* Toby was quiet for a moment. *"I don't know how I'm going to swing that. Say—do you have a Qur'an? I told him I'd get him another."* Toby went on to relate all that had happened since the fire festival and ended by explaining how he had come to be in possession of Ali.

"You know he thinks you're an angel?" Asked Hermano.

"Yeah, I keep telling him not to call me that. He's done it twice in public." Toby laughed again. *"Well, now,"* said Toby, *"let's get down to business. We're in a lot better position than they think we are. They've got you bugged—but we know it. We've got one of their main headquarters bugged—and they don't know it. We know who a lot of their local members are--- including the Sheriff, by the way—and they don't know we know it. They think that they know about you—but they don't know that I exist."* Toby, paused, *"That sounds like a pretty good poker hand."*

"Why don't we think on it until tomorrow night," suggested Hermano. *"Dave Hunt will probably get out of jail tomorrow and we can get the whole group together tomorrow night. These people are ready to fight,"* he added.

"Good," replied Toby, *"I'm supposed to contact Chaplain. Harris tomorrow evening, and there may be some more developments up there by then."* Toby stood in a fluid movement that belied his size. "Does midnight, right here, sound okay?"

"Yeah, that'll be fine," Hermano got up and brushed off the seat of his pants.

"Ali!" Toby called. The boy joined him and they both disappeared into the darkness, toward the west. *"Don't forget the Qur'an,"* Toby called back.

The next morning, Hermano left by the main gate and drove into Fort Worth. He didn't notice the two men in the green Chevrolet pickup that followed, almost a half-mile behind.

"Seven-five-eastbound on 20," said one of the men, holding a CB microphone to his mouth.

As he neared Fort Worth, Hermano veered off to his right to follow old Highway 80. A few minutes later, the pickup swerved to the right to follow. *"Seven-five---"*, the pickup passenger dropped the mike as the left front tire blew out and the pick-up swerved across the median and into the westbound lane.

"Jesus!" Was all the driver had time to say before colliding head-on with an 18-wheeler.

Hermano, still a half mile ahead of them never saw what had taken place behind him. He followed 80 for a few miles until it became Camp Bowie and then turned into the first bookstore that he noticed on his right.

The girl in the red Volvo had picked him up at the intersection of Camp Bowie and River Oaks. When Hermano turned into the bookstore, she picked up her mic. *"Seven-five-Firebrand Bookstore on Camp Bowie,"* she said, turning into the bookstore behind him.

Hermano found several translations of the Qur'an from which to choose, but the prices limited him to two. He chose a hardbound copy with black binding, written in both English and Arabic, and was back on the road to Weatherford in about ten minutes. The slight detour around a terrible-looking accident near the intersection of highways 80 and 20 slowed him down a little, but he was back at the ranch by 10:30.

"Hermano!" A grinning Dave Hunt rushed out of the open garage door to greet him as he walked from the Jeep.

"Dave, they let you out." smiled Hermano, shifting the Qur'an to his left hand. He shook hands with Dave and followed him back through the garage and into the house.

He had cautioned Deirdre the night before about the kitchen being bugged and he found her, Dora, and Bill all sitting on the couch in the den. "Look at all the smiling faces," he said as he sat the Qur'an down on the desk.

"They didn't press charges!" Said an excited Dave as he poured himself and Hermano a cup of coffee. *"That bastard's still in the hospital, and they didn't even press charges."*

Dee got up off the couch and walked over to the desk. She picked up the Qur'an and looked at the title. *"Isn't this the Muslim Bible?"* She asked.

"Well, it's kind of like that." He took the offered cup from Dave. *"Thanks,"* he said. He sat down at the desk.

"Actually, though, they acknowledge all the same prophets that the Christians do. So, the Bible is actually for them, too." "Reverend Hall says that the Muslims don't believe that Jesus is the Son of God," commented Dora.

Hermano Glanced up at Deirdre. Almost imperceptibly she shook her head 'no'--she hadn't told her mom about Reverend Hall, yet.

"Well," Hermano began, looking over at Dora, *"they believe that Jesus is the Messiah. They believe that He's the Word of God. They believe that He's living—that God took Him up alive. And they intend to serve Him on His return. They also believe in the virgin birth—that God put his Spirit in Mary and willed her to be pregnant with Jesus. But—in spite of all this—you're correct. The Qur'an tells them not to call Him the 'Son*

of God'." He paused. *"It's as if God's deliberate intention was to keep the Muslims separate from the Christians until the end—or near the end."*

"Why?" Asked Deirdre.

Hermano shrugged his shoulders. *"Only God knows that,"* he said. *"Look at the state of modern Christianity, though, and that might answer your question."*

"God's reserves," commented Dave, taking a long drink of his coffee.

Chapter 19

At Hermano's request, the helipad lights hadn't been turned on that evening. At various times throughout the day, he had seized opportunities to catch members of the family away from the house and had advised them of the upcoming midnight meeting.

"The house is bugged," he had informed them and had then cautioned them to be careful about what they said indoors.

Shortly before midnight, they had filed out the patio door and, following Hermano, had walked a hundred yards to the north- west. All of them, with the exception of Hermano, were armed.

The faint rumble of thunder could be heard in the west and occasional flashes of lightning near the western horizon announced an approaching storm.

"Señors, senoritas." The child's voice came out of the darkness.

"Your Spanish is getting better, Ali," laughed Hermano. *"Did you bring your guardian?"*

"Yeah, I'm here," Toby's gruff voice came from about ten yards to the right. *"Did you bring our army?"*

They could see the silhouettes of the little boy and his huge companion walking toward them.

"We're all here," replied Hermano.

"Good," said Toby as he stopped a few feet from them. *"Let's sit down and figure out a plan of action."* As the adults sat down in a small circle, Toby turned to the boy.

"OK, mujahedin, time to earn your keep. Make wide circles around us and keep a look-out for the enemy. Stay low and keep quiet." Without comment, the boy disappeared back into the darkness.

"Good news, Preacher," began Toby, *"you're scaring the shit out of those people."*

"What you mean?" Asked Hermano.

"According to the Chaplain, they put some surveillance specialists on you this morning. A couple of guys. They followed you into Fort Worth— and got creamed in a head-on collision with a semi." Toby laughed. *"And that's just the appetizer."* He paused, *"you bought a Qur'an this morning, didn't you?"* He asked.

"Yeah," answered Hermano. *"It's right here."*

"Well, at about noon today, our time, their head satanist in Egypt was assassinated—by the Muslim Brotherhood." He laughed again. *"They think you're big medicine, some kind of white witch. The chaplain said they really freaked. Manticore's shittin' bricks."*

The Hunts had been quietly listening to Toby's report. *"Just who <u>are</u> you guys?"* Asked Bill.

"The wrath of God, son," laughed Toby. *"The wrath of God."* A loud clap of thunder made them all jump. Toby laughed again.

"The Chaplain said that Manticore had a big party, yesterday," he continued. *"You remember that May Day party we crashed in Colorado Springs?"*

"Yes," replied Hermano.

"Well, that was two different factions of the Church of Satan—trying to patch up some differences. What's the organization called, i.d?" He asked.

"I.D.," replied Hermano, *"International Druidism."*

"Well, they're convinced that the Church of Satan was responsible for what happened. And the Church of Satan thinks id did it. Sounds like they're on the verge of some kind of war."

"Beautiful," said Hermano. *"Let's give them a push."*

"Alright!" Exclaimed Toby. *"I. D's pretty much out in the open—not*

as secret as the Church of Satan. They've got some kind of regional head-
quarters in Dallas. Ali and I'll check it out tomorrow. But, let's get back
to you. Manticore wants you real bad. He figures he can produce you and
patch up their family squabble. He's got some real heavy's coming in from
New York. They're flying in on Wednesday—I even got their description
and what flight they're on." He paused, *"Man, I love this. We'll send*
'em back in body bags."

Mainly for the benefit of Dora, Dave, and Bill Hunt, Hermano
said, *"The local members that we know of here are the Sheriff, that*
Jackson woman, the guy Dave hospitalized, the deputy called Hutch,
and Pastor Hall." He heard Dora gasp. *"Can you find out who the other*
members are?"

"Yeah, I'll run a bug on Hall. I think we ought to take out the Sheriff
as soon as possible, though."

"I agree," said Hermano.

"Oh," said Toby, bringing a canvas bag around and laying it in his
lap, *"I've got my 'Sniffer' here."*

"What?" Asked Dave.

"My Sniffer—low-energy output, directional indicator, it detects
bugs. Take it back to the house with you and see if any rooms other than
the kitchen are bugged. Just click it on and if the needle rises above zero,
you've got a bug. The needle goes to its highest when pointed directly at
the bug. Don't pull any of the bugs—we don't want to tip 'em off that
we're wise to them, but it'll let you know which rooms are safe to talk in."

"Good," said Hermano, taking the bag. *"Oh, and here's Ali's*
Qur'an," he said, handing it to Toby. *"You'd better go pretty soon, if*
you want to get out of here before the rain starts."

"Yeah," said Toby as they all got to their feet. *"We'll meet you here*
the same time Wednesday night."

"Wait," said Dave, *"I want to get in on some of the action. How*
about letting me help with those guys coming in from New York?"

Toby was quiet for a moment. *"All right,"* he said. *"Can you get*

*away from the ranch early Wednesday morning—about six o'clock—
without being seen?"*

"*He can go out the way we did yesterday,*" offered Deirdre.

"*Yeah,*" agreed Hermano, "*we'll get him out.*"

"*OK, then meet us at Partners Restaurant on Airport Freeway at
seven a.m. Wednesday.*"

"*Good,*" said Dave, "*I'll be there.*"

"*Well,*" said Toby, "*that about---*"

"*Sir! Sir!*" Ali whispered frantically, scrambling into the circle.
"*Men are on the hill over there!*" In the dim light they could barely see
him pointing to the south.

The lightning flashes were nearer and more regular, and for a
second they could see five men standing on a slight rise about thirty
yards away. They appeared to be looking in the direction of the ranch
house, but during an exceptionally brilliant flash, one of them spotted
Hermano's group. All five wheeled around and raised what appeared
to be rifles.

Hermano raised his right hand and pointed at them. "*No!*" He
shouted.

Simultaneous with his shout, the five men were engulfed in a
brilliant flash of light, immediately followed by an ear-splitting crash.

"*God Almighty!*" Exclaimed Dave.

When their eyes had readjusted to the dim light, nothing could
be seen of the men.

"*God Almighty,*" repeated Dave in a hushed tone. The others, with
the exception of Ali, stood quietly looking at the spot where their
would-be attackers had stood.

Ali leaped into the air with his right arm raised. "*Allah Akbar!*"
He shouted.

"*He certainly is,*" agreed Hermano.

Chapter 20

"Has it started raining, yet?" Asked Dora. She was filling five cups, set in a row on the desk, with coffee.

"No, it's still just thundering and lightening," answered Dee. She was standing at the patio door, gazing thoughtfully out into the night. It was 1:30 a.m., and they had been back at the house for about thirty minutes.

"What you think about all this, Mom?" She asked, still staring into the night.

"I'm having trouble absorbing all of it," answered Dora. *"Reverend Hall. It's hard to believe."* She had finished pouring the coffee. *"Why don't you call the boys, the coffee's ready."*

Dee turned from the patio door and, preoccupied, walked toward the hallway.

"I'll tell you one thing, though," her mom added. *"If Hermano told me that it was daylight outside right now, I'd believe it."*

Dee stopped and turned to her mom. With a wry smile, she said, *"I know it's wrong, Mom—but, he scares me."*

"I know what you mean. But, like you said, it is wrong. It's a real blessing that he came here."

Hermano, Dave, and Bill could be heard coming down the hallway.

"The only bug is the one in the kitchen," said Dave as they entered

the den. They had checked the den as soon as they had arrived back at the house. *"It's in the electrical wall-socket beside the table,"* he added.

"Coffee's poured", said Dora, taking a sip of her own. *"I'm not going to be able to sleep tonight, anyway."* They all took a cup and found a place to sit.

Dora sat down on a reclining chair beside the couch. *"That little boy sure is cute,"* she said. *"Is he—uh, Toby's?"*

"Toby took him away from some satanists," answered Hermano. He had sat down on the couch with Bill and Dave. *"His parents—if they're still alive—live in Afghanistan."*

"Oh," said Dora. She paused for a moment, *"just how big is this— Organization—that we're fighting?"*

"It's--" he paused, *"it's so big that you might have trouble believing me if I told you."*

"She'd believe you," said Dee. She was sitting on the chair at the desk.

Hermano looked at her curiously. He turned back to Dora. *"They control the world,"* he said.

"The world!" Exclaimed Dee. *"Then how can we possibly win?"*

"Because," Hermano said, looking back at her, *"God really **does** exist."*

"For the first time in my life," said Dave, *"I don't have any doubts about that."*

"Are we in—what people call the 'end time'?" Asked Bill.

Hermano turned to Bill and smiled. *"Yes,"* he said. *"And that's why I'm sure we'll win. No matter what the odds **appear** to be."*

"Toby said something about y'all crashing a May Day party," said Dave. *"Isn't that the main Celebration Day for international communism?"*

"Yes," answered Hermano, *"but the Communists merely adopted it as their primary holiday—they didn't originate it. As a holy day, it predates Christianity by a thousand years."*

"A thousand years!" Exclaimed Dora. *"That puts it back to about the time of King David."*

"You know your biblical history pretty well," said Hermano, smiling at Dora. *"Actually, it was one or two generations after King David. You've heard of the Druids?"* He asked.

"They started Halloween, didn't they?" Asked Deirdre.

"Yes, they called it Samhain—summers end. That was one of their four main holy days. Samhain, Lugnassad—in August, Imbolc-- in the winter and Beltane, which the Communists call May Day. The night before May Day is called Walpurges Night, that's when they had their fire-festival."

"This differentiation between May Day and Walpurges Night is a modern thing, though. Both of them together are Beltane. You see, religions whose primary focus is on a god or gods of darkness, begin their day at sundown. So, Beltane began at sundown on what we now call the last day of April and continued until sundown of May first. Walpurges Night plus May Day equals Beltane. It's curious when you consider that Hitler deliberately left the scene on Walpurges Night."

"Are you saying that what we're really fighting here are Druids?" Asked Dave.

"No, not exactly," answered Hermano. *"What we're opposing is more like a marriage of several different groups with a common denominator. The common denominator is that they're all anti-Christ. Under the skin, they're all satanists."* He paused. *"Let me get back to the Druids, though."* Hermano took a drink of his coffee. He looked back at Dave.

"You've heard of the Chaldeans, the Semitic tribes that controlled Babylon, haven't you?" He asked.

Dave nodded his head. *"What you just said is about all that I know about them, though."*

"Well, the Druids were northern contemporaries of the Chaldeans. Except, while the Chaldeans exercised absolute control over their area— southeast of the Mediterranean—for about a hundred years, the Druids

*exercised control over almost all of Europe for a **thousand** years—ending about the time of Christ.*

The Druids, like the Chaldeans, were a priestly corporation. In other words, while there were at lot of pagan religions in Europe, Druids were at the head of all of them—like the Chaldeans were in Babylon.

Julius Caesar even wrote about them when he wrote of his military campaigns. He called their gods by the names of the Roman gods, though—and for good reason. They were the original version of his own gods. Caesar said that the Druids asserted that they were descended from the God Dis—the God of the underworld, associated with the powers of darkness. Well, the Druids called Dis, Belenos. The name we know him by is Satan. The Beltane celebration is in honor of Belenos—or Satan."

"So, May Day is a satanic celebration?" Asked Dave.

"Yes, but I'm not saying that many Communists realize that," said Hermano. *"Their founders did, though."* Hermano turned back to Dora. *"A while ago you asked about how big this organization was,"* he said. *"Organization was a correct thing to call it, but a more accurate word would be Corporation—after the manner of the ancient Druids or Chaldeans."* He paused. *"What **we're** fighting is called 'The Beast',"* he added.

Dee spilled her coffee.

Dave looked at Hermano incredulously. *"You mean we're taking on **the** beast?"* He asked.

Hermano smiled. *"I mean, **God** is taking on the beast."*

There was a tremendous crash of thunder. Waves of rain began washing over the house.

Chapter 21

It was still raining at 9 a.m. when Hermano was awakened by the sound of someone knocking on his bedroom door. He got up and put on his jeans.

"Come in," he called out, grabbing a shirt from the dresser.

"Hermano," said Bill, swinging the door open and walking in. He was already dressed. *"Guess who's here?"* He asked.

"Who?"

"Two deputies. Frank Jr. and that Hutch guy. I answered the door." He paused, *"Hutch acted kind of surprised to see me."* Bill started laughing. *"I guess he was expecting to find a bunch of dead bodies in here. They're having coffee in the kitchen with mom and Uncle Dave, now. I hope, Uncle Dave keeps his mouth shut,".* He paused. *"He winked at me when he was walking to the kitchen."*

Hermano hurriedly put on his shirt and sneakers and followed Bill toward the kitchen.

"Mom's got breakfast goin', it should be ready in a few minutes," Bill said as he opened the hallway door into the old house.

"Hermano, mornin'," said Dave as Hermano and Bill walked into the kitchen. *"The deputy was saying that some prowlers were reported down near Jackson's store, last night. You didn't hear anybody trying to break in here, did you?"*

"No, it would have been hard to hear anything with all the thunder, though," answered Hermano, as he pulled up a chair beside Hutch.

The table was rectangular, with seating space on either side for two, and room for one on each end. Dave was sitting across from Hutch and beside Frank Pierce Jr.

*"I heard a **hell**-acious crash from back to the northwest at about one or one-thirty,"* deadpanned Dave. *"**Hell**-acious,"* he repeated.

"How about the coroner's report on Sam?" Quickly asked Dora, as she walked over from the stove and sat at the end of the table. She glanced at Bill, *"Bill, go tell Dee that breakfast's almost ready."*

Bill hesitated for a moment and then walked back toward the hall door. Hutch waited until Bill had left and then looked at Dora. *"We got it yesterday evening,"* he said. *"I haven't had a chance to read it all, but it states something like 'death due to accidental discharge of firearm'. Apparently he tried to shoot at those wolves from his helicopter and dropped the gun. It went off and a round hit him. He was firing with the copter door open and the gun must have fallen out after it discharged."* He paused. *"He must have tried to touch down once between where the cow was, and where we found the copter. The open door got knocked off there—and he finally came down to stay about a hundred yards east of where the door was."*

Dora got up and hurried back to the stove. Dave's face was strained, but he managed to keep the anger out of his voice. *"An accident, huh?"* He asked.

"That's what the report says," answered Hutch. He took a drink of his coffee.

"Tell me about the activities of the Church of Satan, around Weatherford," said Hermano, looking coldly at Hutch.

Hutch choked on his coffee. After a few seconds, he said. *"The Church of Satan?"* He wiped the coffee off his chin with the sleeve of his shirt. *"I never heard of anything like that around here,"* he said, avoiding Hermano's gaze.

"There are some satanic churches up around Denver," said Dave. *"Cowardly bunch of sneaks. They all ought to be burned at the stake."* He paused. *"There's probably some around here, too."*

"*I don't think we've got a single hippie in Parker County,*" said Hutch, looking down at his empty coffee cup. He glanced over at Hermano. "*I noticed you got Colorado tags,*" he said. "*You visiting here—or what?*"

"*Kind of a working visit,*" answered Hermano. "*I heard you were some kind of free-lance writer,*" Hutch said, studying Hermano more closely.

Hermano smiled. "*Where did you hear that?*" He asked.

Hutch ignored the question. "*I guess –from your question—that you write about satanism.*"

Hermano kept smiling, "*A little investigative writing—a little creative writing. Usually on religious topics. I don't write about flying saucers, though.*" He took a drink of his coffee.

"*We've got to be going,*" Hutch said as he pushed back his chair. He looked at Frank. "*We've still got some stops to make before lunch.*"

"*We'll call you if we find any traces of prowlers,*" called out Dave as they walked back through the kitchen door.

The rain finally tapered off and had stopped altogether by ten-thirty. The night before, Hermano and the Hunts had agreed that it would be best to delay reporting the charred bodies until they were discovered in the natural course of ranch business. So, at five-thirty that afternoon, while they were all eating supper outside on the deck table, Bill paused between bites and studied the northwest sky.

"*It would be normal to check and see why those buzzards are circling,*" he said, glancing across the table at Hermano.

Hermano nodded. "*Yeah, let's get this over with,*" he said, getting up. He looked up at the sky, three turkey-buzzards were lazily circling the knoll where their would-be attackers had been stopped the night before. Dave and Bill got up from the table and followed Hermano toward the helipad.

"*Have you ever noticed how they always seem to circle counter-clockwise,*" commented Dave as he caught up to Hermano.

"I hadn't noticed," replied Hermano. "*In this case, though, that's certainly appropriate.*"

"*Appropriate?*" asked Bill. He was a couple of steps behind his uncle and Hermano.

"*Almost everything about satanism is upside down, backwards or counter-clockwise,*" replied Hermano. "*They're into the opposite of what is right.*"

"*Left,*" said Dave, stopping at the north edge of the paved helipad.

"*Yes,*" smiled Hermano. "*Left is a symbol of theirs, too.*" He stopped beside Dave.

"*This is going to be muddy,*" commented Bill as he walked past where the other two had stopped.

"*It is,*" he said, stopping to roll his pants legs over the tops of his boots. Hermano and Dave did the same.

Trying to keep to the grassy spots, they slowly began making their way across the red clay-like mud to the focal point of the still-circling buzzards.

"*Counter-clockwise was the operative concept behind Hitler's swastika,*" said Hermano. "*He borrowed it from the Hindus or the Babylonians. It's the 'spinning wheel'—clockwise rotation represents the powers of light, counter-clockwise rotation represents the powers of darkness. The Nazi's swastika rotated in a counter-clockwise direction.*" He paused. "*Hitler was a practicing satanist. That's obvious to anyone who understands occult symbolism.*"

"*Speaking of that,*" began Dave, "*you said last night that what we were up against was the beast. Where does the number 666 come in? Who is he?*"

"*Reverend Hall said it was some kind of computer number,*" commented Bill. "*I guess that we can figure that whatever he said was wrong, though.*"

Hermano smiled at Bill. "*Not necessarily. You'd be surprised at the arrogance of these people. But, as far as a computer is concerned, they're only what people program into them.* "Thoughtfully, he stopped at the base of the hill.

"666 is the number that the organization which I called the Church of Satan has accepted as their identity." Hermano glanced at Dave. *"You said something about it being a ' he'. Some people think that. They're convinced that 666 is the number of some particular super-magician."* He paused, *"The power of the beast, though, is an organizational power. Now, there may be an individual who the organization acknowledges with some sort of title of prominence. But without the organization, he's like a queen ant without an ant bed--impotent."*

The three ascended the hill together. They stopped at the edge of a blackened circle which completely covered the flat twenty-foot wide top of the hill. Near the center of the circle lay five crumpled, charred bodies.

"Fire ants," quipped Dave, smiling.

"Let's don't go any closer," suggested Hermano. *"Our tracks indicate that we walked up here and discovered the bodies."*

They turned around and walked back down the slope, in the direction of the house.

"The ritual number for the Church of Satan is nine," continued Hermano *"The magic circle is supposed to be nine feet in diameter-- nine people are the ideal amount for higher order satanic ritual—the Satanic Bible lists their nine commandments—and so on."*

"Why nine?" Asked Dave.

"Well, they've counted—or calculated—the number of the beast. See, satanic ritual relies heavily on astrology and numerology. Particularly numerology." He paused. *"All forms of worship—involving communication with a deity—use numbers as symbols. Numerology is a kind of pseudoscience of numbers. In numerology, all numbers, for whatever reason, can be reduced to a single digit. The single digit is considered to be the essence of the number calculated."*

Hermano smiled at Dave's puzzled look.

"Let me cut to the heart of it," he said. *"Six plus six plus six, equals eighteen. One plus eight equals nine. Nine is the essence of 666. So, the organization that has accepted 666 as their identity has* **counted** *the number of the beast and they use that number for their rituals."*

Chapter 22

"Say," Toby grabbed the arm of a passing waiter. *"Would you tell the boy, here, what's on these burgers."* Ali, sitting across the table in the booth opposite Toby, looked expectantly at the waiter. An untouched burger-deluxe platter sat on the table in front of him. Toby, with a half-eaten burger in one hand, went back to reading his newspaper.

"Yeah, sure." The waiter stood beside Toby and Ali's booth and, with a slight show of indignation, smoothed the sleeve of the arm that Toby had grabbed. He glanced down at Ali's plate. *"Lettuce, tomato, onion, mustard, hamburger patty and bun."* He said glibly.

"Ham-burger?" Ali asked. He looked at Toby.

"Christ!" Toby glanced at the waiter over the top of his paper. *"Tell him what the meat's made of."*

"Oh. Well, beef, of course," said the waiter.

"A hundred percent, right?" Asked Toby, looking back at his paper.

"Yes, one hundred percent beef." The waiter paused, *"is that all?"*

"Yeah," said Toby. The waiter walked back toward the kitchen. Toby lowered his paper and looked at Ali. *"Satisfied?"* He asked with a smile.

"Yes, but--", Ali had picked up the burger but, hesitating, had continued to study it. *"What kind of grease did they cook it in?"*

"It cooks in its own juices," still smiling, Toby shook his head. *"Don't you think you might be going a little too far with all this?"* he asked.

"No, sir," Ali answered. He took a big bite of his burger. He looked at Toby, *"Mrrmph---"*

"Wait 'til you've swallowed," chuckled Toby. Ali quickly chewed and swallowed.

"If I'm going to be a good Muslim, don't I have to do it all?" He asked. *"We're commanded not to eat pigs."* He paused. *"Manticore made me do evil things,"* Ali averted his eyes and looked at his plate. *"Maybe God will forgive me if---if I really try hard."* He glanced up at Toby.

Toby shifted uncomfortably and folded his paper. He set in on the table. *"Ali,"* he began gently, *"I'm not a good enough person to tell people what they should do to make God happy with them."* He paused. Ali was looking at him expectantly. Toby took a quick swallow of his iced tea.

"But it seems to me," he continued, *"that since God knows your heart, and God knows your future—He would have to know if you really meant it when you told Him you were sorry."* Uncomfortable, he picked his paper back up. *"Hermano's the one you should ask about this kind of stuff."*

Toby changed the subject by holding the folded newspaper over the table and pointing to a photograph in the center of the page. *"You know this guy?"* He asked.

Ali leaned over the table and studied the photograph. The picture was of a bearded Arab man wearing a white woolen cap.

"No, who is he?" Ali sat back down and took another bite of his burger.

"According to the article, he's a former Afghan mujahedin—in Dallas trying to raise money for starving Afghan widows and orphans." Toby took a bite of his own burger and leaned back, chewing thoughtfully. He leaned forward and looked at the article again.

"Says his name is Omar Bedawi, the chief of some tribe in Afghanistan", Toby added.

"He's here? In Dallas?" Asked Ali. Excited, he leaned back over the table and looked at the photo again. *"Can we go talk to him?"* he asked.

Toby took a long drink of iced tea. *"Well,"* he said as he leaned back in his seat. *"He's going to give a talk at some mosque here in Dallas, tonight—at eight."* He looked at his watch. *"That's an hour and a half from now."* Toby finished his burger and sat quietly, still thinking. He looked at Ali.

"Do you understand what's going on here, son?" He asked.

"You helped me get away from people who hate God. Now you're helping other people who the satanists hate." He paused, *"Is that not right?"* He looked at Toby expectantly.

"Yes—but it's more than that. The man who had you is a very powerful satanist—with many influential friends." Toby paused, *"and the people who I'm helping now—well, Hermano—is greatly feared by the satanists. They want him very badly."*

"God protects him," said Ali flatly.

"Well, I can't argue with that," said Toby, *"but what I'm trying to say is that the satanists have many ears. Spies that you would never suspect."* He paused. *"If I let you go to that mosque, you would have to be very careful who you talk to—and what you said. The satanists don't even know about me. --well, just be careful."*

"I won't betray you," said Ali solemnly.

Toby gave Ali an old but reliable pocket watch that he kept in the glove compartment and dropped him off in front of the downtown Dallas mosque shortly before eight. He had told him that he would drive back by the front of the mosque at 11 o'clock that evening in case the people there wouldn't help him. *"I've got a good feeling about this, Ali,"* Toby had told him, *"But if anything should go wrong, and you should also miss me at 11 o'clock—then make your way back to the Hunt Ranch. Go by the same way that you and I went before."* Toby had then handed him a $50 bill. *"Just in case,"* he had said.

By 8:30, Toby was slowly cruising past the North Dallas Center for Druidic Research. Located in the prestigious Turtle Creek Road area, the center sat fifty yards west of the road—behind a lush and well-manicured lawn. He and Ali had thoroughly checked out the area earlier in the day. The Center's driveway left Turtle Creek and bordered the lawn on the north, ending in a surprisingly small parking lot directly behind the structure. The three-story block like white marble building, looking more like a Masonic Lodge than anything else, had no windows and only two doors. The front door, with the words '*Mur Ollavan*' chiseled directly above it in large block letters, opened onto a ten-foot square porch. The porch, though, was apparently no more than an ornament—there was no sidewalk and it was bordered on three sides by the lush immaculate lawn. All visitors obviously came and went by the back door.

The Druidic Center was the only structure on the heavily wooded block, and after Toby had rounded the corner to leave Turtle Creek, he turned into an alley which ran behind the Druids' parking area. There was a large trash dumpster, which sat near the alley at the southwest corner of the parking lot and Toby parked a few yards short of that.

Satisfied that he was out of sight of the Center, Toby doused his lights and turned off the ignition. Opening the glove compartment, he removed a tight-fitting pair of leather riding gloves and put them on. He then reached over into the back floorboard and picked up a five-foot long roll of canvas. Laying it on the front seat, he smiled and deftly removed the sword.

"*Well, Henry, ready to go to work?*" He whispered as he grabbed the sword's handle with one hand and quietly opened his door with the other.

The parking lot, though well-lit, was cut out of a thick grove of scrub oak. Toby carefully and quietly made his way through the trees and emerged from the grove beside the southwest corner of the building.

He was almost fifty feet from the back door, located near the center of the structure. The door, made of some sort of dark, heavy-looking wood, was well-lit, as was the whole parking lot. There was no porch or protective awning, only a solitary light fixture above the door that extended out about five feet and curved down to illumine the entrance.

The rest of the parking-area was lit by lights affixed to four tall lamp posts which were situated at the four corners of the lot. Standing near the corner of the building, Toby was almost directly underneath one of them.

He glanced out at the parking lot. Five cars. There were apparently several people still inside the center—but Toby had no way of knowing how many. He carefully walked a few feet into the parking area to get a better look at that door. If it was locked, it looked impregnable.

He stopped midway between the corner and the door and about ten feet from the wall of the building. He looked at the cars and then back at the door. He would have to try and hide behind the cars and catch them as they left the building. It was chancy, but that looked like the best option. He had just started to step in the direction of the cars, when he heard a clicking sound come from the direction of the door. Someone had just unlocked it.

He hurried back to the wall but was unable to move toward the corner before the door swung open. It opened out-in the direction of Toby, so he was temporarily out of sight of whoever was exiting the Center.

Hugging the wall and moving purposely, with a fluidity unusual in so large a man, Toby moved to get as close to the opening door as possible. He stopped immediately behind it.

"There should be a small wooden wedge laying just outside the door," the voice came from inside the building, *"prop it open with that."*

"Yeah, I see it," replied the man on the other side of the door.

"Put the two larger boxes in the trunk and the two smaller ones in the back seat," the first voice called out. It sounded farther away.

"Okay," the outside man called back. He wedged the door open at slightly more than a 90-degree angle.

Upon hearing retreating footsteps in the parking lot, Toby carefully looked around the edge of the door. A tall slender man, dressed in a business suit, was walking toward the trunk of a brown Lincoln Continental. He was struggling under the apparently heavy load of a large cardboard box. Every few feet, on his fifty-foot walk to the car, he would stop and set the box down, stretch, pick up the box, and continue for a few more feet. Toby, expecting the man to get a hernia, grimaced each time he picked up the box.

Deciding to chance it, Toby quietly stepped around the edge of the door and peered into the building. All that he could see, besides the three boxes which sat just inside the door, was a well-lit hallway which went straight toward the center of the building. A closed door was at the other end of the hallway, twenty feet from where Toby stood. It and the back door were the only doors in the hall. The dark-paneled walls were unbroken except for a panel of three electrical switches near the entrance and another panel of switches at the other end of the hall. Toby ducked back behind the door.

After a few seconds he heard approaching footsteps coming from the direction of the car. Gripping the sword handle with both hands, Toby waited. When he heard sounds of the man straining under another load, he whirled around the door.

The man, ten feet away, apparently heard the sound of Toby's movement. He stopped dead in his tracks. It was too late, though. As he turned his head—Toby struck. Henry's blade completed its powerful arc on a horizontal line even with the man's Adams' Apple. His head flew off to bounce in the general direction of the center of the parking lot. Like a rag doll, the rest of the body crumpled over the cardboard box, soaking it in blood.

Toby, after cleaning the blade on the seat of the man's pants, turned back toward the door. He quickly pushed the two smaller boxes out into the parking lot and kicked out the wooden wedge. While the door was swinging shut, he flicked the first electrical switch down—the parking lot lights went out. He flicked the second switch and noticed the porch light go out just before the door swung shut. He figured that the third switch must be for the hallway lights. Leaving that switch untouched, he hurried toward the inner door.

As Toby transversed the hall he kept his eyes fastened on a rectangular window, one foot wide by two feet high, which was centered in the upper half of the door. He could see some light behind it, but he couldn't see any movement. Stopping at the door, he stooped down and peered through the window.

Toby gasped. The sight beat anything that he had ever seen. In the center of the building, towering three stories high, was a huge, gnarled old oak tree. Apparently the whole Druidic Research Center had been built around the tree.

Just outside the door where he stood was a five feet wide concrete walkway which circled the tree. Between the tree and the walkway Toby could see fifteen to twenty feet of freshly laid squares of green grass.

Even though the building itself was square in shape, Toby could see that the inside was laid out in a circle. Five evenly spaced doors, counting the one Toby was behind, were interspaced around the circular walkway. Looking at the wall on the other side of that tree, Toby realized that all the office space was on the ground floor. There wasn't any second or third floor. Except for the branches of the tree, the space where a second and third floor should have been was nothing but empty air.

Bending down and looking up through the window, Toby could see the twinkling stars beyond the branches of the great oak. The building was nothing more than a huge greenhouse with a few offices. Toby looked either way through the window—the four other doors were all closed. The only sounds that he could hear were the incessant twittering's of some small brown birds which were jumping nervously from branch to branch in the oak tree.

Toby frowned. There didn't seem to be any way to determine where the other people were. He looked at the doors again. If he went to the left and somebody came out of a door to the right, or vice versa, he could end up chasing them round and round that damned tree. He straightened up and sighed.

Glancing over at the electric wall switch panel, he noted only two switches—which he assumed would be the hallway and the concrete walkway. Still frowning, he had begun turning back to the window when, with a start, he looked back up into the corner. A metal box, painted brown to blend in with the hallway wall, was nestled into the corner above the light switches. Smiling, he reached up and opened the circuit breaker box.

All the lights in the center went out simultaneously. Toby opened the inner door and quickly stepped out into the hallway, letting the door swing shut behind him. Standing with his back to the wall a couple of feet to the left of the hallway door, Toby didn't have long to wait. He could hear doors opening on either side and masculine voices conversing—more in irritation than alarm.

"The breaker box is in the hall—I'll get it", came a voice a few feet to Toby's left.

Toby, his eyes not yet adjusted to the dark, waited until he could hear the man's approaching footsteps. Then, grasping the sword handle with both hands, Toby stepped out from the wall and, slashing in a downward arc, whirled to his left. He felt a jar as the blade, with a crunching sound, cleaved the Druid almost in half. The man didn't utter a sound as he fell to the walkway.

"What was that?" The question came from almost ten or twelve feet behind the fallen man. Toby hooked the toe of his boot under the man laying at his feet and kicked him over the side of the walkway. He landed on the grass with a loud thud.

"Frank?" The voice came back.

Toby lunged in the direction of the voice and began slashing to his left and right. He hit the wooden wall two or three times, but he connected with flesh at least a half-dozen times. Toby figured he had downed three more men by the time he had moved twenty feet. Not a single one of them had cried out.

The lights had been out for little more than a minute, but Toby's eyes were already beginning to adjust to the dark. He was fairly certain that he could see the forms of three men standing between the hallway door and the first door to the right. Carefully stepping over the bodies between himself and the hallway, Toby hurried to get between the men and their only exit.

"What's going on?" One of the men asked. There was a hint of panic in his voice. *"Who's that?"* Apparently their eyes were also adjusting to the dim light.

Passing the hall door, Toby slowly moved toward them.

The twittering birds in the oak tree were in a state of panic. Their chatter filled the hollow innards of the building with a sound of terror that was almost tangible.

Thrusting forward, Toby lunged for the first man. The blade ran him through above his midsection and buried almost to the hilt. Toby yanked the sword back out and shouldered the falling man over the edge of the walkway.

The second man, who apparently realized what was going on, turned to run but collided with the third man. They both fell in a tangled heap on the walkway.

Toby was on them before they could get to their feet. Slashing downward, Toby began forcing the second man back into the third. He continued slashing and thrusting until they were both still.

Toby stopped and straightened up. Breathing heavily, he leaned against the wall for a few seconds. The birds seemed to have calmed down a little, and the only sounds were their more subdued twitter and his breathing.

Toby walked back into the hallway and threw the breaker switches. He blinked as the center was once more bathed in light.

All the men on the walkway and the inner lawn were dead, but to make sure he hadn't missed anyone, Toby thoroughly searched the remainder of the building. Apparently he had gotten them all.

When he was satisfied, Toby walked over to the man who was closest to the hallway door and laid him out flat on the concrete walkway. Then he reached into his own hip pocket and pulled out a business sized envelope which had been folded in half. He had been saving Deputy Wally Byrd's invitation to Manticore's party for just such an occasion. Smoothing out the envelope, he carefully slid it under the dead man.

Chapter 23

"Doesn't make much sense to me, Sheriff," Dave pointed his flashlight at one of the charred bodies. He and Bill had accompanied Sheriff Blocker, all carrying flashlights, back to the blackened top of the hill—northwest of the ranch house. *"See the barrel of the gun sticking out from under that body over there? That's an AK-47. Whoever heard of prowlers or country-store burglars carrying AK-47s?"*

Noncommittal, the sheriff just stood staring at the bodies.

"I guess it's a good thing for us that they decided to stand on this hill." Dave panned his flashlight around the top of the hill. *"Have you ever seen such a big lightning strike?"* Smiling, he glanced at the Sheriff.

"Lightening," the Sheriff repeated.

"Naw, I think it was the wolves—they must have got some flame throwers," quipped Bill. Dave laughed and slapped him on the back.

"Well, better them than us, huh Sheriff?" Asked Dave. *"Sheriff?"* Dave looked around for the Sheriff and saw him, flashlight in hand, walking back down the hill in the direction of the house. *"Hope it wasn't something we said,"* chuckled Dave.

"Don't track mud in the house," called out Dora. She was sitting on the couch with Reverend Hall when Dave and Bill entered the den through the patio door. Deirdre, seated at the desk, was bent over the opened family Bible.

"We left our boots on the deck, Mom," answered Bill as he slid the door shut behind them. *"Where's Hermano?"*

"I thought he was with you—he's outside, somewhere," said Dora.

"He's around front—meeting some television news people," interjected Deirdre. She never looked up from the Bible.

"What are you reading, Dee?" Asked Bill as he walked over to the desk. He peered over her shoulder.

She glanced up at him and then continued reading. *"I'm looking for the part about someone who 'brings fire down from heaven' or something like that,"* she replied.

Reverend Hall pursed his lips. *"That would be in Revelation,"* he said. *"13, 13."* He paused. *"It's about the false prophet—let's see, 'He performs great signs, so that he even makes fire come down from heaven on the earth in the side of men.'"*

"No, that's not it," Deirdre said without looking up.

"How about the two witnesses?" Asked Dora. *"if anyone tries to harm them, fire comes from their mouths and devours their enemies.'"*

Dee, Dave, and Bill all turned to look at Dora, who shifted uncomfortably. *"I read it this morning,"* she said sheepishly.

Dee smiled at her mom. *"What I was looking for was in the Old Testament,"* she said. *"It's right here."* She looked back at the Bible and began reading, *"'Elijah answered the captain, 'if I am a man of God, may fire come down from heaven and consume you and your fifty men!' Then fire fell from heaven and consumed the captain and his men.' That's the one I was looking for,"* said Dee. She turned and looked at Reverend Hall.

"Isn't Elijah supposed to come back in the end-time?" She asked.

"According to Jesus, he already came back," replied Reverend Hall, *"in the person of John the Baptist."*

"Is there a limit on how many times he can come back?" Asked Dee. Her tone bordered on sarcasm. Reverend Hall pursed his lips.

"I don't believe a little lightning means that the end of the world is here," he stated dryly.

"That's what they said to Noah," quipped Dave.

A few minutes later, Hermano slid open the patio door. *"There are at least fifteen or twenty news people on their way out to that hill,"* he said as he walked in and slid the door shut. *"The Sheriff's with them."* He glanced at Dora, *"There's supposed to be live coverage on channel 5's ten o'clock news,"* he added.

"I've got to be going," said Reverend Hall as he stood up.

"Oh, don't run off, Reverend Hall," said Dora. *"The news will be on in ten or fifteen minutes."*

"Thanks, but I still have a stop to make," he replied as he walked to the patio door. He slid it open. *"Goodnight, all,"* he called out as he hurriedly walked across the deck.

Hermano reached out and slid the door shut. Then he turned to the Hunts and held his right index finger against his lips, signaling them to be quiet. He walked across the room and into the hallway and returned in less than a minute with Toby's 'sniffer'.

He turned it on and pointed it at the couch. The needle started bouncing.

Hermano motioned for Dora to get off the couch. After she had, he began panning the sniffer back and forth across it. He stopped near the spot where Reverend Hall had been sitting and then began panning up and down. He paused at the front-edge of the couch seat and laid the sniffer behind him on the coffee table. He bent down and stared at the black and brown patterned fabric. Without looking up, he motioned for the others to join him.

When they had, he pointed to what looked like the cloth-covered head of a large pin. They all nodded in agreement and then followed Hermano over to the desk. He grabbed a pad of paper and a pen. He wrote, *"I think we need to get rid of this bug—even if it seems suspicious to them."*

The Hunts all nodded in agreement.

Hermano thought for a minute and then wrote; *"Water or coffee will probably short it out. ---Dee, pour a cup of coffee slowly on the bug. --- Dora, just before she does it, say something like,' look out! You're going to spill that coffee!'---OK?"* Having finished writing, Hermano looked at Dee and Dora.

They smiled and nodded in agreement.

After they had gone through with their charade, Hermano again tested with the sniffer. This time the needle never moved from the zero.

Hermano smiled. *"They can't be <u>sure</u> that you really didn't just spill some coffee,"* he said, looking at Dee.

"You know," said Dora, *"I never really believed it about Reverend Hall til now."* She paused thoughtfully. *"Well,"* she shrugged her shoulders, *"let's watch the latest from the Hunt Ranch on the news."* She walked to the other side of the room and flicked on the television.

"We switch now to live coverage with our man on the scene— Jerry Barlow," the female newscaster was saying.

"This must be it," said Dave, taking a seat on the couch beside Bill. Deirdre sat down in the recliner and Hermano turned around and leaned against the edge of the desk.

"No, this is channel 8 –in Dallas," said Dora as she reached for the remote to change the channel.

"Just a minute," said Hermano as the picture changed to that of a bizarre looking fire shooting out the top of a three-story white building.

"Jerry Barlow on the scene at the Center for Druidic Research on Turtle Creek." The camera panned from the building to focus on a slender well-dressed man in his late twenties. Standing a good distance from the building, he reported that the fire department had only just arrived. Except for a single back door, there was no way for the firemen to get inside to fight the fire, and water was going to have to be hosed onto the roof.

"This could take some time, Jane," he said. The camera panned back

to the building. *"I've seen a lot of fires,"* he continued, *"but I've never seen anything like this. And to add a touch of the macabre to an already bizarre scene—the headless body of a man was found in the parking lot near the back door."*

The picture changed back to the female newscaster, *"We'll try to bring you an update on this story later in the newscast,"* she said. *"In the Middle - East today---"*

Dora changed the channel back to 5 where they were reporting on an upcoming City Council election. She turned around and raised her eyebrows, *"The Druidic Center,"* she said

"Toby?" Asked Dave, looking at Hermano.

"No doubt." Hermano smiled. *"He sure does have a flair for the dramatic, doesn't he?"*

They sat through five more minutes of political reporting, a report on the Middle East and a rehash, without benefit of live coverage, of the fire at the Center for Druidic Research. Then the reporting turned to sports coverage.

"What happened?" Asked Bill, getting up from the couch. *"Why didn't they do the report from the ranch?"*

"Somebody managed to squash it," replied Hermano. He paused, *"They'll have a reasonable excuse, though,"* he added.

"Is there anything this—organization—can't do?" asked Dora. She was sitting on the desk chair.

"They can win some battles," replied Hermano, looking down at her, *"but they can't win the war."* He scooted farther back on the desk and sat cross-legged. *"This—organization—has members in every segment of society. Members who can't be connected but work together for their common---"* he paused, *"evil."*

He turned his head to look at Deirdre. *"With the old women at the truck stop and the young couple at the store, you experienced the very beginnings of their psychological warfare.*

The organized Church of Satan is a behavioral psychologist's dream-come-true. And there are behavioral psychologists in it—tops in

their field." He paused again, *"experts in psychological warfare. And they are no more than advisers to the real manipulators—the 'Manticores' of the organization. Imagine,"* he continued, still looking at Deirdre, *"if things hadn't changed after the incident at the store, every time you left the house you would encounter people and situations which would yank you from one end of the emotional spectrum to the other. There would be bizarre confrontational episodes, overheard conversations that deliberately reflect things occurring in your life. Traffic accidents—or near accidents—would occur almost every time you got on the street.*

There would be trouble with any big organization that you come in contact with. Particularly banks, but also electric companies, phone companies, the police, the Postal Service—anything having to do with the government."

Dora frowned. *"Roger, our attorney, called today,"* she said. *"He said that he was just notified that the IRS was going to do an audit on us."*

Hermano nodded and continued, *"As a part of the organization is beating you down with contrived personal situations, another part can be chopping your legs out from under you materially—financially."* He paused. *"And if, at some point, you cry 'conspiracy'? Well, that's simply a further manifestation of your obvious paranoia."*

Dora leaned back in her chair and looked at Hermano skeptically, *"From your perspective as a, uh, a servant of God, exactly what do you think this organization is?"*

"Let me answer that, to begin with, by pointing out an error in translation in the last verse of chapter thirteen in The Revelation of Jesus Christ. *Whereas most English translations say that the number of the beast is the number of a man, the single Greek word that they translated into 'a man' should actually be translated into, simply, 'man'."* Hermano paused and looked around at his new friends. *"The* organization *that we're going to war with, is called 'The Beast'."*

"God Almighty!" Exclaimed Dave.

Hermano smiled. *"Yes,"* he said, *"fortunately for us, He is."*

Chapter 24

The large north-south thoroughfare that dissected DFW Airport was heavily congested with traffic, as it always was on weekday mornings. Wednesday was the worst day, though, and 9 a.m. was the worst time. And it was at precisely 9 a.m. on Wednesday morning when five men in a light blue Ford sedan approached the toll booths to exit at the southern end.

Each of the several lanes of traffic had its own toll booth. Most of the lanes had lines of fifteen to twenty cars stacked up behind the booths. One lane, though, the third and fourth from the right, had five or six fewer cars than the others. As he approached the booths, the driver of the Ford changed lanes to get into the shorter line.

"You bastard!" He exclaimed. An old station wagon had just whipped into the line in front of him. The driver jerked his right hand up to pound the horn—but hesitated. There was a sticker on the back bumper of the station wagon that read, *"Honk if you love Jesus."* He lowered his hand and frowned.

"Where exactly is Weatherford?" One of the men in the back seat asked. There were two other men in the backseat, all three were dressed in business suits.

The man on the passenger side of the front seat twisted around to lean with his back against the door. He threw his left arm over the top of the seat and looked at his three companions in the back. *"About fifteen or twenty miles on the other side of Fort Worth,"* he replied. *"We'll take you over there to check it out this afternoon. You've got reservations at the Blackstone Hotel in Fort Worth—we'll drop you off there first. You can freshen up after your flight. Congressman Burton will drop by the hotel and talk with you some time before lunch."*

"Look, we want to get this over with as soon as possible," one of the other men in the backseat said.

The driver glanced around. *"We're just chauffeurs,"* he said.

"Yeah," the man on the passenger side agreed. *"You'll have to talk over strategies with Burton."*

They were coming up on the toll booth and conversations stopped as the driver rolled down his window.

"You got any change?" He asked the man sitting beside him. *"It's hard to get to my wallet with this seatbelt on."* He stopped beside the booth.

"I think so," the man replied, leaning back to put his hand in his right front pocket.

The station wagon in front of them, already having paid and gone past the booth, halted nearly twenty feet beyond where they were stopped. A man with short hair and a beard, wearing a bulky car-coat, opened the back door on the driver's side and got out.

Leaving the door open he walked toward the toll booth waving some dollar bills in his left-hand. *"Miss! Miss!"* He shouted. *"We gave you a twenty."* He waved the money again, looking at the booth attendant. *"You gave us change for a five."* He stopped between the booth and the Ford.

Turning around to the driver of the Ford, he said, *"You didn't honk."* Before the driver had a chance to answer, Dave pulled his right hand out of his pocket and tossed a grenade through the open window. He turned and sprinted back to Toby's station wagon.

Just as Dave dove into the back seat of the wagon, the Ford exploded in a ball of fire. The door swung shut when Toby floorboarded it, and Dave raised up to stare incredulously at the scene behind them.

"*Wow!*" He exclaimed as they sped away. "*Nobody could have gotten out of that.*"

"*Good,*" said Toby. "*Damn good.*"

"*Isn't that Dave?*" Asked Deirdre as she stood up to gaze in the direction of the bunkhouse. She, Dora, and Hermano were having lunch at the poolside table.

"*I think so,*" replied Hermano. He had turned his head to look at the distant man, walking toward them across the northeast pasture.

They all raised their arms to return the man's exuberant wave. He had apparently spotted them sitting near the pool.

Five minutes later, out of breath, Dave plopped down in a chair beside the table. "*Whew,*" he said. "*Got any more grub?*"

"*I'll make you a sandwich,*" said Dora, standing up. "*What's that you've got in your hand?*" She asked, looking at the long, rectangular piece of white paper that Dave was still clutching in his right hand.

He flipped the paper over. "*Honk if you love Jesus*" was printed across it in big black letters.

Dora smiled. "*Dave?*" She asked. "*You _are_ Dave?*"

Dave returned her smile. "*Toby gave me this as a souvenir.*" He paused, "*He doesn't like identifying stickers on his car. He put it on this morning so that he could play with the heads of those satanists at the airport.*" Dave smiled at Hermano.

"*He swerved his car real close to the front-end of the car of the satanists to see if they would honk.*" He started laughing. "*That guy is unreal,*" he said.

Hermano smiled. "*We watched the noon news,*" he said. "*Was that fireball at the toll booth the satanists?*"

"*Yeah. Like Toby said—we sent 'em back in body bags.*"

"*Here's something you probably didn't know. Do you know who three of those men were?*" Asked Hermano. Dave shook his head 'no'.

"The news described them as employees of Roth-Unicorn. Some sort of executives."

"Roth-Unicorn!" Exclaimed Dave. *"Are you serious?"*

Hermano nodded, still smiling.

"Who's Roth-Unicorn?" Asked Dee.

The smile disappeared from Dave's face. He looked at Dee, *"When I was a POW, the cage that I was kept in was made by Roth-Unicorn."* He paused, *"That name still pops up in nightmares now and then—Roth-Unicorn."* He looked back at Hermano.

"Does that—the three guys being employees—does that mean that Roth-Unicorn is part of the, uh, satanic organization?"

"I would say so," replied Hermano.

"Looks like the chickens are coming home to roost," remarked Dora as she turned and walked toward the patio door. *"I'll get your lunch,"* she called back to Dave.

"Just a minute," replied Dave. *"Before I forget, does Reverend Hall have church services on Wednesday night? I told Toby that I thought he did."*

Dora stopped a few feet from the table. *"Sunday morning, Sunday evening, and Wednesday evening. Wednesday services start at seven o'clock."* She paused, *"why does he want to know?"*

"He wants us all to go. Bill, too. I think he wants us to have an alibi." He raised his eyebrows.

"Lord, doesn't he ever rest?" Dora smiled as she turned to continue on toward the patio door.

"Doesn't seem like it." Answered Dave. *"Anyway, we're all supposed to be seen somewhere between seven and eight o'clock tonight."*

"Sheriff Blocker?"

The Sheriff, sitting behind his desk, looked up from some shift schedules that he had been busily rearranging. *"Yeah,"* he said, *"what is it?"*

The deputy, who was standing in the doorway, nodded toward the Sheriff's telephone. *"Line 1,"* he said, turning to walk back toward the front desk.

Sheriff Blocker punched a button on the telephone and picked up the receiver. *"Yeah,"* he said, *"this is Sheriff Blocker."*

"Sheriff," the voice began, *"I don't know how to say this, but— uh—I've given it a lot of thought and—uh –I got ahold of some stuff that I think I'd better turn over to the police."*

Sheriff Blocker continued to work on his scheduling as he held the phone to his ear. *"Yeah, what kind of stuff?"* He asked.

"Well," the voice hesitated, *"it's a—kind of a –diary or something."* There was a long pause. *"I'm visiting relatives in the area,"* the voice went on, *"when they were all out of the house the other day I—uh—kind of started meddling around. This diary—it's, uh—they're in some kind of Church of Satan or something. This diary has all kinds of weird stuff in it."* There was a pause. *"Is there a family around here called the Hunts?"*

Sheriff Blocker put down his pen. *"Just a minute,"* he said. He got up and quickly walked over and shut the door. He walked back to the desk and, still standing, picked up the receiver.

"Sorry," he said. *"The Hunts? There's a family by that name that has a ranch north of here. Are they in that Church of Satan, too?"*

"No, but they're mentioned in this diary. That's why I called. It looks like the Church of Satan is going to try and kill them." There was a pause. *"It doesn't say who the other members are—except for the leader of their group. Do you know a Reverend Hall?"*

Sheriff Blocker frowned, his stomach was knotting up. Bending over, he eased around the table and sat back down in his chair. *"Not personally. There's a preacher here in town by that name, though."*

"Well, according to this diary, he's head of their group," the voice went own, *"how about if I just mail this thing to the Police Department or Sheriff's Department—I'm leaving tonight."*

"No!" Sheriff Blocker said quickly, *"if someone's life is in danger, we shouldn't waste time with the mail."* He paused, *"I'll tell you what.*

I'm going to be in the office late, tonight. Why don't you just drop by on your way out-of-town? The only ones here'll be just me and whoever is on duty at the desk."

"*Okay,*" the voice said. "*I'll call before I come by—sometime after supper. If you're not there, I'll leave it with whoever is at the desk.*" The phone went dead as the caller hung up.

Sheriff Blocker leaned back in his chair and took a deep breath. Letting it out with a rush, he leaned over the shift schedule and, grabbing a pen, scratched out the name that was already filled in for that evening's desk duty. In its place, he wrote the name '**Hutch**'.

Church services that evening began promptly at seven o'clock. Counting Hermano and the Hunts, there were only twenty people present. And, not counting Hermano and the Hunts, none of them appeared to be younger than sixty.

As a cuckoo-clock—located somewhere in the offices behind the pulpit--announced the hour, Reverend Hall mounted the stage to stand solemnly behind the podium. He pursed his lips.

"*I wonder if Judas puckered like that?*" whispered Dee. She glanced at Hermano, who was sitting beside her-- next to the center aisle.

Eyes twinkling, he barely managed to suppress a laugh. "*Was that a cuckoo clock?*" He whispered incredulously.

Holding her mouth tightly shut and ducking her head, she started shaking with barely contained laughter. Keeping her head down, she covered her face with both hands.

Dora, who was sitting immediately to Dee's left, elbowed her. "*Shhh!*" She said.

"*Tonight's sermon,*" began Reverend Hall, "*will be from the Book of Revelation. The end, ladies and gentlemen,*" he looked at Hermano and the Hunts, "*is **near**!*"

Toby slammed the door shut. A startled Sheriff Blocker glanced up from his paperwork.

"Sheriff? The deputy said to come on back," said Toby as he walked toward the front of the desk.

"Are you the guy that called?" Asked Sheriff Blocker as he leaned back in his seat.

Toby, wearing a long overcoat, reached casually into his right coat pocket. *"I'd like to have mailed this, but, like you said, we shouldn't waste time."* He whipped his hand out of his pocket.

Sheriff Blocker's eyes opened wide at the sight of the silencer-equipped, long-barreled .22 caliber semi-automatic pistol. Toby fired three quick shots and three red spots appeared in the center of Sheriff Blocker's forehead. His head jerked back in his seat and then he pitched forward over the desk.

Toby turned around and walked back toward the door. Still holding the gun in his right hand, he stuck his left hand into his hip pocket and pulled out a handkerchief. Draping the handkerchief over his hand he turned the doorknob and opened the door. He stepped out and then reached around to wipe off the outside doorknob. Sticking the handkerchief back in his pocket, he walked toward the front desk.

Hutch, the deputy on duty, was sitting with his back to Toby. He was holding a telephone to his ear with his left hand and writing on a notepad with his right.

Toby, unseen, walked silently up behind him. He placed the barrel of the .22 automatic behind Hutch's left ear and fired off three more quick shots.

Without even pausing to see the effect, he continued on toward the back door. He took his handkerchief back out and put the gun away. Using the handkerchief to open the door, he casually wiped off the outer knob and let the door swing shut behind him.

Toby walked a block to the south of the Sheriff's Department and climbed back into the station wagon. His mind was already on his next project and he figured he had about forty-five minutes to complete it.

He had already checked out Reverend Hall's house and had been relieved to find that it was fairly secluded. It was a wood frame house with a couple of out-buildings, located on the south edge of Weatherford. The nearest neighbor was nearly a block away and Toby felt certain that he could get in and out of Hall's house without being seen.

"Are you saying that we shouldn't do anything but sit and wait?" Asked Hermano.

Reverend Hall gave him a cold look as the small congregation turned to look at Hermano. *"What I'm saying is that all of God's people are going to be transfigured out of here before any of the really bad things come to pass,"* replied Reverend Hall. *"I didn't mean we shouldn't do **anything**. It's our commission to spread the Gospel to all the world. We should preach and pray,"* he said, and liking the sound of it, repeated himself, ***"preach** and **pray."***

Hermano's eyes narrowed, *"Remember the Alamo,"* he said flatly.

"Huh? What?" Reverend Hall had a puzzled look on his face.

Hermano smiled, *"I always remember **John 18:36** by the year 1836—remember the Alamo? The battle was fought in 1836."* He paused. *"In **John 18:36** Jesus says that his servants would fight if his kingdom was of this world. In the book of Revelation, when the Seventh Angel sounds, the kingdoms of the world are declared the kingdoms of our Lord and His Christ."* He paused. *"Then a command is given to those referred to as 'my people'. It's a command to take vengeance. To whom is the command given, if all of His people are already gone?"*

Reverend Hall's face was red, and his knuckles were white as his grip tightened on the front edge of the podium. *"We're not supposed to take vengeance!"* he spat. *"We're supposed to return **love** for persecution."*

He relaxed his grip as he swept his gaze over the rest of the congregation. *"When one of the disciples asked Jesus if they should bring fire down from heaven to destroy their persecutors, Jesus was offended and said that they did not know 'what Spirit they were of'."* He looked smugly at Hermano.

"And yet—at the 'transfiguration'—Jesus was advised and comforted by Elijah, who had done that very thing," replied Hermano. *"The spirit that Jesus was talking about to some of his original disciples, was the demeanor necessary to complete the 'great commission'--an almost two-thousand-year job. According to Scriptures, the spirit of **justice** and **righteous indignation** is characteristic of God's people in the 'end time'. And, like you said, the end **is** near."*

"Amen!" Exclaimed Dave.

Chapter 25

"Do you mind if I join you?" Deirdre was carrying two cups of coffee. She sat one down in front of Hermano.

Hermano had been sitting alone at the table near the swimming pool for the past half-hour. He looked up at Deirdre and smiled.

"Please do, but I'm afraid that I'm not very good company, tonight."

"I haven't been good company for the past couple of days," replied Deirdre, sitting in the chair to Hermano's right. *"That's why I wanted to catch you alone."* She paused and sipped her coffee. *"I want to apologize for the—distant way I've been acting. What happened Monday night just blew my mind. That lightning was the most frightening thing that I'd ever seen. After that I—I didn't know how to act around you."* She paused. *"What I mean is—I've never been around anyone that I've felt was,"* she paused again, *"beyond being human."*

Hermano, holding his cup in both hands, took a sip of coffee. He looked at Deirdre. *"What happened Monday night,"* he began, *"was God's work, not mine. That lightning strike was as much a surprise to me as it was to you. I'm—I know it sounds strange to hear something like this in this day and time—but, I'm a servant of God. And God—well, He acknowledges His servants with actions like that lightning.*

But, I'm just a man. With a man's thoughts and weaknesses. I understand what you're saying, though. And I don't blame you." He paused. *"Even though I understand—the way you've been acting, it really—well, hurt my feelings."* He set his cup on the table and reached over to take

Deirdre's hand. He looked into her eyes. *"I think I'm falling in love with you,"* he said softly.

Deirdre's eyes filled with tears. She gripped Hermano's hand tightly. *"I **know** I'm falling in love with **you**,"* she said.

"Wait a minute—wait a minute. Not while Uncle Dave's here." Dave slid the patio door shut behind him and, smiling, walked toward the table. *"How does that go, Hermano? 'A time for love, a time for war, a time to reap, a time to sew---a time to **kick-ass**!' No offense,"* he added quickly.

"You should have seen the 10 o'clock news," Dave continued excitedly, taking the seat opposite Deirdre. *"I can tell you why Toby wanted us to have an alibi. He blew away the sheriff and Hutch, right in the sheriff's office."* He paused, *"and it was clean—according to the news they don't have the foggiest idea what happened. No witnesses."*

"Right at the Sheriff's Department?" Deirdre asked incredulously.

"Yeah," Dave replied, grinning broadly. *"While we were at church. According to the news, it happened a little after seven o'clock. Man! That Toby's a regular dynamo."* He paused, *"I'm glad he's on our side."*

Hermano gently released Deirdre's hand and sipped his coffee. *"I'm glad it was clean,"* he said, *"but our enemies will figure we had something to do with it."* He stared quietly out into the night for a few seconds. *"I think we'd better pick up the tempo,"* he said. He looked at his watch.

"Toby should have called the Chaplain for his nightly report by now," he said. *"Later on, when we meet with Toby, we'll have to talk strategy."*

"Oh, speaking of that," said Dave. *"Just before the news, Dora, Bill, and I were talking. It seems to us---"*, he glanced over at Dee, *"we didn't leave you out on purpose, Dee, you just weren't there when it came up. Anyhow, it seems to us that we're either going to have to go all-out and try to beat these people, or they're certainly going to destroy us. Well, the bottom line is this. We're going to get ahold of all the cash we can lay our hands on and give it to you and Toby to use against these people."*

"No, I really don't want---" began Hermano.

"Just a minute", interrupted Dave. *"It's **our** money and we're going to use it. You two can use it more wisely than we can, though. I've got a lot of shady connections in Denver—I can get any weapon you want to name. But I don't know the places that need to be hit or the kinds of weapons that need to be used. You two have the knowledge and skills—let us supply the material."*

Hermano looked at him closely and nodded his head. *"Okay,"* he said. *"But what we really need now are bodies—people willing to help. And no matter how many guns you---"*

"Señors, senorita," as if on cue, the boy's voice wafted out of the shadows beyond the helipad.

Dave pushed back from the table and reached for the pistol he had tucked under the belt of his jeans. Dee motioned for him to be still.

"That's Ali," she said. She stood up and peered out into the night. *"Si, muchacho,"* she called out with a laugh. *"Estamos aqui."*

Hermano glanced from the helipad back to Dave. *"Toby said that he had been left with some Muslims?"* He asked.

"Yeah. And that's about all that he said about it." Dave kept staring in the direction of the child's voice. *"There's some men with him,"* he said, standing up. *"None of them is big enough to be Toby."*

The dim shapes of a child and three adults could be seen walking toward them across the helipad. The three adults stopped near the center of the pad and the boy continued on alone. He stopped, still in the shadows but plainly visible now, between the helipad and the patio deck.

"They're afraid that somebody might be watching you," he explained.

"Who are they, Ali?" Asked Hermano as he got to his feet.

"Three Muslims. One of them married my cousin," replied Ali, proudly. *"One of them is the Imam at a mosque in Dallas and the other one is a friend of my cousin's—uh—her--"*

"Husband?" Prompted Hermano.

"Yes. He's the friend of my cousin's husband." He paused, *"They want to talk to you. They want to help."*

Hermano thought for a moment. *"Tell them we'll act like we're walking back into the house. We'll turn off all the outside lights and then walk back out in the dark to talk with them."*

"Okay." The boy turned around and walked back toward the three men.

Hermano, Dave, and Dee walked casually across the deck to the patio door and went inside. A few seconds later, the deck lights and then the lights in the den went out. The patio door slid back open and Hermano and all the Hunts filed out. They walked quickly across the deck and joined their three visitors, who were standing motionless on the helipad.

"I'm Hermano." Hermano had stopped about three or four feet in front of the three men. The man in the center turned to the one on his right and spoke something in Arabic.

"My cousin's --husband doesn't speak English," explained Ali. *"His name is Omar."* He reached over and tapped the arm of the man in the center. When the man looked around, Ali said something in Arabic. The man held out his hand to Hermano.

They shook hands. The man to Omar's left then held out his hand. *"I am Ahmed,"* he said.

After he and Hermano had shaken hands he continued, *"I am Imam at the mosque in downtown Dallas."* He motioned toward the man on the other side of Omar. *"That is Abdul. He has been accompanying Omar on his tour—as translator,"* he added.

Hermano held out his hand. Abdul hesitated, but then grasped Hermano's hand with both hands and shook it vigorously. *"I am honored,"* the man said, *"Ali has told us about the---lightning."* He laughed nervously and quickly withdrew his hands.

Omar spoke for a few seconds to Ali, who then turned to Hermano. *"He said---,"* Ali started snickering. *"He talks funny,"* he explained. *"Omar said that he is a hunter who has only been hunting rabbits in a---valley,"* he paused, *"but now he has a chance to hunt goats on the mountaintop. He wants to help you fight Manticore.*" He paused again, as if searching for the right words. "*It's for the honor of our tribe.*"

"*Tell him that Manticore's place is like a fort. And he has many guards.*" Hermano paused, "*there is also the chance that he could make a hero out of Manticore. Manticore could say that for some noble reason Arab terrorists are after him.*"

Ali turned to Omar and began translating.

"*Tell him that if we can't bring Mohammed to the mountain, we'll bring the mountain to Mohammed.*" They all jumped at the voice from the shadows and the Arabs wheeled around to look behind them.

"*Mr. Toby!*" Ali shouted. He started to bolt in the direction of the voice but then caught himself and turned to his Arab companions. Waving his arms excitedly and chattering in Arabic, he pointed to Toby, whose silhouette was just becoming discernible as he approached from the north. Another, smaller figure was walking beside him.

"*I've got a lot of news,*" said Toby as he and his companion stepped onto the helipad, "*so I thought I'd better come out a little early. Is there a safe room in the house where we can all talk?*"

"*The den,*" suggested Hermano. "*There was a bug in it —but we shorted it out.*"

"*We were all in and out of the house this evening, though. I'll run back in and check it out again,*" offered Dave. He turned and hurried back toward the house.

"*Hermano, you remember Chaplain Harris,*" said Toby as he and his shorter companion joined the group.

"*Peter!*" exclaimed Hermano. "*It's good to see you're Okay.*"

"*This is the most exciting time of my life,*" replied Chaplain Harris enthusiastically, "*I couldn't be feeling any better.*" He shook Hermano's hand vigorously, "*I had to get here fast when---*"

"*Ali,*" interrupted Toby quickly, "*who are your friends?*"

"*This is Omar,*" said Ali, motioning toward the bearded Arab. "He married my cousin." He paused and then added, "*he doesn't speak English.*"

"Ah, the man in the picture. Tell him I'm glad to meet him," said Toby. Ali turned to Omar and spoke a few words in Arabic.

Looking at Toby, Omar stood a little more erect and spoke in Arabic.

"He says that he is honored to finally meet a warrior in this country." Ali paused, *"He says that any man who fights the Jihad is his brother."*

"Tell him I also admire him and his mujahedin," replied Toby. Ali spoke a few words in Arabic and Omar grinned broadly.

"This is Ahmed, the Imam at the mosque where you took me," continued Ali, pointing to the man at Omar's left.

"Glad to meet you. I hope Ali hasn't been too much trouble," said Toby.

"His company has been most refreshing—and enlightening," replied Ahmed. *"For a twelve-year-old boy to have such courage and—determination, has shamed many of us. Omar made the cut, and Ali—poured on the salt."* He paused, *"I and my people wish to join you in your jihad."*

"That's---," Toby could be heard taking a deep breath.

"A blessing," finished Hermano.

Ali had just introduced Toby to Abdul when Dave rejoined them. *"It's all clear,"* he announced.

They walked across the deck and filed into the still-darkened den. Toby and Dave, who had hung back a few paces behind the others while Toby whispered some quick instructions, were the last ones in. Bill closed the door and pulled the drapes as he turned on the lights.

"I need to put this 'sniffer' up," said Dave. He scooped it up from the coffee table and continued on through the hallway door.

"Bill, there are some folding chairs in the garage. Would you get them?" Asked Dora.

"I'll give you a hand," offered Chaplain Harris. He followed Bill through the garage door.

Five minutes later, the half-dozen folding chairs had been set up in the den. Just as they were all taking seats, Dave reentered from the hallway. He was carrying a large gray rectangular case with a handle on top.

"This is the only reel-to-reel tape recorder we've got," he said, looking at Toby. *"It has built-in speakers,"* he added.

"Good. That'll do," replied Toby. Holding a rolled-up length of canvas, he had taken a seat on a folding chair between Ali and Abdul. Omar and Ahmed were just sitting down to Abdul's right.

"Chaplain Harris, would you mind putting on that tape? See if you can find the part that's about Ali," said Toby. He glanced at Chaplain Harris who had sat down on the other side of Ali.

Chaplain Harris jumped to his feet and, reaching into his jacket pocket, pulled out a square, flat metallic box. *"You bet,"* he replied and hurried over to join Dave who was setting up the tape recorder on the desk.

Toby leaned forward and looked at Ahmed, seated to his right at the end of the row of chairs. *"Ahmed, would you explain to Omar that this tape is a recording of a conversation that took place in Manticore's office—in Vail, Colorado. It was secretly made last night. And,"* he paused, *"as you hear it, would you translate the conversation for him?"*

"Yes, of course," replied Ahmed. He immediately began talking to Omar in Arabic.

"Abdul," said Toby, straightening back up. *"Did you come over to the U. S. with Omar?"* Toby laid the rolled-up length of canvas across his lap.

"No, but we're from the same tribe," replied Abdul. He had been fidgeting in his chair as he watched Chaplain Harris thread the tape. *"This tape is about Ali?"* He asked.

"He's mentioned," Toby paused, *"so, how did you come to be Omar's interpreter?"*

Abdul was still watching Chaplain Harris. *"What? Oh, uh--I'm a graduate student in this country,"* he stammered. *"I wanted to help in some way, so when I heard that Omar was coming I asked to be his interpreter. We're from the same tribe."*

Chaplain Harris, watching the footage-counter as he ran the tape fast-forward, glanced at Toby. *"Do you want me to start playing it as soon as I get there?"* He asked.

"Without mentioning <u>critical</u> names, you might explain to everybody why you're down here, first," suggested Toby.

Chaplain Harris nodded and continued watching the counter. After a few seconds he clicked it off and turned around. The row of chairs, all facing the patio, were arranged perpendicular to the hallway-end of the couch. They were slightly to Harris's left. Hermano was sitting on the end of the couch near Chaplain Harris' empty chair, and Deirdre and Dora, looking expectantly toward Chaplain Harris, were sitting beside him.

Dave and Bill, who had been conversing quietly near the hallway door, split up.

Bill disappeared down the hall, while Dave walked across the center of the room to lean with his back to the patio door-jamb.

"Every night," began Chaplin Harris, *"I've been giving a report to Toby. About the conversations that had taken place in Manticore's office that day. Last night, since I was running low on food, I'd left the house a little early in order to walk to a supermarket before Toby's phone call. As it turned out, I was out of the house—away from the recorder—for well over an hour. When I got back to the house it was about 9:30. Manticore's usually not in his office after nine, at least he hadn't been the few nights that I've listened. Anyway, when I walked into the house, I could hear—over the tape monitor—Manticore shouting at somebody.*

I didn't even bother to put the groceries away, but just put them on the desk and sat down to listen. Manticore was shouting at someone over the telephone. I never did hear the name of the person he was talking to, but whoever it was is a member of I.D.. He was apparently calling from Dallas. Judging from Manticore's end of the conversation—the I.D. man had apparently accused Manticore and the Church of Satan of killing some Druids and burning one of their buildings in Dallas.

Manticore denied it and tried to blame it on you people—I mean, on Hermano and the Hunts. But I don't think the guy believed him. Anyway, Manticore ended the conversation by saying that he was flying down on Thursday to take care of the matter, personally. He said that he was already planning on coming down, anyway." Chaplain Harris paused, *"The past few days I hadn't heard him say anything about going to Dallas. So, after he left his office a few minutes later, I ran the tape back and played the part that I had missed when I was making my report."* He glanced back at the tape recorder. *"The part that I missed is what I'm about to play. Before I'd listened to this, I had figured that I would simply report on Manticore's upcoming trip when I reported to Toby tonight. But when I heard this, I decided that I'd better not chance waiting that long.*

I hitchhiked to Denver, woke up a pastor who's a friend of mine, and borrowed plane-fare. Then, after he'd driven me to the airport, I caught the first flight out this morning—to Dallas."

"He woke me up pounding on the door at three o'clock this afternoon," said Toby. He glanced at Hermano, *"I own a little house in Dallas,"* he explained. *"It's usually not much more than a home address, but I spent the night there Tuesday night, and had gone back for a nap this morning. Chaplain Harris had the address."*

"Don't ever land at the Dallas-Fort Worth Airport without cab fare," said Chaplain Harris. *"It took longer to get from the airport to Toby's house than it did to get from Denver to Dallas."* He looked at Toby. *"Do you want me to play the tape now?"*

"Just a minute," said Toby. *"What Chaplain Harris had,"* he glanced at Hermano, *"was a good reason to get to Ali or Omar as soon as possible.*

So, since I had to be in Weatherford by 6:30 or 7:00, I dropped Chaplain Harris off by your mosque at around five o'clock," Toby said, glancing at Ahmed. *"He was supposed to try and locate Ali or Omar and wait for me to get back. Well, he didn't locate them, but he **did** spot a carload of guys watching your parking lot.*

After I got back, he had no sooner pointed out those guys to me, when we spotted the four of you coming out the back door of the mosque." Toby raised his eyebrows and glanced from Ahmed to Omar. *"That carload of men spotted you, too,"* he said.

Ahmed paused in his translation to Omar and looked at Toby. *"Did they follow us?"* He asked.

"Yeah, they followed. When I figured out where you were going, I speeded up and passed them and you between Fort Worth and Weatherford.

Chaplain Harris and I got out to the spot where Ali and I had been entering and leaving the ranch property about ten or fifteen minutes before you did." He glanced around at Ali and smiled. *"You sure got a good memory, boy. I was afraid you'd get lost."*

"I remembered—no sweat." Ali was beaming.

"Anyway," Toby continued, turning back to Ahmed, *"we watched while you parked and walked off toward the ranch. Then, about five or ten minutes later, that carload of guys pulled up and five of them got out. They checked out your car and then took up positions around it. One of them drove their car about fifty or a hundred yards back down the road and parked it."* He paused, *"they're out there waiting, now. This tape will help explain why they're out there."* He glanced at Chaplain Harris. *"Okay, Chaplain,"* he said.

"Just a moment," interrupted Ahmed. He was listening to Omar who was speaking rapidly in Arabic. When Omar stopped speaking, Ahmed looked at Chaplain Harris. *"Omar has asked if you are Imam—uh, chaplain of some Christian organization that is helping in this. He's been listening to us talk about organized Satanism all day— and he can't believe that the faithful of this country aren't organized to fight it."* Ahmed paused, *"**Do** you represent an organization?"*

Chaplain Harris nervously ran his hand back through his gray hair. His cheeks reddened as he cleared his throat, *"I—uh, I'm ashamed to say that I don't know of any Christian organization that is willing to fight,"* he paused, *"save for the people in this room."* Chaplain Harris sighed as he waited for Ahmed to translate what he had said to Omar.

Omar scowled and spat out a short sentence in Arabic. Ahmed turned back to Chaplin Harris. *"It's a—uh—slang expression. He— uh—America isn't what he thought it was,"* he explained lamely.

"Tell him it isn't what any of us thought it was," said Toby. *"Go ahead and play the tape, Chaplain."*

"---don't care what their excuse is," a voice was saying. *"You tell them that their primary job is to get their people to the polls. Canfield is our man, regardless of what he says to the television cameras."* They heard a crash as the telephone receiver was apparently slammed down.

"That's Manticore," said Chaplain Harris.

For the next few seconds they could hear paper being shuffled around and then the ringing of a telephone.

"Manticore." Manticore sounded irritated. *"Who? Oh, yes. What do you have, Harvey?"*

"That's Harvey Mattox—Director of the CIA. He's called twice since Sunday", interjected Chaplain Harris.

"Are you sure?" Manticore was excited. *"How did he get down there?"* There was a long pause.

Dave, suddenly alert, straightened up by the back door. Toby glanced back over his left shoulder to see Bill leaning against the hallway door-jamb. Bill was holding his right arm slightly behind him. Toby winked and turned back around.

"Bullshit!" Manticore exclaimed. *"He didn't just **happen** to stop-in where some Afghans were visiting. Did you find out?"* It was quiet for a moment and then Manticore chuckled. *"Traveling with them?"* He paused. *"Translating for whom?"*

Abdul shifted uncomfortably. His right hand began inching up toward the open flap of his corduroy jacket.

Toby was watching him out of the corner of his eye. Figuring that Abdul was probably wearing a shoulder-rig, Toby discreetly slipped his right hand under the canvas and gripped the handle of the sword.

Omar, his eyes angry-slits set above a clenched jaw, slowly turned his head to look at Abdul.

"Great," said Manticore. *"Can this 'Abdul' get ahold of the kid?"*

Pandemonium broke out in the Hunt's den. Abdul whirled to his left and pushed Toby over backwards in his chair. As Toby fell, Abdul leaped to his feet, pulling a snub-nosed revolver from a shoulder holster.

Bill crouched and brought one of his dad's .357 Magnum's up into firing position. His gun was leveled at Abdul's chest, but before he could fire, Abdul pitched forward, sprawling across Toby's legs. A long dagger was embedded up to the hilt in his back.

Omar was standing where Abdul had been a second before. Wild-eyed, he uttered a single Arabic word and spat at the lifeless body laying in front of him.

"Untranslatable," dead-panned Ahmed as Omar bent over and retrieved his knife.

"Sorry we had to do it this way," said Toby as he pushed Abdul off his legs. He looked at Ahmed. *"But we were afraid you wouldn't believe us if we just told you that Abdul was a traitor."* Toby got to his feet as Ahmed translated to Omar.

*"I **got** the drop on him,"* said Bill wistfully as he stuck the .357 in his belt.

"Lord, Lord, Lord," said Dora. She, Deirdre and Hermano were all standing in front of the couch. Dora looked at her son, *"I'm glad it didn't have to be you---that did it,"* she finished.

"Let's drag him outside and listen to the rest of Manticore's phone call," suggested Toby as he grabbed Abdul's feet and began dragging him toward the patio door.

Chapter 26

After Toby had returned, they all sat back down while Chaplain Harris rewound the tape a few feet. He punched "play".

"Can this Abdul get ahold of the kid?" Manticore asked. There were a few seconds of silence. *"Well, you tell him he's got until midnight to-morrow night. If he hasn't managed to grab the kid by then, I'm sending some people into that Mosque to kill the kid and anybody he might've talked to. Either way, I'll be down there on Thursday to help hush things up. ---Yes. I'll meet with you and Burton both. ---What? ---Probably at his house—Thursday night. ---I'll talk to you after I get down there."* There was a clatter as the phone was hung up.

Chaplain Harris, still standing by the desk, reached over and clicked off the tape deck.

"You people amaze me!" Exclaimed Dee. She was leaning forward on the edge of the couch, glaring around the room. *"There is a **dead** man lying in the backyard, half a dozen killers are prowling around out there somewhere—and you people just go along your merry way like everything was normal."*

"The girls got a point," said Toby. *"We ought to at least have a guard posted outside the house."*

"I'll go," volunteered Bill, who had been sitting in Abdul's vacant chair. Winking at Dee, he got up and quickly exited through the patio door.

Ahmed, who had been listening to Omar speak in Arabic, looked at Dee and smiled. *"Omar says that he is glad that he wasn't the only one who had noticed this. He also said that he is glad that this isn't normal here. It **is** normal in Afghanistan."*

"Where is their car parked, anyway?" Asked Dave.

"All the way up past the northwest corner of your property," answered Toby. *"There's a dirt road that makes a ninety-degree curve there and just touches your property. They're parked on the dirt road—a few yards from the curve."* He paused. *"I seriously doubt that the people watching the car know anything about you people. They'll wait at the car."* Toby looked at Dee.

"We have to share information and get organized as quickly as possible," he continued. *"The Church of Satan is about to come down on you folks like a ton of bricks. Usually they work slow and methodically maintaining secrecy is their first rule. But—Manticore's losing it. He's beginning to panic—ordering an attack on a Mosque!*

*And that was before he knew about the Druid Center in Dallas, the snuffed hit-team at the airport or the Sheriff and Hutch. Their 'thing' is about to be exposed and he'll know it. You know what they say about how dangerous a wounded beast is. We **can't** be distracted. We have to get ready for anything they might do and at the same time keep the initiative."*

"Ahmed, how many men can you raise by tomorrow evening?" Asked Hermano. He was sitting at the end of the couch beside Dee.

Ahmed thought for a minute, *"Fifty,"* he replied. *"Perhaps more."*

"Good," said Hermano. *"We can supply them with guns."* He looked at Toby. *"The Hunts have decided to finance our—war. Do you know of some place where you can get weapons by tomorrow night? Dave says that he has the connections—but they're in Denver."*

"I can get them—AK-47s and M-16's. You're talking about $50,000, though," said Toby.

"I'll have a hundred thousand for you by 10 o'clock in the morning," offered Dora. Sitting beside Dee, she had been quietly taking it all in. She leaned forward, and with an intensity not seen in her before,

looked from one of the companions to the next, letting her gaze linger on each one for a second or two.

"Those people murdered my husband," she said. *"Now, they're going to want to murder my children."* She paused, *"I'm happy to supply the money, but I want you all to understand—I don't intend to just sit here and watch."* She looked at Toby. *"You get one of those guns for me,"* she said.

"Yes, ma'am!" exclaimed Toby, smiling broadly.

Omar, who had been listening to Ahmed translate, slapped his knees and laughed. He said something back to Ahmed. Ahmed smiled and looked at Dora. *"He says that you are mujahedin,"* he said.

They talked tactics for the next hour, and then Toby, still holding the rolled-up canvas, got slowly to his feet. *"Whose car is that parked out on that dirt road?"* He asked, looking at Ahmed.

"It's mine," replied Ahmed.

"Well, one of us will have to run y'all back to Dallas. You'll have to say that you let Abdul use your car." He paused and looked around at the rest of them. *"I think we'd be better off not messing with those guys back at the car,"* he said. *"There's no sense in risking casualties when we don't have to."* He looked at Dave. *"I'm going to take Abdul's body and carry it back close to the car,"* he said. *"In an hour call the Sheriff's department and tell them you were driving down that dirt road where the car's parked and spotted half a dozen armed men. Tell them you thought you saw a body lying beside the road."*

Dave grinned, *"Consider it done,"* he said.

*"Where is **your** car parked?"* Hermano asked, looking at Toby.

"There's a makeshift gate near that corner of the ranch," said Toby. *"We pulled through there and parked on the other side of the pasture. I don't think my car can be seen from that road—even in the daytime. I'm not going to be able to get it out for a while, though."* He paused. *"I'm going to need a ride to Dallas, too, come to think of it. Well, let's worry about all that after I lug Abdul's body out to that dirt road."*

Toby was back in an hour and a half. Dave had relieved Bill and was keeping watch near the still-darkened helipad when Toby returned.

"Toby?" Dave's voice was little more than a whisper.

"Yeah. It's me," answered Toby. He stopped near where Dave was standing. *"Did you call the sheriff's department?"* He asked.

"Yeah, an hour after you left. And then they called the Texas Rangers. That was just before I came out here. Have they showed up yet?"

"I don't know. I'd like to have stuck around and watched the action—but I didn't figure we had the time."

"Did you manage to get Abdul's body close enough to be found?"

"Yeah. I left a little bonus, too." He paused, *"There was only one man watching the satanists' car. I managed to sneak up close enough to lay that gun that I popped the Sheriff and Hutch with right beside it. I wiped it down. It can't be traced,"* he added.

Dave laughed. *"Beautiful,"* he said.

"I don't think we need to worry about posting a guard, yet," said Toby as he started for the house. *"Let's go inside and get this show on the road."*

"Okay," said Toby as he wearily got up from his chair. *"If everybody's got their assignments straight, we'd better head on back to Dallas. I'm bushed."*

"One more thing," said Hermano. He was sitting on the edge of the desk. *"Did you manage to bug Reverend Hall's house?"*

"Oh, yeah." Toby winced, *"I'm glad you mentioned that. We've got a problem there."* He paused, *"I managed to bug it Okay—uh, the room that the telephone is in. Some kind of den or something. But I didn't have a place to receive what the bug picked up. I improvised—but it's going to be a major hassle."* He paused.

"Hall has two old out-buildings that sit back of his house—kind of off to the side. He keeps a lawnmower and different kinds of garden tools in one, but the other's just full of junk. I hid a receiver hooked up to a portable cassette recorder in the one that's full of junk. It's in an old cabinet that's full of paint cans.

It's voice-activated, but the tape's only good for three hours of record-ing. Somebody will have to sneak in there and change it, tomorrow." He looked at his watch, *"I mean, today."*

"We can take care of that," offered Dora. She was sitting with Dee and Bill on the couch.

"Okay, then. We'd better get a move on," said Toby, glancing around at the others. Ali was sound asleep on the recliner.

"Why don't we leave Ali here," suggested Toby. *"I think he'd be safer."*

"I agree," said Ahmed, who then turned and spoke to Omar.

"So does Omar," he added.

A few minutes later, Toby, Chaplain Harris, Ahmed, and Omar began walking across the northeast pasture toward the bunkhouse. Dave, pushing his motorcycle, was following close behind.

They had decided to load Dave's motorcycle in the back of a six-passenger pickup that was kept behind the bunkhouse and drive the truck to Dallas. They would have to cut some fence, but there was a way out of the far-northeast pasture that would put them on the upper end of Mustang Road and from there they could go north and take a roundabout route to Dallas.

Toby, still carrying his rolled canvas, paused to look toward the east. The first hint of dawn was on the horizon. A new day was beginning.

Chapter 27

"Why did he only dig on this side of the house?" Asked Ali.

It was two o'clock in the afternoon and he and Hermano were standing near the tailgate of a pickup parked pointing south, fifty yards west of the ranch house. The pickup, an old blue Chevy with an 8-foot bed, was loaded 2 feet deep with 4 x 8 sheets of three-quarter inch plywood.

Hermano grabbed the rear corners of the top sheet and slid it out. Ali managed to grasp the front of the sheet and, together, they swung it over to cover the north end of a straight twenty feet long by four feet deep trench. The trench ran parallel to the right side of the pickup.

"You can't see it from the house," replied Hermano, straightening back up, *"but on the other side of the house there's a road."* He stepped back to the tailgate. *"On the other side of that road there's a house. Satanists are in that house—trying to watch what happens at the ranch,"* he paused. *"We don't want them to see what we're doing."* He grabbed the corners of the next sheet and pulled it out.

"Overlap it about two feet," he said as Ali took ahold of the front. *"We'll use three sheets for each trench and leave an opening of three feet on the other end."* They swung the plywood over the trench.

"When Bill finishes digging trenches," he continued as he walked back to the tailgate, *"he'll come back and cover the plywood with the dirt that he dug up."*

"How many trenches?" Asked Ali.

"Seven," replied Hermano as he grabbed the end of the third sheet of plywood. *"Five on this side of the house and two beyond the helipad."*

After they had laid the last sheet in place they climbed into the pickup and drove fifty yards to the next trench.

"Are you a Muslim?" Asked Ali as Hermano put on the emergency brake and killed the engine.

Hermano started to open his door but paused to turn around and look at Ali. *"I worship the God of Abraham,"* he said. *"I believe that Jesus is the Messiah. And I also believe that Mohammed was a Prophet of God."* He paused, *"if you accept that I'm a servant of God—it only confuses things to label me."* He paused again. *"Do you understand what I mean by label?"*

"Yes," answered Ali, smiling broadly. *"You're a Muslim."*

Hermano chuckled and opened his door. He had just stepped out when he saw the Hunt's Lincoln speed up the driveway and slide to a stop near the front door of the ranch house.

It stayed motionless for a few seconds and then spun out, bouncing across the pasture in their direction. A few seconds later Dora came to a skidding stop beside the pick-up.

"Dee's gone!" She exclaimed as she leaned across the seat and lowered the passenger window.

"Gone? What do you mean?" Asked Hermano. He bent down and apprehensively peered through the window at Dora.

"I mean she just disappeared. God! What if they got her?" The tremor in her voice betrayed the fact that she was just barely managing to control her emotions.

"Calm down," said Hermano. *"Tell me exactly what happened."*

"After we met Dave and gave him that money, we decided to stop for lunch. After lunch we went by Reverend Hall's.

I stopped out of sight of his house and let Dee get out. I was going to keep him occupied for a few minutes while she snuck back and changed that tape—we had brought a new cassette with us." She paused, *"He was there, alright—in his house. I talked to him for about fifteen minutes—inside his house-and then I left.*

I was supposed to pick up Dee at the same place where I dropped her off—but she wasn't there. I parked for a few minutes, and when she didn't show up I drove down the road the other way from the house. I thought she might have got her directions mixed up—she wasn't there, either. I drove back and forth a few times and then drove straight here."

"Let's go back," said Hermano. He opened the passenger door. "*Come on, Ali,*" he called out as he climbed in.

Ali, who had already walked around to Hermano's side of the pick-up, scrambled into the back seat of the Lincoln just as Dora spun out. She wheeled the Lincoln around and bounced back across the pasture to the driveway.

Their speed was approaching 50 miles per hour by the time they intersected the driveway, going in the direction of Mustang Road. Dora roared down the driveway and was only a few yards short of the road when Hermano leaned forward in his seat and peered to the side.

"*Just a minute,*" he said quickly. "*Here comes one of the Sheriff's cars.*" They slid to a stop at the driveway's entrance and waited for it to pass.

"*Maybe we'd better tell them,*" suggested Dora.

"*I think---,*" Hermano was looking intently at the car as it approached. "*Yes! It's Dee. Thank God!*" He exclaimed.

Dora took a deep breath and, letting it out slowly, leaned back in her seat.

When the patrol car began slowing to turn into the Hunt's driveway, Dora straightened up and shifted into reverse. Cutting the wheel, she backed a few feet into the pasture to allow it to get by.

Frank Pierce Jr. was driving, with Dee sitting on the passenger side of the front seat. As he passed, Frank motioned for them to follow him to the house.

"*Uh-oh,*" Dora said softly.

Frank and Dee had just gotten out of the patrol car when the Lincoln came to a stop behind them. Frank, looking at Dora, stalked back toward the Lincoln as she opened her door.

"*Mrs. Hunt, I'll tell you what I told your daughter. When a mom drives up to a house and goes inside. And then her daughter walks out of the woods beside the house—carrying a tape cassette. And then the daughter* **sneaks** *into a shed with the cassette. And a couple of minutes later comes out of the shed carrying a different colored cassette. And I know the mom and daughter suspect the man in the house with having something to do with Mr. Hunt's murder---. Then it doesn't take Sherlock Holmes to figure out that--, 'Hey! They've got his house bugged!'*"

"*And how did you just* **happen** *to see all that, Frank Pierce?*" Asked Dora as she slammed the car door behind her.

"*That's the same thing I asked, Mom,*" said Dee. She had walked back to stand, smiling, beside the passenger side of the Lincoln.

As he and Ali opened their doors, Hermano glanced back and whispered, "*Ali, don't say* **anything** *about Toby.*" Ali nodded.

"*Hermano, you look pale,*" teased Deirdre.

"*I want to hear that tape, Mrs. Hunt,*" Frank was saying. Dora didn't answer.

"*Look, I'm on your side,*" pleaded Frank. "*Please. Let me help. I know something big is going on out here and,*" he paused, "*I figure you folks are the good guys.*" He glanced at Ali, who had just gotten out of the Lincoln.

"*Did you know an Arab guy was killed up on Meadowlark Road last night?*" Frank asked, looking back at Dora.

"*Buenos Dias,*" said Ali.

Dee jerked her hand to her mouth in a futile attempt to smother a laugh.

Hermano smiled and looked across the top of the car at Dora. "*Dora,*" he said, "*I think we ought to let him listen to it. After all, he could have taken her to the Sheriff's Department.*"

"*I'm doing this on my own,*" said Frank, looking at Hermano. "*I don't know who to trust at the Sheriff's Department. My grandma was at church last night,"* he continued, still looking at Hermano. *"You know—when all you people were alibiing yourselves? She said that if you'd start a church—she would join it."* He paused and smiled at Hermano. *"That woman's ready to fight,"* he said. *"And so am I."*

"Let's walk around to the den," suggested Dora. *"There's a cassette player in the desk."*

The first hour of the tape consisted of nothing more than the sounds of Reverend Hall talking about church renovations with two of his church's elders. They had apparently accompanied him home after last night's church services.

After they had left, the next sound was the ringing of a telephone.

"Reverend Hall." The man sounded irritated.

"Yeah. Oh, Kyle. I didn't recognize your voice." There was a pause.

"Good. Could you tell if they were all in the car?" Another pause.

"Five. Yes, I know it was dark."

"Okay, that's all of them. Call me if any of them come out." There was a click as a receiver was put down.

Dee leaned over to whisper to Hermano, who was sitting beside her on the couch. *"Kyle is the name of Mr. Jackson's son,"* she said.

Hermano nodded. *"That's what I figured,"* he replied.

Ali was sitting beside them on the couch while Dora and Frank were both sitting on chairs by the desk. Frank, who was sitting on one of the folding chairs, glanced around at Hermano and Dee.

*"There were **five** of you last night, weren't there?"* He asked.

Dee nodded her head.

"Somebody's watching your house," he said.

The next sound that came from the tape was that of Reverend Hall's television.

"The ten o'clock news," said Dora.

The top news story was that of the Parker County Sheriff and one of his deputies being shot-down in the Parker County Sheriff's office.

"Oh, no!" They could hear Reverend Hall's exclamation.

After the news program had moved on to the next story they could hear Reverend Hall dialing his telephone.

"Mr. Marston, please." Reverend Hall's voice was strained. There was a long pause.

"This is Hall." Another pause.

"Yes. Yes, I understand, but I--"

"The Sheriff and---"

"Okay, yes, sorry." There was the sound of him hanging up the phone.

"Somebody doesn't want him to talk over the phone," said Frank.

There was apparently a long delay between the telephone call and the next sound because Reverend Hall sounded half asleep when he could be heard saying, *"Just a minute, I'm coming."*

A sound like that of someone knocking could be heard. Apparently, whoever it was was becoming impatient.

"Millwee!" Reverend Hall sounded surprised. *"What are you doing over here? If anybody should---"*

"Shut the door, damn it!" It was an unfamiliar voice to all of them. They could hear the door slam shut.

"There's too much shit going on over here. Marston was afraid to talk to you on the phone. He sent me over." There was a pause and then they could hear the same voice continue, *"there's going to be a mass—Friday night. High priests and above. Bring your station wagon—we want to take as few vehicles as possible. Eight other people will ride with you."*

"Where?" Asked Reverend Hall.

"You nine will meet at Lenore Appleby's. You know where she lives? --Good"

"Where's the mass? Isn't this kind of sudden?" Asked Reverend Hall.

"Yes, it was just decided this evening---after what happened at the

Sheriff's Department." There was a pause. *"Manticore's going to be there."*

"Manticore!"

"Yeah-- three sacrifices, too."

"Three! How are we going to do that on such short notice?"

"It's being done, don't worry about that. The sacrifices will be coordinated with an attack on the Hunt Ranch. We're going to end this once and for all."

"Where's the mass?" Reverend Hall asked again.

"Do you remember Rustler's Cove at Possum Kingdom Lake? You were there last October, weren't you?"

"Yes."

"Well, be at the same gathering place by ten o'clock Friday night."

"We'll be there. Would you like some coffee or something?"

"No, I got two more stops to make." There was a pause. ***"Be there."*** The voice repeated. Then there was the sound of a door opening and shutting.

After that, Reverend Hall turned on his television set and the sound of some late-night movie ran out the remaining footage of the tape. As Dora began to rewind the tape, Frank stood up and shook his head.

"The world's gone crazy." He said. He turned around and looked at Hermano. *"I **really** want to join you people,"* he said. *"If you don't let me, I'm going to try and do something by myself."* He paused, and then added, *"Cops have souls, too."*

Chapter 28

Hermano and Ali heaved the last sheet of plywood over the seventh trench and climbed back into the pickup. They pulled forward a few feet to give Bill's tractor room to push the dirt over the most easterly of the back two trenches.

"When will they be here?" Asked Ali.

"Dave told Mrs. Hunt that they should be here by nine o'clock," replied Hermano. He looked at his watch, *"It's seven o'clock now,"* he paused. *"They're going to be dropped off at the northeast corner of the Hunt's ranch. Dave will guide them across the pastures from there."* He smiled at Ali.

"Gettin' hungry?" He asked.

"Can you hear my stomach?" Asked Ali.

Hermano laughed. *"Just a minute,"* he said. He opened the pickup door and, standing on the running board, motioned to Bill that they were going to the house. Bill waved and Hermano got back into the truck.

Looping around to their right, Hermano drove past the helipad and swimming pool to park on the grass-- parallel to the driveway. He and Ali got out of the pick-up and walked through the raised garage door to enter the den from the garage side.

Bill joined them a few minutes later and at around eight o'clock they were all treated to homemade chili.

"I sure am getting tired of eating in the den," said Dora as she set the

bowls on the desk. She bent down and slid the tray under it. *"Come and get it,"* she said. *"Chuck-wagon supper."*

They had just finished eating when the front doorbell rang. Bill, with his dad's .357 magnum stuck in his belt, went toward to the door while Dora and Dee picked up the supper dishes. Hermano and Ali were standing at the patio door gazing out across the darkened swimming pool and helipad. The lights had been left off and they couldn't see anything, but Hermano had cracked the door open so that they could at least hear footsteps if anyone walked across the deck. It was after eight-thirty and they expected Dave and the others at any time.

A couple of minutes later, Bill came back into the den, followed by Frank Pierce Jr. Frank, who was still in uniform, was carrying several large rolled pieces of paper.

"I got the Palo Pinto County maps," he said, waving them at Hermano. *"I labeled Rustler's Cove on all of them."*

Hermano turned around and smiled. *"That was quick,"* he said.

"I know a deputy over in Palo Pinto-- a Christian guy," he added. *"He didn't even ask what I wanted them for."* Frank walked over and laid the maps on the desk. *"I know that area around Possum Kingdom real well."*

Hermano walked over toward the desk. *"If you want to help—I mean, really be involved in this, then I think you'd be most useful here at the house. Just a minute,"* said Hermano quickly, as Frank started to object. *"Here, you would be a police officer witnessing a group of armed satanists attack someone's home. There, you would be witness to an armed attack against a religious minority."* He paused, *"You tell me—where would you be most useful to us?"*

Frank sighed. *"I see what you mean,"* he said. *"Okay, what time do you want me out here?"*

"*Well, why don't you drop by sometime tomorrow morning,*" suggested Hermano. "*We'll make plans for tomorrow night, then.*"

"*Okay,*" Frank started back for the hall. He paused in the doorway and looked back at Hermano. "*I can change that tape for you—you know, at Reverend Hall's. Maybe sometime just before sun-up.*"

"*That's a good idea, thanks,*" replied Hermano.

"*I'll walk Frank to the door and explain where the recorder is hid,*" said Deirdre. She accompanied Frank back down the hallway in the direction of the old house.

Frank had been gone for about ten minutes when Ali turned away from the patio door. He looked at Hermano who was bent over the desk studying one of Frank's maps.

"*I heard a car door close,*" Ali whispered. A couple of minutes later, a grinning Dave slid open the patio door and stepped in---he slid the door shut behind him.

"*I feel like Lawrence of Arabia,*" he said.

Hermano smiled. "*I take it that everything went well?*"

"*Better than you can imagine,*" replied Dave excitedly. "*We've got seventy or eighty guys out there past the helipad. We've got so much equipment that we had to go ahead and drive a couple of loaded-down pickups onto the ranch. I drove in front—without lights. We had to cut some fence—but that was the only problem.*" He nodded toward the helipad, "*They're all taking a breather back by the pickups, now.*"

"*Is Toby with them?*" Asked Hermano.

"*Yeah—oh, I'm supposed to signal him if it's OK to come in.*" He reached over and flicked the deck lights on and off, then he turned back again, "*It **is** Okay, isn't it?*"

"*Frank Pierce Jr. left a few minutes ago,*" replied Dee as she got up off the couch.

"*Yeah,*" said Hermano. "*It looks like we added one more soldier to our ranks here while you were gone.*" As Hermano began explaining how they had come to recruit Frank, the patio door slid open again and Toby stepped in.

After they had all greeted him, Toby slid the door shut and smiled. *"What a day,"* he said. *"We'd better get these men positioned before we start talking."*

"There's no hurry," said Dora and she entered the den from the hallway. *"We found out their plans---they're not going to attack until tomorrow night. How about a bowl of homemade chili?"*

"That sounds good, ma'am, but—what do you mean you 'found out their plans'?"

Hermano recounted the afternoon's events, ending with Frank's delivery of the county maps.

"Christmas came early," commented Toby. He was obviously excited. He took a deep breath, *"Still, though---what if Hall found the bug and the whole conversation was just to throw you off guard?"* He paused, *"I'd better billet the men,"* he said.

"I'll show you where the trenches are," offered Bill.

"Thanks," Looking toward the others, Toby shrugged his broad shoulders, *"doesn't hurt to be careful,"* he said.

"That's the best chili I ever ate, ma'am," said Toby appreciatively. He set the empty bowl on the desk.

"Oh, why thanks. Would you like some more?" Asked Dora. She had been sitting at the desk as she replayed the Reverend Hall tape—skipping the insignificant parts—for Toby.

"Thanks, but that filled me up." He paused, *"Is that all the tape?"* He was looking at Hermano.

"Except for the sounds of a late-night movie," replied Hermano. He was sitting on one of the folding chairs between Omar and Dave. Ali was sitting on the other side of Omar, next to the couch, while Bill and Dee had gone to their respective rooms a few minutes earlier to get cleaned up. Ali had been translating the tape for Omar.

"Well," said Toby, walking back to the couch. *"This kind of changes*

things. For the better," he added. *"I think Christmas really **has** come early."* He sat down on the couch, beside Ali's chair.

"Ali," he said, *"ask Omar if he understood what was on that tape."*

Ali turned to Omar and they spoke for a few seconds in Arabic, then Ali turned back to Toby. *"Yes,"* he replied, *"and he says that he would rather be with the ones who attack."*

Toby sighed and, leaning back on the couch, thought for a minute. *"What do you think, Hermano?"* He asked.

Hermano leaned forward and looked at Toby. *"I think we should find out how many of these guys are American citizens,"* he replied. *"If there's enough, it would be better if American citizens attacked and foreign nationals— as our guests—helped defend the house."* He paused and looked at Omar as Ali translated. *"Ali, tell him that here at the ranch our enemies will come armed and expecting a fight—but at the lake they will be mostly unarmed. We could use an experienced soldier here."*

While Ali was translating, Toby glanced at Dave. *"Dave, there's three or four guys sitting at the table on the patio. One of em's name is Addel. Would you ask him how many American citizens we've got?"*

"Yeah, be right back." Dave got up and hurried out the patio door.

"Omar says that you know how to talk," said Ali, smiling at Hermano. *"He says that if you have enough American citizens, he will stay here."*

"Toby," began Bill. Wearing clean clothes, he had just walked back into the den. He was standing by the door to the hallway. *"Dad and I used to fish in Rustler's Cove—and I've hunted all around that side of the lake, too."*

Toby looked around at Bill, but just as he started to say something, Dave came back in through the patio door.

"Addel says that twenty-five or thirty of them are citizens," said Dave as he slid the door shut behind him. *"Six of them are black—they were born and raised in the area."*

"Good," said Toby as he looked back around at Dave. *"How well do you know this 'Rustler's Cove'?"* He asked.

"It's been a long time—I remember the name, but that's about it."

*"Look, I **need** to go,"* Bill protested.

Toby looked over at Dora, who was sitting at the desk. She sighed and shrugged her shoulders.

Bill looked over at his uncle Dave. *"How old were you when you went to Vietnam, Uncle Dave?"* He asked.

"I'm not arguing with you, kid," laughed Dave. *"Besides, it might be more dangerous here than there."*

"Okay, you're going," said Toby. *"Now, tell me what the terrain is like over there."* He got up and accompanied Bill and Dave over to the desk to look at one of the maps.

"Say, where's Chaplain Harris?" Asked Dee. Barefooted, she walked in from the hallway and plopped down in the recliner.

"He stayed in Dallas with Ahmed—that Imam," Toby replied. *"They're going through that stuff that I got at the Druid Center and listening to the tapes that Chaplain Harris brought from Vail. They're going to try and cook something up with that stuff—they've both got a lot of connections."*

"Oh! Bill?" Dee sat bolt upright and looked at her brother. *"With so many things going on I forgot to mention it earlier—but Frank said that you could pick up the helicopter, any time. It's at Mockingbird Field— south of town."* She paused. *"He said that both doors are on it –no sign of any bullet holes."*

"A helicopter," repeated Toby, straightening up. He thought for a moment. *"Dave, would you get a couple of those 'stingers' out of the pick-up?"*

"Sure," Dave replied. He started for the patio door.

"Stingers?" Asked Hermano.

Toby looked around at him and smiled. *"Stinger missiles,"* he said. *"Ground-to-air, shoulder launched missiles. We've got four."*

"You can't tell much from this," said Bill. He was still leaning over the desk studying the map. *"It shows you where it's at, but that's about*

all. There are some gullies that it doesn't show, and it doesn't have the island."

"Island?" Asked Toby. He looked back at the map.

"Yes, sir," Bill pointed to a spot at the northwest corner of the lake. *"There's the cove. It's about thirty yards wide and maybe a hundred and fifty yards long. The mouth of it narrows to about ten yards –the map doesn't show that, either. Anyway, about fifteen or twenty yards from the end of the cove there's a little island—about ten yards across. There's a bunch of scrub oak and brush on it. The water's about waist-deep between the island and the end of the cove."*

"Where do you think they'll hold their shindig?" Asked Toby. *"They need a big open space—pretty flat."*

"Probably right there at the end of the cove," Bill pointed on the map. *"There's a huge flat slab of sandstone that starts right there at the waterline."* He paused. *"That's the only big flat open space around there. There's a lot of scrub-oak and mesquite all over that area."*

"What kind of access is there?" Asked Toby.

"Well, it's pretty much inaccessible." Bill moved his finger slightly to one side of the cove. *"And there's actually a small cove right here,"* he continued, *"and another one about the same distance on the other side. Those two little coves mark the end of two pretty deep ravines that run parallel to Rustler's Cove on either side. The ravines go about three or four hundred yards beyond the end of the cove. There's a fairly steep grade on the other side of the sandstone---so, the farther you go back, the deeper the ravines get. The grade ends at the face of a thirty- or forty-foot cliff—real steep. That's about fifty or a hundred yards behind the sandstone."*

"Hmmm," mused Toby. *"How do you think they'll get in there?"*

"They won't drive. The nearest road is a couple of miles—and there's lots of ravines worse than those two." He paused, *"They could land a helicopter on that sandstone easy enough."*

"Reverend Hall was told to drive his car out," muttered Toby, almost to himself. *"Could they park at the top of that cliff?"*

"No, I'm telling you—you'd have a lot of trouble getting near it, even

in a four-wheel-drive vehicle. It couldn't be done in that station wagon of Reverend Hall's."

"That must not be the gathering place," said Dora. She leaned forward in the desk chair and studied the map.

"What do you mean?" Asked Toby.

"Well, on the tape, that man told Reverend Hall that the mass would be at Rustler's Cove and then he said to be at the gathering place' at ten o'clock." She paused. *"I got the feeling when I heard that, that he was talking about two different places."*

"They could get there by boat," suggested Bill.

*"Probably helicopters **and** boats,"* said Hermano. *"I doubt if they'll risk landing more than one or two helicopters, though. All the lower level people will probably come by boat and get everything ready. Then Manticore, Burton, maybe that CIA guy, and people like them will probably come just before it starts. In a helicopter—or helicopters."* He paused. *"The people they're going to sacrifice will probably be brought in by helicopter, too."*

The door slid open and Dave came back in. *"I laid two of those stingers on the deck—behind the door,"* he said. *"And don't forget, your sword's in the pickup, too."*

"Yeah, thanks, Dave." Toby straightened up and grinned at Hermano. *"Let them bring their helicopters,"* he said.

"Sword? Do you actually use a sword?" Asked Dee. *"Why?"*

Toby, slightly embarrassed, looked back at the map. *"It's a long story,"* he mumbled.

"You ought to see it," said Dave. *"Straight out of the Middle Ages."*

*"**Could** I see it?"* Asked Bill. He looked at Toby.

Toby hesitated a moment. *"Yeah, I guess so,"* he said, and then glanced at Dave. *"Would you mind bringing it in?"* He asked.

A few minutes later, Dave came back carrying a rolled length of canvas.

"Oh, that's what you were carrying last night," commented Dora. She looked from Dave to Toby, who was still bent over the map. *"I'm glad you didn't use it in here."*

Toby straightened up and took the bundle from Dave. Laying it on the map, he began to unroll it. *"Yeah,"* he replied, *"Henry can be a little messy."*

"Henry?" Dee got up from the recliner and walked over to the desk. *"You named it?"*

Toby glanced around at Dee. *"Well, not exactly. The name's on the handle — in French or Italian or something."* He pointed at the raised letters.

Hermano, Omar, and Ali all got up and walked over to join them at the desk. Hermano leaned forward and looked over Bill's shoulder at the sword.

"I-N-R-I," he read aloud, looking at the handle. Abruptly straightening back up, he took a deep breath and let it out slowly.

"It's an antique," explained Toby. *"Supposed to have been used in the Crusades."*

"You figured I-N-R-I was a foreign word for Henry?" Asked Hermano.

"Yeah. ---well, that's what I thought til recently." He paused, *"Some satanist really went nuts a few months ago when he saw it, though. He started me thinking that maybe it meant something else."*

Hermano took another deep breath and nodded his head. *"If he knew what it meant, I'll bet he **did** go nuts."* He paused, his eyes filling with tears. *"It's the initials for four Latin words. <u>Iesus</u> <u>Nazarenus</u> <u>Rex</u> <u>Iudaeorum</u> ---Jesus of <u>Nazareth,</u> <u>King</u> of the <u>Jews.</u> It's the inscription that was fastened above Jesus's head when he was crucified."*

Toby, smiling thoughtfully, slowly began to wipe down the blade with a white cotton cloth. *"Well, then, it's about time for a little payback, isn't it?"*

Chapter 29

"What's all that for?" Asked Dee. It was lunchtime and she, Dora, Ali, and Hermano were standing around the patio table where they had been busily preparing, and individually wrapping roast-beef sandwiches. Dee was looking at Bill, who had just driven across the pasture from the bunkhouse in a heavily loaded short bed truck. It was piled five or six feet high with an assortment of lumber.

Bill climbed out of the truck and began untying the ropes that he had used to secure his load. *"Uncle Dave said to pile this up by the patio door,"* he said. *"We're going to board-up all the ground-floor doors and windows—after dark."*

"Want some lunch?" Called out Dora. *"We've got two hundred roast beef sandwiches, here."* She laughed. *"I'm glad they remembered to bring food,"* she said. *"We had the roast beef, but –four hundred slices of bread?"*

"Did Toby manage to get any sleep?" Asked Hermano. He laid the last sandwich in one of two boxes which were sitting beside the table.

"Yeah, about four hours. He and Uncle Dave left through the north pasture a couple of hours ago." He paused. *"I think he wanted to pick up a bunch of stuff and talk to that Chaplain. They're supposed to pick up the American citizens at the northeast corner at around seven."*

"Need any help?" The voice came from the east end of the house, near the garage door. They all turned around to see Frank Pierce Jr.,

dressed in jeans, boots and a Western shirt, walk around the corner of the house. He was carrying a small brown paper sack. He held it up.

"The tape from Reverend Hall's house," he said. *"Nothing new as far as the situation here goes, but there's some good information on it."* He stepped onto the patio and walked over to the table. Laying the sack down, he stared at the two boxes full of sandwiches.

"Good Lord!" He exclaimed. *"Are you going to throw sandwiches at them?"*

Dee laughed. *"These are for people who want to help us,"* she said. *"Want one? - Roast beef."*

"You're more of an optimist than I am," he said, still looking at the boxes.

"Frank," Hermano said quickly, *"we need to be able to get you back out here without you being seen. Bill's going to pick up the helicopter in a few minutes—can he meet you somewhere and fly you back out here?"* He paused. *"The helipad can't be seen from---the road."*

"You mean from that Jackson house, don't you?" Asked Frank with a smile. *"I told you that there was some good information on that tape. Hall called every member of his group last night—told them to get good alibis for tonight. Nine local calls and five long distance. I spent all morning figuring out who they all were."* He opened the sack and pulled out a folded sheet of paper. *"The membership list,"* he said. *"The long-distance ones were easy—I just got a record of his long-distance calls from the phone company. The local ones, though—that took quite a while. Fortunately, he has an old rotary dial phone."* He paused. *"I bet I listened to him dial those numbers thirty or forty times apiece. I figured them all out, though."* He slid the paper back into the sack.

"I'm pretty sure it's complete. Oh, and here's an interesting fact. All the flying saucer reports we got on May first were from people on that list."

"So, they're not attacking with local people," observed Hermano. He and Frank both began walking over to help Bill with the lumber.

"Apparently not," answered Frank. He grabbed one end of a short

stack of 3/4" plywood. With Hermano on the other end, he backed toward the patio door.

"*How about Silas's airfield?*" Asked Frank.

"*For Bill to pick you up?*" Hermano synchronized his movements with Frank's as they set the stack down on the near side of the patio door.

"*Yeah, I'll make sure I'm not tailed. I can park my pick-up down the road from the airfield.*"

"*That sounds good.*" They walked back to the truck. "*Did you hear that, Bill?*" Asked Hermano.

"*Yeah, how about three o'clock?*" Bill looked at his watch. "*That's three hours from now.*"

"*Three o'clock it is,*" answered Frank. "*Say, do you have an extra rifle? I don't want to walk to the airfield carrying one –I forgot to bring mine with me,*" he added.

"*I'll let you borrow one of mine,*" answered Dora. "*Do you prefer an M-16 or an AK-47?*"

"*Station one, this is base.*" Hermano, sitting at the desk, was speaking into the microphone of the large base-radio console, which occupied most of the desk's surface. Frank and Ali were standing on either side of him while Dora and Dee, leaning forward on the couch, were going over the action of an AK-47. The rifle was laying on the coffee table in front of them.

"*Station one is clear,*" the heavily accented voice came back over the radio console.

"*Station two, this is base,*" Hermano said, holding the microphone close to his mouth in an effort to be heard over the racket of hammering and sawing that reverberated through the house.

"*Station two is clear,*" quickly came back.

"*How many stations?*" Shouted Frank.

"Twelve here and twelve with Toby," Hermano shouted back. He turned back to the microphone. *"Station three, this is base."*

"Station three is clear."

The den grew considerably quieter as the last plank covering the patio window was nailed into place. One of the young Arab men, hammer in hand, turned around and smiled. *"Fort Hunt,"* he quipped.

"Guess what was on the radio just now?" Asked Bill. Carrying an AK-47, he entered the den through the door from the garage.

"What radio?" Asked Dee.

"In the Lincoln. --I was just putting it in the garage," he added.

"What was on it?" Asked Dora. She glanced up from the coffee table.

"On the news they were talking about the 'cult wars'," he replied. Smiling, he walked on over to the couch.

"The Cult Wars? What does that mean?" Asked Dee. *"They weren't talking about us, were they?"*

"No. The Temple of Set—in Los Angeles—just burned to the ground. Ten or twelve members burned with it. This morning, something called the Church of the First Blood in Newark, New Jersey, was blown up. There's been a bunch of other things, too," he added.

"The British ambassador was killed yesterday—on his way to the UN building in New York," said Dora. She picked up the AK-47 and slammed in a clip. *"Somebody spray painted pentagrams on the side of his car,"* she added.

"Well, it's after seven o'clock—I've got to be going," said Bill. Gently pushing his mom's assault rifle aside with one hand, he bent over and kissed her on the top of the head. She laid the gun back on the coffee table and stood up to embrace her son.

"Please be careful, Billy," she said.

"I'm just flying the chopper, Mom. It'll probably be more dangerous here," he said, gently pushing away and turning back toward the garage.

"Dee, would you follow me through the garage and lock the outer doors?" he asked, slinging his own AK-47 over his shoulder.

"Station twelve is clear," came over the console. Hermano laid the microphone on the desk.

"Well, the stations are all set," he said. *"Now, we wait."*

Dee walked back in through the garage door and, turning around, locked it behind her. *"I just happened to think of something,"* she said. *"That bug in the kitchen—can't they hear all the hammering and stuff?"*

"I took care of that," replied Dora. *"I took a portable TV in there and turned the volume up real loud."* She smiled, *"I also hollered something like,' Bill, would you repair those cabinets, now?'"*

"Mom!" Dee laughed. *"I'm beginning to think I never really knew you at all."*

"Why didn't you tell me about all your help when I was out here earlier?" Asked Frank as Hermano pushed his chair back from the desk.

Hermano looked up at him. *"If something had happened, and you didn't show up—we'd have to wonder if all this was still a secret. No offense,"* Hermano added.

"No. No offense," replied Frank. *"It's just that—for a few hours there, I felt like I was on my way to help defend the Alamo."*

Hermano laughed, thought for a few seconds, and then laughed again.

Chapter 30

"Toby?" Dave, accompanied by two other men, pushed through some brush a few yards to the west of where Toby was standing. Toby, like all the others, was wearing a black ski mask, but his size made him easy to distinguish, even in the dark. In low tones, he was talking to a group of five or six men who were gathered around him

"Yeah, Dave. Is everybody in position?" Toby looked around to watch Dave approach.

"Yeah. Eight guys near the mouth of the north ravine. Two on the other side of the north ravine—even with where the mass is being set up. Two on this side of the south ravine, even with them. And the three of us. We'll secure the top of the cliff—I think there's two guards up there."

"Good. Has everybody got their ski masks on?" Asked Toby.

"There was a lot of grumbling 'til I told them that the whole thing was going to be videotaped." Bill paused. *"Did our frogman make it, yet?"*

Toby chuckled. *"He called in a few minutes ago. His teeth were chattering so much that I couldn't understand what he was saying. I finally made out that he was saying that the water was like ice."*

"He's probably scared shitless—if I was laying on that little island with nothing but a video camera—I would be." Bill paused, *"Ahmed might not have been so gung-ho if he'd known his son was going to be in a position like **that**."*

"Yeah, well—there wasn't much choice. He's the only one who'd ever done any skin-diving." Toby paused, *"He said his video equipment stayed*

dry. And he's got a good view. He said he's about thirty or forty yards from some kind of altar that they've set up. He said he counted six guys there."

"Six there, two on the cliff, two at the lip of the cove—on the other side. How about on this side?" Asked Bill.

"Two near the lip of the cove on this side," replied Toby. *"There's probably a few cruising around out there on the water, too."* Toby turned and looked toward the east. They were standing just inside the tree-line, about thirty yards from the beach—but reflected moonlight was all that could be seen on the surface of the lake.

"How about boats?" Asked Dave.

"They've already checked in. All three of them are tied up to the bank about a mile northeast of here." Toby looked at his watch. *"The guys on the other side of the cove know how to take-out the guards with those silencers, don't they?"*

"Yeah. They wanted to use knives, but I told them not to chance it—that this was why we brought the pistols." Dave patted his right hip. *"I've got mine here."*

"You got that M-16 with the night scope?"

"John here does," he motioned toward one of the men standing behind him. *"John was a sniper in 'Nam."*

"Okay," Toby said, looking at the tall black man behind Dave. *"John, your shot will signal the beginning of our attack. Wait til the last minute—but don't let them harm any of their captives."*

"Yes, sir."

"And no prisoners." Toby turned back to Dave. *"You stressed that didn't you? **No** prisoners."*

"I stressed it," replied Dave. *"No prisoners."*

"We'll take out the guards when we're sure they're all there." Toby paused, *"I'll contact you on the radio—but until then, maintain radio silence."* He paused again, *"Well, it's 10 o'clock. Y'all better get moving back around to that cliff."*

"Okay", said Dave. *"Good luck."* He and his two companions turned and disappeared back through the brush.

"No such thing as luck," mumbled Toby.

"Do any of you want to watch the 10 o'clock news?" Asked Dee. She got up from the couch and stretched. Dora was sitting beside her, studying a checker-board which was flat on the coffee table between herself and Ali.

Ali, sitting cross-legged on the floor, reached up and hopped a checker halfway across the board. He scooped up three of Dora's red checkers.

"Crown him," he said gleefully.

"Beginner's luck," teased Dora. She looked up at Dee. *"Turn it on if you want to, dear,"* she said.

Hermano and Frank, both sitting at the desk, were deep in conversation and neither of them even gave any indication that they had heard Dee's question.

"Y'all want to watch the news?" She asked a little louder, looking in their direction.

"Base," the whisper came over the console. *"Base—Station seven."* The voice sounded urgent. All conversation in the den ceased abruptly.

"This is a base," replied Hermano. He held the microphone close to his mouth and spoke softly. Frank reached over and turned up the volume on the console.

"Some cars are on the road. A man opens the gate," the whisper came back.

"Okay," said Hermano. *"Stay out of sight and call us back when they come in. Try to see how many people there are."* The voice didn't answer.

Hermano leaned back in his chair and looked over toward Dee and Dora. *"We should have reviewed radio procedure,"* he said. *"I hope he understood me."* He paused. *"Station seven is in the northwest corner— by Meadowlark Road."*

For the next three or four minutes no one in the room said a word. Dee, Dora, and Ali walked over and stood quietly beside the desk.

"*Base,*" the whisper made them all jump. Hermano jerked the mike back to his mouth.

"*This is base,*" he said.

"*They parked in the pasture. Six cars. Five or six people in each car.*"

"*What are they doing?*" Asked Hermano.

"*Standing in a group—talking. Lots of guns.*"

"*Call me back when they start moving. Try to count them—but don't let them see you.*"

"*Okay,*" came back.

Hermano sighed and smiled at the others. "*Well, here we go,*" he said.

"*Hey, isn't—-somebody's car still in that pasture?*" Asked Dee. They had all agreed not to mention Toby's name in front of Frank.

"*All our vehicles are behind the bunkhouse,*" replied Hermano.

"*Base,*" the voice sounded excited, "*this is station seven.*"

"*This is base,*" replied Hermano.

"*They're moving. At the house.*" There was a pause, "*Thirty-six men—and women. Two stayed at the cars.*"

"*Okay, stay away from them. Get by the outside fence and wait for station six to join you. You two will take out those guards when the fighting starts. I'll tell you when.*"

"*Okay,*" came back.

Then, "*Station six, this is a base.*"

"*Toby!*" The man came crashing through the underbrush from the direction of the beach.

"*Don't make so much racket,*" cautioned Toby impatiently. "*What is it?*"

"*Boats—going—in the cove.*"

"*How many?*" Asked Toby.

"Six —big boats. With cabins," he added.

Because of the ski mask, the others could sense, rather than see, Toby's smile. *"Well, here we go,"* he said casually.

Toby, hefting his sword, quickly led the seven men, single file, across the mouth of the ravine. They stopped when they had reached the cover of some trees on the other side. Toby turned to face them. *"Hassan,"* he said softly, *"you and Ameed take those silencers and work your way up close to the two guards on this side of the cove. Be careful, and don't do anything until I tell you."* He paused, *"You got your radio?"*

"Yes." One of the men held up a two-way radio.

"Turn the volume down low—we don't want to tip 'em off." Two of the men separated from the group and carefully began making their way toward the lip of the cove. They were both carrying long black pistols—held at the ready. Assault rifles were slung over their shoulders.

"The rest of you men stay here until I give the word to advance to the forward positions." He paused, *"Where's the radio?"*

"Here." One of the men held it up

"Good," said Toby. *"Remember, no prisoners."* Toby turned and, like a single-minded grizzly, disappeared into the woods.

From where Toby and his group had been standing, it was well over a hundred yards to the sandstone slab. Though the scrub-oak and thick brush hid the slab from Toby's view, he could hear voices while he was still more than fifty yards away. The voices conveyed a sense of urgency, rather than the cordial revelry that had been so much a part of the Fire Festival. Toby stopped for a few seconds to listen and then continued on. He smiled grimly. Their situation was about to go from bad to worse.

The red sandstone slab was square in shape, with each side approximately a hundred feet in length. The heavily wooded tree-line to either side of the slab was twenty feet away, but there were only a few scattered trees between the slab and the cliff, fifty yards to the west.

Toby stopped behind a six-foot high domed rock at the edge of the woods, roughly even with the little island. He pushed some brush aside at the water's edge and, leaning on the rock, peered out into the clearing. The whole area was well lit with over a dozen Coleman lanterns, strategically placed around the slab.

Six cabin-cruisers were tied up on the other side of the little island. The guests were apparently using the cabins for changing rooms, because every couple of minutes a black-robed figure would exit a cabin and hop over to the shore. There were already between thirty and forty people on the slab, and Toby could see at least ten or fifteen still in civilian clothes standing around on the boat decks.

There was no movement on the little island and Toby figured that Ahmed's son had probably burrowed into the sand under the brush like some kind of clam. He smiled at the thought and eased back from the brush.

Stretching up, he peered over the top of the rock. He jerked his head back down quickly. A man was leaning with his back against the boulder on the other side. He was apparently watching the southern tree-line.

Toby leaned back toward the cove and gently pushed the brush back aside. He studied the opposite bank as well as he could, trying to discern if there was a corresponding guard on the other side. He couldn't see anyone, but the cabin cruisers obscured part of his view. He eased back against the rock. They had been uniform with their placement of guards all the rest of the way around, so he figured that there was probably one over there, too. Stooping over, he began searching the ground on his side of the rock for something to stand on. There was ample light to see by, but there didn't appear to be anything at hand larger than football-size.

Exasperated, he straightened back up and leaned against the rock. The rock was right at the water's edge, so he couldn't get the guard by going around it that way. And several trees were growing so close on the south side that getting to the guard from that direction would be both time-consuming and risky. With his back against the boulder he sighed and slid slightly down—to a sitting position.

With a start, he straightened back up and turned around. He had just sat on something. How could he have missed it, he wondered. He bent over and felt down near the base of the boulder. Nothing. Still stooping, he slid his hand up the smooth surface of the rock and realized that what he had sat on was a knobby protrusion about three feet up from the base of the boulder. He smiled and, looking up at the sky, gave a thumbs-up sign.

Turning back around, he slid to a sitting position and stretched his legs out in front of him. Laying his sword across his lap, he peered at the luminous hands on his watch. Eleven o'clock. He leaned his head back against the rock. Any time now, he thought. He gazed over the tops of the trees into a night sky that was almost startling in its clarity. There were a lot of elements—a lot of movements—that had to merge perfectly for this mission to be as successful as he wanted. Toby frowned. He wasn't happy with the feeling of responsibility that he had, and he wasn't happy with the idea of depending on the actions of other people.

Still looking up, he narrowed his gaze and tried to concentrate on a point beyond the stars.

I know You're there, he thought. You're so big and I'm so—small. I probably wouldn't be bothering you, but—these people that came with me and the ones at the ranch—they're willing to die for You. They really love You—and--well, so do I.

Toby dug his heels into the ground and pressed his back against the rock. A sudden rushing feeling had caused him to feel dizzy. Suddenly a distant star had come into focus—then a closer one— and then a closer one –then a planet—then the Moon—then a huge meteorite blazed out of the eastern sky to leave a long luminous trail that dissected the sky from east to west.

Simultaneously, Toby could hear the distant thump, thump of an approaching helicopter. He squeezed his eyes tightly shut and re-opened them, trying to regain his equilibrium. Shaking his head, he got to his feet and turned around.

Chapter 31

The helicopter-a tall, large-bellied Bell came in low over the cove. It's nose to the west, it hovered for a few seconds over the other side of the slab.

Toby leaned his sword, point down, against the side of the rock. Then, in a single fluid movement, he was standing on the little ledge. Hugging the surface, he eased up and bent over the top.

The guard, still leaning with his back against the other side of the rock, was watching the helicopter.

Toby leaned forward and grasped the man's neck with both hands. Heaving backwards, Toby yanked him up and over the rock. Never loosening his grip, Toby twisted around and landed—knees first—in the middle of the man's back. The man went limp, but Toby kept squeezing for a full minute. Then, with a final burst of strength, Toby leaned forward and dug his fingers into the man's throat. He could feel cartilage snapping under the pressure of his grip.

Toby slowly got to his feet and cautiously peered over the rock. Apparently, no one had noticed the disappearing guard. The chopper was on the ground and a door had been slid open on the right side. At least sixty or seventy black-robed figures, like some bizarre color-guard, solemnly stood in a semi-circle around the door.

One by one, six red-robed figures disembarked from the helicopter. Their hoods were down, and Toby immediately recognized Manticore and Congressman Burton from pictures he'd seen in newspapers. The other four also appeared to be middle-aged and, though they looked familiar, Toby couldn't put a name on them.

After the six had begun mingling with their black-robed colleagues, three small children---one at a time---were dropped from the chopper onto the sandstone. Half a dozen satanists were standing below to grab them, but one high spirited little boy, no more than five years old, broke and ran toward the rock where Toby was concealed. One of the satanists caught the boy before he'd gone more than fifteen or twenty feet and, flinging him around, tossed him back with the others.

Toby gripped the handle of the sword tightly and tried to figure out some way to distinguish that particular hooded satanist from the others. He wanted to deal with that one personally.

"Damn!" He said under his breath. They all looked alike. Toby unclipped the radio from his belt and, crouching down, brought it up close to his mouth. *"All units—this is A--sound off in order."*

As the helicopter lifted, his men began to report in.

"Unit B in position," came a raspy response.

"Unit C in position."

"Unit D in position."

The helicopter, staying low, flew back across the lake to the east and was completely out of sight by the time the last unit reported in.

"Unit L in position."

"This is unit A," said Toby. *"Take out the guards."*

Toby kicked the dead satanist out of the way and sat back down on the little ledge. He held the radio close to his ear and waited. The wait was less than a minute.

"Unit B', uh, uh, they're dead."

Toby shook his head impatiently.

"Unit I--Mission accomplished."

"Unit E –Mission accomplished."

"All units," Toby said, *"move to forward positions. Units G, H, and*

I--listen up. There was a guard at the tree line on this side of the cove. There's probably one on your side, too. Tell your men."

"Unit H, 10-4."

"Unit G, 10-4."

"Unit I, 10-4."

Toby got back up and turned around, looking across the top of the rock. It appeared that they didn't intend to waste any time. Around the altar, a large circle was being formed by the black-robed people. The red-robed men, their hoods up now, were already inside the circle, solemnly proceeding to the altar. The high-spirited little boy, kicking and thrashing, was being dragged along between two of them.

Toby tried to spot the other two children but couldn't. Apparently they were being held beyond the circle, toward the cliff.

As soon as the red-robed men had reached the altar, the little boy was roughly flung up there and held down on his back. One of the men disrobed him while the other four positioned themselves at the four corners of the altar---each pinning down an arm or leg of the child.

The fifth red-robed man stood at the head of the altar, facing the cove. He held a long-curved knife in his left hand. *"Blessed be!"* He shouted, looking around at the circle of high priests.

"Hail Satan!" Came the response.

He spread his arm's, extending them high over his head. *"Lord Satan---hear our prayer,"* he said.

"Hail Satan!" Responded the black-robed circle.

"Accept the sacrifice of this child---one of those beloved by the usurper!" The man shouted.

"Hail Satan!" Responded the crowd.

"Deliver our enemies into our hands!" The red-robed man shouted, waving his arms. *"Help us to **kill** them!"*

"Hail Satan!" Pleaded the crowd as they joined hands.

"Help us to work as one!" The red-robed man lowered his right arm

and raised his left, still holding the knife extended straight up over his head. *"Help us to be your **Lucifer**, oh mighty Satan!"*

"Who was that, Mom?" Asked Dee. Dora, with a puzzled look, had just hung up the telephone.

"That was Roger," answered Dora, as she walked back toward the couch. *"Our attorney,"* she said in answer to Frank's inquisitive look. *"I---I think he was checking to see if we were all home,"* she said, frowning. *"I led him to think that we all were."* She paused. *"Surely not Roger, too?"* She asked, looking back at Hermano. He was seated at the desk with the radio mike in his hand.

Hermano raised his eyebrows. *"I don't know,"* he replied. *"But I don't believe in coincidence. I'd never trust him again."* He added.

"No," said Dora, *"I won't."* She picked her AK-47 up off the coffee table.

"The windows in the upstairs back bedroom of the old house aren't boarded up," said Dora as she started for the hallway. *"I can get a good shot at the swimming pool deck from the east window."*

"Just a minute, Mom," said Dee as she picked up her own rifle. *"I'm coming, too."*

Frank watched them walk down the hall and then turned to Hermano. *"I think I'll go down to the other end of the hall and kind of keep an eye on the staircase. You know, watch their back. I'll keep the door propped open so I can watch both ways."* Grabbing his own M-16, he hurried off down the hall. Ali quietly took the seat beside Hermano.

"Base," the voice came over the console.

"This is base," Hermano replied.

"They're past the trenches. Walking one by one," the voice advised in a whisper. *"They're going at the—at the pool,"* he added.

"Okay, thanks." Hermano paused. *"Station twelve, base."*

"This is station twelve," came the immediate reply.

"Tell Omar that he's in charge out there. Fire on his command."

"Okay," replied twelve.

Hermano took a deep breath and, letting it out slowly, leaned back in his chair. He held the microphone near his mouth and waited for the first sound of gunfire.

The seconds seemed like minutes.

Dee looked over her mother's shoulder. They had pulled a mattress off the bed and had used it to cover the lower third of the window. Dora's AK-47 rested over the top edge of the mattress. Dee leaned against the window frame to her mother's left and quietly aimed her gun down at the half dozen men that were gathered in front of the patio door. The lights were out in the bedroom and the women remained unnoticed. Dee clicked off the safety.

One of the men, hearing the click, whirled to look behind him just as gunfire was heard from the west side of the house. Dee squeezed the trigger.

As Hermano glanced impatiently toward the boarded-up patio door—a diagonal line of bullet holes appeared in it. All hell broke loose outside.

Hermano snapped his head back around, *"Stations six and seven —take out those guards!"*

"Okay," came back.

Dee's first shot was only a split second ahead of her mom's. Together, they took the men on the patio completely by surprise. A couple of them tried to run toward the garage, but they were downed before they even realized where the fire was coming from. For the men on the patio, it was all over within three or four seconds. Five lay on the patio deck, and one floated, face down, in the pool.

"We'll have to drain the pool, again." Shouted Dora.

"Listen!" Said Dee, as they both stopped firing. The sound started low and rose to a crescendo that echoed across the ranch.

"Al—l—lah Ak—bar!"

The red-robed man turned the knife point-down and grasped the handle with both hands.

"Come on," muttered Toby, looking toward the cliff, *"Come on, John."*

The red-robed priest suddenly arched his back and pitched forward as if he'd been hit in the back with a sledgehammer. As he fell across the little boy, the knife clattered harmlessly to the foot of the altar. Three rifle shots echoed through the clearing as the two red-robed men beside the head of the altar were propelled into their two companions at the foot. All four sprawled on the ground between the alter and the cove.

The little boy, now free, kicked and pushed the still body of the priest off him and jumped from the altar. He ran for the rock behind which Toby was hiding.

Automatic weapon's fire was coming from the tree-line on the other side of the cove, but, because of the boy, no one was yet firing from Toby's side. This had the effect of causing the entire group to flee toward the southeast tree-line.

Toby hurried around the trees beside his rock and, gripping the handle of the sword with both hands, stepped out into the clearing. Two of the satanists had already beat the little boy to the rock and Toby's first action was to wheel on them and lash out with the sword. The nearest he cut almost completely in half. The other tried to leap over the rock but stepped on his robe and fell against it instead. Toby ran him through.

The little boy had frozen, ten feet short of the rock, and was staring, open-mouthed, at Toby.

"Run for the woods, boy!" Shouted Toby and motioned toward the trees to his left.

Still wild-eyed, the little boy dashed for them and was soon out of sight. Automatic weapon's fire erupted from the southern tree-line.

Toby walked purposefully toward a satanist who had just run off the sandstone slab and, seeing Toby, had stopped. Toby raised his sword.

*"Welcome to **hell**!"* He shouted as he swung the big blade. The woman's head and hood flew different directions as her body lurched back and sprawled across the red sandstone.

Toby stepped over her as he ran toward the altar. One of the two red-robed men who had been at the foot of the altar had gotten to his feet. He had pulled out a small revolver and was aiming it toward the cove. Toby could see Ahmed's son, waist deep in water, pointing the video camera at the red-robed man and wading toward the shore.

Toby lunged and slashed downward, severing the man's arm at the wrist. The pistol, with the unattached hand still gripping it, fell to the sandstone. Toby's momentum carried him past the man and by the time he had turned around, someone else had already finished him.

There was one red-robed man still alive and he was just getting to his feet as Toby approached him. Holding the sword with one hand, Toby grabbed the man with the other. The satanist tried to wrench away, but Toby flung him back against the altar. A man wearing a black ski mask ran up and pinned the satanist while Toby yanked back the hood.

"Manticore!" exclaimed Toby. *"God's given **you** to **me**! Hold him down!"* Another man in a ski mask ran up and assisted the first in pressing Manticore back against the altar. Toby took a step toward the head of the altar and, turning, raised the sword high with both hands.

"No!" Screamed Manticore. *"No! I can give you anything! Every---"*

Toby swung the sword with such force that—after decapitating Manticore—it knocked a huge wage-shaped chunk out of the altar, itself. Weakened, the stone altar cracked across the middle and crumpled inwards.

Chapter 32

"It's nice to feel comfortable in here again," said Dora. Pulling out a chair beside Bill, she joined the three television reporters, Dee and her son at the kitchen table. She had just re-filled all of their coffee cups.

Dee, sitting with her back to the front hallway, was at one end of the table. She looked at the two reporters to her right and glanced at the one sitting at the other end.

"This room's been bugged since the beginning of this," she explained. *"We always had to be real careful about what we said in here."*

"It's not, now," Bill put in quickly, *"That was taken care of a couple of hours ago."*

"How, exactly, are you going to run this interview?" Asked Dora. She blew softly across the top of her cup and took a sip.

"Well, live interviews are always a little—unpredictable," answered the older of the reporters. Gray-haired and rosy-cheeked, his appearance reminded the Hunts of Chaplain Harris. An internationally recognized network commentator, he was obviously in charge. He looked across the table at Dora.

"Generally speaking, though," he said, *"it will be in three segments. The first segment will be from Opossum Lake—where all those people at a black mass were killed last night."*

"Possum Kingdom," corrected Bill.

"Yes," He looked at his notes. *"Possum Kingdom. The next segment will be our live interview, here—and some shots taken outside the house*

earlier. Then the third segment will be an interview—also live—with your Chaplain Harris and a Muslim Imam. It'll be broadcast from a mosque in Dallas." He paused. *"That's about as much as I know about it. I was handed a suggested outline for the interview as I boarded a plane in Washington, and—other than that—all I know about what's been going on here is what I've heard in news reports."* He glanced at the young man sitting to his right. *"Everything set up?"* He asked.

"Yes, the lighting's fine. Since you'll be seated for the entire shot, I'll use a tripod—for the minicam." He nodded toward where he had set up the minicam near the back door.

"Good," said the commentator. He glanced at his watch. *"It starts at nine,"* he said, *"Five minutes—do you mind if we turn on your television?"* He asked, glancing at Dora.

"I'll get it." She got up and walked around to the television.

"This first segment is supposed to last for almost 30 minutes," he said, looking at a clipboard that was laying on the table in front of him. *"So we've got about half an hour before we go on."*

Dora turned on the television and then quickly filled everyone's cup. The special program began just as she took her seat.

"The following one-hour news special-edition has scenes of graphic violence that may not be deemed suitable for children." A voice on the television said as the words **"Parental Guidance"** flashed on the screen.

The words gradually faded out to be replaced by a ground-level view of what appeared to be a waterfront camping area. It was night-time, and in the foreground black-robed people could be seen walking from right to left—on the surface of a large stone slab at the water's edge. They were all hooded and appeared to be loosely gathering around a reddish-colored stone altar in the center of the slab.

"Ladies and gentlemen," a voice from the television was saying, *"for the past twenty or thirty years, rumors have been circulating about a sophisticated, powerful, secret organization of satanists. Until two or three years ago—not many people took those rumors seriously. Ladies and*

gentlemen—the videotape that you're now watching, will forever dispel any doubts about the existence—and power—of the organized Church of Satan. This videotape was made last night at a Texas lake called Possum Kingdom in Palo Pinto County—about sixty or seventy miles west of Fort Worth. There is no sound—but, as they say—a picture is worth a thousand words."

A large Bell helicopter, without running lights, could be seen landing beyond the stone altar. The black-robed people hurried over to gather around it, but because of the low camera angle, nothing but the fringe of the black-robed people could be seen.

The picture changed to a shot, apparently taken from the same place, of a widely spaced circle of robed satanists. Within the circle, on the other side of the altar, five hooded red-robed characters could be seen advancing toward the altar. The back two were dragging a small, struggling boy between them.

They positioned themselves around the altar and, yanking the clothes from the little boy, pinned his arms and legs down. One of them stood at the head of the altar and—while apparently saying something—held a knife straight up in the air. Grasping the handle with both hands, he prepared to thrust it down into the little boy.

Dee gasped. *"Oh, no!"* She said, covering her eyes.

As if he had been hit from behind, the man with the knife fell forward over the little boy. Almost simultaneously, the two red-robed men at the other end of the altar, also as if they'd been hit, sprawled in the direction of the camera. In little more than a second, all five red- robed men were down.

The camera angle changed as if the cameraman had just stood up. He panned to his right. Beyond some boats that were tied up to the shore, several men dressed in black and wearing ski masks were slowly walking out of the woods. They were all calmly and method- ically firing automatic weapons at the rapidly dissolving circle of black-robed people.

The picture began bouncing around as if the cameraman was

running—the focus panned back toward the altar. A red-robed man had just gotten to his feet and was bringing up what appeared to be a small pistol. He pointed the pistol in the direction of the camera and began to take aim. Suddenly, something big and black streaked in from the camera's left and the picture froze.

"We stopped at this frame so that you could see what's happening," The voice came from the television. *"The big black thing is a man—and the flash of light is a sword. I'm told it's called a* **broadsword.***"*

The picture continued and all that could be detected was a bright downward flash of light as the big black form rushed across the screen. The red-robed man was still standing there—except now he was extending the stump of his right arm, rather than a gun.

"All right!" Exclaimed Bill, clapping his hands together.

The man, blood spurting from the end of his arm, pulled the stump back slightly and then pitched forward. A diagonal line of bloody holes had appeared in the front of his robe.

One of the other red-robed men started to get to his feet and was immediately snatched up by the huge bear of a man with the broadsword. While another man in a ski mask held the red-robed man back against the stone altar, the big man yanked the red hood back, exposing the satanist's face. The picture froze.

"This man, ladies and gentlemen," the voice came from the television, *"is Pierre Manticore, former Secretary of State, industrialist, and adviser to every President of the United States for the past thirty years."*

The picture continued. A third man in a ski mask ran up and assisted in holding Manticore back against the altar. The big man stepped to the side to get a better angle, lifted the sword in both hands and swung downward with such force that the altar broke in half.

"Wow!" Bill said excitedly.

The picture panned to the left and picked up seven to eight men in ski masks advancing toward fifteen or twenty black robed people who were fleeing to the right of the cameraman. The cameraman followed the pursuit and it soon became obvious that there was no escape—the black robed people were stopped by a twenty-foot sheer cliff. They were mercilessly slaughtered by the men in ski masks, who all appeared to be armed with automatic weapons.

Then began the long process of the cameraman going to each of the dead satanists and filming the hood being removed. This went on for about ten minutes, with a television commentator supplying the name and occupation of each dead satanist.

Then, when he was about half through, the camera panned upward and the helicopter that had brought the red robed men could be seen hovering about two hundred feet over the tiny island at the mouth of the cove.

A fiery streak shot up from the top of the cliff and the helicopter exploded in a huge ball of fire.

The commentators voice broke in, *"That, ladies and gentlemen, was a ground-to-air missile."*

"A.B.D.," commented Bill authoritatively.

All three reporter's heads snapped around to look at Bill.

"What? What was that?" Asked the gray-haired reporter.

"Anti-Broomstick Device," quipped Bill. Dee and Dora laughed uproariously.

The gray-haired commentator looked at the Hunts curiously and then turned back to the TV.

The next picture was a continuation of identifying the dead satanists. After another five minutes the camera panned back to the tree line. The large man with the sword was walking out of the woods leading a little boy by the hand. The boy was naked, but they were soon joined by another masked man who was carrying the little boy's clothes. As he dressed, two other little children ran over to join him.

The cameraman had apparently been approaching the children and the masked man when all of their heads could be seen to snap up. Something in the sky had caught their attention. The picture on the television screen went blank and then switched to live coverage at the lake.

"We figure that a friendly helicopter was approaching at that point," said the gray-haired man. He eyed Bill. *"You have a helicopter, don't you?"*

"My dad had a helicopter," answered Bill. He nodded toward the TV. *"That's live?"* He asked, changing the subject.

The cove area was well lit, and several police officers could be seen scattered about the clearing. A reporter was standing in front of the broken altar, looking at the camera.

"Eighteen elected government officials---," the reporter was saying, *"Five **supposedly** Christian ministers---six nonelected government officials---four psychologists,"* the reporter was reading from a list. *"Nine college professors---three heads of major corporations---four commissioned military officers---several small- business owners."* He looked up from the list. *"And there are still many bodies that remain unidentified. The video which you just watched,"* he went on, *"along with the three children seen in the video, were found in a van parked in front of the offices of channel 8, an ABC affiliate in Dallas. Copies of the video were also given to the local NBC and CBS affiliates, the Palo Pinto County Sheriff's Department, The Dallas Morning News, the Texas Rangers, and the FBI. All the videos were hand delivered, but no one seems to know who delivered them.*

The van which contained the children and one of the videotapes is registered to Central US Avionics—a company largely owned by Congressman Burton, one of the dead satanists." *"And,"* the news reporter glanced off to his right and then looked back at the camera, *"if you think that this is merely a higher level of the 'Cult Wars' that we've been hearing about all week, I'd like to introduce to you a local Sheriff's Deputy named Frank Pierce, Jr.."* The reporter looked back to his right. The camera panned in that direction and picked up Frank, in civilian clothes and a cowboy hat, walking toward the broken altar. Frank smiled and waved uncomfortably to the camera as he stopped beside the reporter.

The reporter looked back at the camera but held the microphone in front of Frank. *"Mr. Pierce,"* he said, *"would you tell our viewers—what was the purpose of the black mass that was held out here last night?"*

Frank cleared his throat. *"The purpose of the mass was to pray for success in murdering some people who were trying to expose their organization. All these people out here were high priests and above."* Frank paused. *"This black mass was supposed to coincide with an attack on a ranch—about 40 miles east of here."*

"And, as I understand it," the reporter leaned toward his microphone, *"you were present at that ranch when it was being attacked?"*

"Yes. Inside the ranch house." He paused, *"I was off duty, though, Uh, I mean I was out there as a friend of the family more than as a deputy."*

The reporter jerked the microphone back. *"I see,"* he said, and looked at the camera. *"While this mass was in progress—some thirty or forty armed satanists attacked a small ranch near Weatherford, Texas."* He paused. *"Apparently, they thought that they were getting some kind of satanic power from what was going on out **here**."* He turned and looked at the broken altar and then back at the camera.

"We now take you to Jim Preen at the Hunt Ranch in Weatherford, Texas. --Jim, what did the satanists find so lethal over there?"

In the kitchen, the cameraman had gotten up and positioned himself a couple of minutes before the Hunts were to be on the air. The camera had been pointing towards Jim Preen, but when the other reporter had asked what the satanists had found so lethal—as they had gone live, the cameraman swiveled the minicam to point at Dora and Dee. Much to their embarrassment, he held the shot for several seconds while the younger of the reporters jumped to turn down the volume of the TV. Then he panned to Jim Preen.

Jim laughed. *"I'm afraid they had a lot more to worry about than these two attractive young ladies, Walt. ---I'm standing here in the kitchen of the Hunt home with Dora, Dee, and Bill Hunt,"* as Jim talked, the camera slowly panned back to the Hunts, *"who, along with a few of their friends, ---in true wild-west fashion—fought off a band of marauding satanists last night."* He held the microphone over toward Dora, who was frowning, and looking at him as if she thought he was crazy.

"Did this remind you of something your ancestors might have experienced, Mrs. Hunt?" He asked.

"My ancestors burned witches at the stake, Jim. They would have been ashamed of the state this nation is now in. Gangs of satanists attacking people's homes and snatching children off the street. My ancestors would have been against Texas joining the Union if this sort of thing had been going on back then." Dora, obviously just getting warmed up, leaned forward—but Jim pulled the microphone back.

"How did you happen to be prepared for such a large-scale attack?" Jim asked quickly, pointing the microphone at Dee. Dee looked into the camera.

*"A **real** Christian found out that the Church of Satan was after our family. He and his friends came to help."* She paused. *"The people who we thought were our friends—turned out to be our enemies."* She paused again, *"One of those dead satanists over at Possum Kingdom was the minister of our church."*

"Yes, I heard something about that," said Jim. *"You must have really felt alone—until these <u>friends</u> showed up."*

"I'll say! That organization—that's what the Church of Satan is, an organization—anyway, that organization can grind you into the ground. Lots of powerful people with lots of connections—all secretly working together to destroy you." She paused. *"You can imagine."*

"Yes," answered Jim. He glanced down at his notes. *"Who, uh--who were the people who came to help?"* He asked.

Dora put her hand on Dee's arm before she could speak. *"We better not mention names—except Frank, who already told you he was here,"* said Dora. *"We're not sure what sort of legal problems we'll run into, yet."* She paused. *"I'll say this, though. Christians and Muslims worked together-- to defeat a mutual enemy."*

Jim Preen looked quickly at the cameraman and made a motion

with his index finger across his throat. The man turned off the mini-cam and lowered it.

Jim looked at Dora. *"We've got to get in a clip that we shot earlier outside the house before they switch to the Dallas segment",* he explained.

"Is that it?" Asked Bill.

"Well, for this program," answered Jim as he got up from the table. *"You'll probably get a belly full of reporter's questions in the next couple of weeks, though."*

Dora pushed her chair back from the table and stood up. She glanced at Dee, and then at Bill. *"Y'all want to finish watching this in the den?"* She asked. She smiled at Jim Preen as she walked for the hallway door. *"Do you mind letting yourself out?"* She asked. *"It's been a long day and I think we'll relax awhile—back in the den."*

Jim Preen smiled and waved as he got to his feet. *"Sure thing,"* he said. *"Thanks for the interview."*

Chapter 33

The TV in the den was already on when Dora, Dee, and Bill all walked in. Hermano was sitting at the desk chair, which was swiveled around facing the television, and Dave, his boots off, was sitting on the couch with his feet propped up on the coffee table.

"Get those feet off my coffee table," said Dora, feigning anger as she slapped at Dave's feet. He jerked up to a sitting position and put his feet on the floor.

*"This thing hasn't mellowed **you** any,"* he teased.

"That coffee table is one of the only things downstairs that doesn't have a bullet hole in it," Dora laughed as she sat down on one of the folding chairs.

Dee and Bill sat down on either side of their mom and Dee glanced over at Hermano. *"Have we missed anything?"* She asked. Hermano looked around at her and smiled.

"You just missed two beautiful ladies on TV," he answered.

Dee returned his smile. *"You'd better look out—or I'll come over there and embarrass you,"* she said.

"Shhh," said Dora. She was looking at the TV. A picture of Chaplain Harris, Ahmed, Ali, and Omar—all sitting on the same side of a rectangle table---had just come on. Each of the four had a separate microphone sitting in front of him. Chaplain Harris, sitting at the far left, was speaking into his.

"They agreed to do an exclusive interview with this network only if

Chaplain Harris could run the interview—live," Bill said. *"I'm surprised they agreed to it,"* he added.

"For an exclusive on a story this big?" Dave interjected. *"I'm not surprised."*

"Shhh!" Dora repeated, leaning forward.

"---young boy could have been involved in this?" Chaplain Harris was asking—looking at Ali.

Ali took a deep breath and sat up straight. He looked at the camera, *"I'm from Afghanistan. Because we were starving, my parents had to sell me. Then I was given---as a gift---to Pierre Manticore. He used me for--"* he paused, *"evil things. He worshiped Satan."*

"This brave young man," said Chaplain Harris, *"at great personal risk, escaped from Manticore and ended up taking refuge with the Hunts."* Chaplain Harris looked back at the camera. *"The Hunts were already having a serious run in with the organized Church of Satan."* He went on to explain about the May Day cattle mutilations and Sam Hunt's murder.

"To anyone who is knowledgeable about the power of organized satanism—both the Hunt's and Ali's situations would have appeared hopeless." He paused, *"Look at the types of people who were killed at that mass. Government leaders—industrialists—judges—police officials—pastors. All bound to gather in a secret organization that will do—literally—anything to further the goals of the organization. They can and do crush anyone who gets in their way."* Chaplain Harris looked steadily at the camera as he narrowed his eyes.

"Yes," he said, *"their situations appeared hopeless. And—their situations might have been hopeless, if not for some real Christians, and some real Muslims. People willing to do more than talk."* He paused and looked at Ahmed.

"My brother—Peter Harris—speaks for all of us," said Ahmed. *"If we call ourselves Muslim or Christian—we are one family."* He paused, *"You have an expression in this country—'we'll either all hang together, or else, we'll certainly hang separately'."* He paused, again. *"Today,*

we announce the birth of an organization—an organization of believers—Christian and Muslim—dedicated to fighting and winning against satanism.

Like the first shot fired in your Revolutionary War—someday, what has occurred in Texas over this weekend, will be known as 'the shot heard round the world'."

The screen went blank. The Hunts and Hermano kept looking at the TV, but after a few seconds, when it came back on, it came on to regularly scheduled programming.

"They didn't give any kind of address or phone number," observed Dee. *"What if people who were watching should want to join with us?"*

"If they're serious about joining—they'll make the effort to get in touch with them," said Dora. *"I think they didn't give an address or phone number on purpose."*

"I think you're right," agreed Hermano.

"Wait a minute," said Bill, looking around at the rest of them. *"I thought it was finished. Didn't we **win**?"*

Hermano looked over at the Hunts and raised his eyebrows. Dora turned to smile at her son.

"We got off to a real good start, Billy," she said. *"But the only thing that's finished here is our indecision."*

"The most critical part of a race is coming off the blocks," said Dave as he began putting on his boots. *"Like your mom said—we got off to a **real** good start."*

Dee, perking up as if she had just remembered something, began looking around the room. *"Where's Toby?"* She asked. *"I thought he was still hiding-out back here."*

Dave chuckled as he got to his feet. *"He found Frank's list."* He chuckled, again. *"Did Bill tell y'all what Toby did with that bug that was in the kitchen?"* He asked.

"The tiny smashed pieces of it are back on the patio," he said. *"But before Toby smashed it, he held it close to his mouth and said---'**You're next**'."*

About the Author

The author, formerly a professional investigator in Texas, had cause to thoroughly investigate the organized church of Satan when he learned that they were responsible for the abduction and murder of a little girl in Denton, Texas. Receiving no help from local law enforcement, the author determined to make himself an expert on Satanism and the elements of "magic" ritual. May Day, A Curse in Black and White is the fruit of that endeavor.

Printed in the United States
By Bookmasters